W9-ACU-676

Just
Trust
Me

Just Trust Me

Judy Markey

MIRA®

MIRA®

ISBN 0-7783-2062-6

JUST TRUST ME

www.MIRABooks.com

Printed in U.S.A.

First Printing: August 2004
10 9 8 7 6 5 4 3 2 1

For my parents, Johnny and Lois Lindheim

ACKNOWLEDGMENTS

Well, first off I just have to thank that Jean Naggar. Such an agent. For twenty years she has provided giant doses of candor and support—two of my favorite things.

Thanks also to MIRA's Valerie Gray, who asks all the right hypothetical questions. And to computer guru Kelly Conwell, who has all the right technical answers.

Then there are all the people I badgered with questions while I was writing this—questions about Italian grammar, the running of restaurants, insurance rules, criminal law and offenses of the federal sort. Thank you to Christie Kempf, Ron and Trisha Miller, Diane Quackenbusch, Herb Goldberg and that nice Secret Service agent who spent valuable government time with me, and made me swear I would never tell his name. My lips are sealed.

Lastly there are all my girlfriends, who read, critiqued and what-ifed the early drafts of this book: Chris Paschen, Kathy O'Malley, Elizabeth Berg, Carol Anshaw, Johanna Steinmetz, Phyllis Isaacson and my very best girlfriend—the one I married—Tommy Collinger.

It is easy to tell a lie, but it is impossible to tell only one.
—Unknown

1

Chapter One

When Kate Lerner read the letter from her extremely detestable ex-husband saying that he had less than a year to live, she decided to help herself to a second mound of mashed potatoes.

No way was she going to try to handle this news bulletin on an empty stomach.

Kate Lerner was one of those women who made you nuts. At forty-three she could devour triple servings of mashed potatoes, greasy chicken, lardy fruit pies and still slide into her size-six jeans. She had no starter wrinkles—except for a couple of great crow's-feet around gray-green eyes—and her thick chestnut hair hadn't even faded, much less gone to salt-and-pepper. If Kate hadn't been such an all-around funny/edgy/smart/complicated/embracing person, you'd have to hate her.

But she was all of the above, which no doubt accounted for her consistently respectable radio ratings as one half of the David and Kate Show, which aired on a small Chicago FM station. Kate was so well-adjusted, she didn't even mind that David Weiland got top billing, in *spite of the fact that he was the new member of the equation. For almost a decade Kate had co-hosted the* Samantha and Kate Show *with her feisty best friend Samantha Marquist. Two years ago Sam decided to bag the brutal Chicago winters, as well as the pressure of having to maintain a good personality every day for four hours on the air, and moved to Sonoma County to do some apprentice cooking at an old friend's restaurant. Theirs had been the saddest of split-ups.*

Unlike Kate's split-up with Richard, the aforementioned ex-husband. Their split-up was toxic. Richard Farley may only have been Kate's starter ex-husband (yes, there were two), but he was the only ex-husband who, fifteen years after the divorce, still had the power to curdle her insides just by showing up in a half-page letter. Particularly a letter like the one sitting in front of her.

> *Dear Kate:*
> *Here's what I know...*
> *I know you probably still hate my guts.*
> *I know I was a schmuck for having walked out on you and Danny and never sending you a dime.*
> *I know that according to several doctors, I'm going to die within the year.*
> *I know I've made a shitload of money.*
> *I know I've got an interesting proposition for you.*
> *Call me...*
> *Richard*

Son. Of. A. Bitch.

It was amazing. There I was at my kitchen table, in the very same baggy blue sweater I'd had on that Sunday night fifteen years ago when Richard disappeared on Danny and me. I took a second helping of my Boston Market mashed potatoes and reread a piece of paper that I could not have imagined would ever exist.

A letter from Richard S. Farley.

The man who'd fathered my son, but was a little too busy to come to the hospital the night that very son was born. On that night Richard was otherwise engaged. He was with the young redheaded reporter he'd hired to temporarily replace me in the newsroom. Apparently she was replacing me elsewhere as well. First *at* my mike, then *under* my husband—with Richard all the prepositions were interchangeable. Richard was a player. I knew that when he first hired me as a weekend reporter on WKIX.

So for a long time I stayed away from him. For at least three years. Until one night, I didn't. By then I'd been promoted to a weekday shift, and there was definitely a lot more time to be exposed to the old Richard Farley charm. The man was hard to ignore—he was smart, he was quick and he was excellent to look at. Blue eyes, black curly hair and a smile that would make a spy hand over his bomb recipe.

Here's what happened that night. We went for drinks; we skipped the dinner; we went to bed. Hardly original. Hardly politically correct either, given that Richard was my boss. So, we thought we'd make things more kosher by falling in love and getting married.

Brilliant.

Oddly, station management never hassled us. Instead we started hassling each other—five or six months into official married life. Bickering escalated to fuming, and fuming escalated to silent treatments, and silent treatments exploded into screaming matches. But then a confusing thing would always happen. The screaming matches—and I'm not proud of this—would frequently evolve into hot, sweaty sex.

I'd never believed that could happen between two people. It always seemed like a movie ploy from the "you're so cute when you're mad" days. It also seemed completely spineless on my part. If I was furious, why couldn't I stay connected to my fury, instead of letting my hormones boss me around? But with Richard my hormones always got in the way. And he knew it. He knew it was the one sure way we could always find our way back to each other. But then the cycle would start again.

By the time Danny was born, in month eleven of our ill-fated union, and in spite of the powerful sex, a fair amount of goodwill—not to mention love—had irrevocably eroded away. But then, sleeping with your wife's on-air replacement while she is giving birth can definitely be hard on goodwill and love.

Six months later, Richard and I unraveled for good. One night I picked up Danny from his day-care lady, came home and found a strange little purse flask of cheap hair spray on our bathroom sink.

I didn't use hair spray. Richard didn't use hair spray. Thus, I considered the hair spray a bit of a problem.

Richard was due home later that night from two days in Washington, D.C. where he'd attended a meeting for radio program directors from around the country. He walked in; I held up the hair spray; he pleaded complete ignorance. But something was rotten in Denmark. I found it the next morning. I went into his jacket and pulled out his plane ticket.

Apparently Richard had not flown back to Chicago the day before at nine in the evening as he'd told me. He'd flown in at nine in the morning and had been home all day frolicking in our marital bed with some woman who used cheap hair spray. But then, of course, he apparently was too cheap to get a motel. The perfect couple.

I harbored not a shred of ambivalence. I told him to move out. He made some great speeches, but Richard was a born cheater. I knew if I stayed with him, my life would turn into a bad country-western song. Nope, I decided at age twenty-eight to cut my losses. I'd collect my child support and get a job at another station.

Only I didn't have to. Richard left first. Not just the station. He left the country. We were divorced on a Wednesday and by that Sunday, the first day he was supposed to pick up Danny, according to our expensively hashed out joint custody decree, the man had completely vanished. It was as if I'd been married to Houdini. It took almost a year for hired detectives to find out where he was. And where he was, was in Vancouver, safe from me, my lawyers and the arm of the U.S. law. I equivocated for a while, but it became clear that going after him would have been cumbersome and way too expensive—both financially and psychologically. I couldn't afford fury.

So that was it. Danny and I never heard from him again. Until now. I read and reread the now gravy-stained letter that basically said, "Hi. I'm dying. I'm rich. I've got an interesting offer for you." Somehow it didn't sound like the movie version of "interesting offer" was going to be a musical.

Of course, who said I was going to call him at the number on his letterhead to find out what the offer actually entailed? I'd spent the better part of two decades despising this person, if not actively, at least passively. Why would I want to reengage with a man capable of behaving as despicably as he had? What could he possibly say that would make it wise to listen now?

I stretched out my legs and wiggled my feet in the stripes of pinky-yellow light slanting across the kitchen's wood floor. It was early June and the benefits of daylight saving were finally kicking in. It was after eight and still light enough to see the clumps of peonies and irises exploding in my backyard. I've always loved flowers—Delphiniums, Queen Anne's Lace, lush, startling Datura. It didn't matter, they all brought me such pleasure out there in my garden.

The doorbell rang and as I walked through the living room to get it I picked up an empty Domino's pizza box. Danny must have ordered it before leaving for his part-time job. He was doing data entry at some insurance company for ten dollars an hour. Not bad for a high school junior.

Tim was the one ringing the doorbell. He's my second ex-husband. And quite the opposite from the rich, disappearing, currently dying first ex-husband. Tim was a model ex-husband, not to mention he was the father of my second child, the glorious seven-year-old Sarah Rose, whom he was returning to the premises at precisely the designated hour.

I opened the door to the two of them. Sarah was holding his hand and jumping up and down, pleading, "Mommy, Mommy, my gerbil is sick, and I'm scared to leave her alone at Daddy's, 'cause he's going on a trip, so we brought her here, and she's in the car, and can we have her with us until Daddy gets back? Please, Mommy, please?"

Tim grinned his "is she darling, or what" grin, shrugged his shoulders, and said, "I tried to call you with this, but you didn't answer your cell, so I figured if this was a problem for you, I'd take the gerbil back. She's in the car and I'll only be gone two days, so…"

"Tim, it's no problem," I sighed, wondering at what age a

woman is finally sprung from menagerie-land. I have a friend at the station whose twenty-two-year-old college graduate son decided that a good thing to spend his first grown-up paycheck on was a three-foot-long iguana.

Sarah leaped into my arms, kissing my face all over and said, "Oh Mommy, I love you, I love you, I love you!" Then she and her six pounds of red curls ran back into her room to clear some space for the ailing gerbil.

It was hard to say no to Sarah Rose. She'd been through a lot in her short life. Not only did Tim and I divorce when she was only two, but a year later, she knocked into a can of lit Sterno under some chocolate fondue and badly burned her right arm and the right side of her jaw and neck. She'd spent months in the hospital and already had undergone three operations. There would be at least five more along the way to her being full-grown, and we'd already used almost two-thirds of our insurance policy benefits. How we would pay for the rest of her treatment was a constant source of worry. Had we been in a managed care plan, there wouldn't have been a limit. But Sarah was locked in with these Houston burn specialists and our insurance topped out at two million.

And though the financial part was scary, the Sarah Rose part was not. Sarah had a great attitude—long on strength and deep on confidence. It was amazing how undaunted she was by the scars she bore. Granted, they weren't disfiguring, but they were plenty visible. One covered nearly sixty percent of her upper arm, and the other about twenty percent of her neck and jaw. My concern, of course, was for those years when she'd be confronted with all the mean-spiritedness of adolescence, but to date, she had handled her situation with great equanimity.

A lot had to do with her daddy. Tim Wuthrich was a terrific man. No wonder I married him. By then Danny was six, and during the four years we'd been on our own, a lot had changed. He'd had to adjust to not having a daddy, we'd had to adjust to moving to an apartment and I'd had to adjust to having a much smaller bank account.

It wasn't just the money I'd wasted on the private investigator trying to find Richard. I'd also managed to lose the entire seventy thousand dollars I'd made from selling our house. I'd been in a bit of an I-am-woman-hear-me-roar phase and had decided I could be a brilliant financial investor. I decided very wrong. I was a disaster. Such a disaster that I'd considered leaving the radio show with Samantha because the pay we were getting was not much better than that of a city schoolteacher. Sure we were in radio, but we were hardly a number one station and we were never going to make big money at WKIX.

For Samantha, money wasn't a problem. She had the security of a trust fund from her grandmother.

But for me, it was an issue. I made the choice to stay, because it was work that I loved and I learned from. And I decided to supplement my income with freelance textbook editing. Most of the time I couldn't get to it until eight or nine at night, and while it wasn't lucrative either, it was steady. Editing was actually how I met Tim.

He taught philosophy at DePaul University and had written a book called *The Ethics of Lying*. Most of the books I worked on were either dry or pretentious, but I found his to be very readable and very provocative. In fact, I liked it so much, I invited him on the show.

When he showed up for the interview, I was a bit surprised.

His author picture on the back cover had been decidedly furrow-browed and professorial. But in person the man was easygoing and very funny.

A few weeks later on our first date he actually had me doubled up laughing. We were eating oysters at Shaw's raw bar and he was explaining how he and his best friend had been stuck on a road trip once and were forced to share one motel room.

"There was one king-size bed and two heterosexual guys," he said, taking three empty oyster shells from his plate and placing them on the table to illustrate what he was saying. He pushed the two smaller shells to the right to represent the guys and set the one long one to the left to represent the king-size bed. "So where do you think the two guys slept?"

I smiled back at his brown eyes behind his glasses, picked up the two smaller shells and placed them on top of the long shell. "Is this a trick question or something? They slept in the king-size bed of course."

"Ahh, Kate Lerner, you have much to learn about my gender," he said gently, while lifting one of the oyster shells off the big pretend bed and placing it a huge distance away from the other two. "The answer to the one king-size bed, two heterosexual men quandary is that they flip for the bed and the loser gets the floor."

"Why?" I laughed, incredulous at the idea.

"Because we'd be awake all night making sure we didn't accidentally roll into each other. Guys are hairy and disgusting. We emit horrible body noises. Why would anyone want to sleep in bed with a guy?"

Of course, only three months later I was sleeping in bed with the very guy who posed that question. Tim, too, had had a fast, awful first marriage, and he was genuinely interested in doing it right the next time. Preburned as we were, Tim and I moved toward each other very cautiously, but over the next year all three of us fell in love. Tim and I with each other, he and Danny with each other and Danny with Tim and me as an entity.

And I guess it was that entity thing that killed us in the end. Both of us had been through these cataclysmic divorces. His first wife had to be hospitalized three times during their marriage because of chronic pill addictions and emerged from the third hospitalization with a clean bill of health lasting all the way back to their kitchen when she pulled a knife on him.

So, bruised as we were by the excessive behavior of our ex-spouses, I think we became hell-bent on being kind and neutral with each other. We didn't fight, we didn't *point out* and we didn't acknowledge any of the rough moments that would have allowed for normal flare-ups in the course of a marriage. Instead we became so intent on preserving the "we" of us, that we mutually erased the "I" that comprises any healthy "we." We became a Stepford couple—yielding, beige and perfect.

But not so perfect we didn't recognize, even with Danny and Sarah Rose in our presence, that we'd each almost extinguished the best parts of ourselves. A year of therapy and lots of tears and discussion forced us to conclude we were unable to be together without each losing ourselves in the process. So sadly, civilly, we unhitched nearly five years ago.

And, like I said, Tim sets the curve for terrific ex-husbands. The checks are on time, the pickups and deliveries are on time, and as fabulous as he is with Sarah, he has still kept the great connection he has always had with Danny. For all the reasons I love him as an ex, I think I love him most for that. Danny almost always goes to Tim's with Sarah, on trips with Tim and Sarah, and

Tim goes with me to teacher conferences for both children. Even though we never went through any legal adoption, Tim has truly been Danny's only real dad. And he has been a superb one.

"Is it okay if we put this in her room?" he asked, standing outside the screen door with the ailing gerbil in a cage.

"Sure. What do you think? Are we about to host a tragic gerbil funeral in the next few days?"

"Nah. Sorry to report, I don't think it's anything fatal. I know how you feel about rodents, and that this isn't your favorite hostessing assignment, but it's only for a couple days. When I pick Sarah up Thursday night, I'll get the cage, too. When is her play again? Next week?"

"Wednesday and Thursday at 2:00. Sarah wants one of us to be there each day, so which do you prefer?"

"Thursday. I teach on Wednesday."

"Fine." We were still such cooperators. "Hey, I've got something astonishing to tell you. Go put the cage in Sarah's room and then come back. I wouldn't want you to drop it when you hear who's dying."

"Who?"

"Someone who's been as good as dead anyway."

Chapter Two

Tim was not one bit happy that Richard had written to me. Nor was he one bit curious about what Richard's offer might be.

After Sarah Rose went to bed, he stuck around another half hour. "For God's sake, Kate, you know this is a man with no moral center. Who knows what he is going to propose?" He reached into the cabinet where I kept the pretzels—just where I did when we were married.

One of the great things about divorcing Tim was his insistence that I keep our stucco bungalow on Chicago's near North side. It was cramped, and something was always screaming for repair, but we had a huge oak tree in back and a sweet front porch for people watching. Two weeks ago he'd come over to help me put the green wicker furniture out there, then Sarah Rose set up her lemonade stand on the sidewalk, and that was the official opening day for our summer.

"Tim, I have no idea what he's going to propose. I just think it seems a bit shortsighted on my part not to hear what's on his mind." I uncorked a half-full bottle of Trader Joe's finest six-dollar Chardonnay and emptied it into two glasses.

Picking his up he said, "It's not because he's dying, is it?"

"Is what?"

"I mean, you're not thinking of calling him because he's dying, are you?"

"Well obviously it will be easier to call him before he dies, rather than after. But if you're asking do I feel sorry for him, the answer is no. He's been in my s.o.b. category so long that I'm not about to let him slide into the zone of cheap sentimentality. If you're asking do I find his dying something of a compelling factor, the answer is, well, yes, on some level. It does seem to be the final thing a person can do. If you're asking do I think his knowing he is dying means he's a changed man, I'd have to say, probably not. But I won't know unless I talk to him, right?"

"Right," he said, running his fingers back through his formerly red, currently reddish hair. "But not knowing isn't necessarily bad. Ignorance may not be bliss, but it can help you avoid some destructive behavior. What does Karen say?"

Karen is my twin sister who I tell everything to. She and Tim have always been crazy about each other.

"I haven't told her yet. She's on a bike trip up in Wisconsin somewhere and her cell doesn't work."

"Well, why don't you pretend your phones aren't working either," Tim said dryly, "then it will be that much easier not to call him."

The weird thing is that the next morning at work, I played Tim's role in the very same conversation with David, and David was playing my role. David Weiland is an interesting human specimen. Great heart, quick wit and deep reservoirs of insight into human behavior. I've been surprised at just how quick the "click" came about in our partnership.

Samantha and I had been genuine real-life girlfriends—even before we were put on the air together. She had worked in TV, but just hated the part where you had to be in full makeup at five in the morning and the boss would periodically "suggest" that you update your hair, or get your lips inflated. So radio was perfect for her. It offered the glorious Wizard of Oz factor that we've all come to love and enjoy. Tell the listeners you're gorgeous…and you're gorgeous. Or tell them you're young…and you're young. Or, best of all, don't tell them anything, and let them invent you. If you check out the radio hosts around America, you will see a disproportionate number of extra-large white guys with extra-large egos in jobs they could never have gotten in the appearance-oriented corporate world.

David Weiland, however, was one of those radio exceptions. He looked even nicer than he sounded. And he sounded plenty good. I remember the first time I saw him, how taken I was by his looks. David is tall, trim and has the most arresting liquid black eyes I've ever seen on a human. His grin is tilted—great teeth—and his light brown hair hasn't even given a thought to thinning. It's catalog-guy hair—thick and wind-blown. Granted, when we met for the first time it was outside on the street and the wind *was* blowing, but even inside, David's hair is always a little rumpled. I like that. He's not a guy with gel and moisturizer in his medicine chest. Not that I look in medicine chests, but you never know what a person might have in there. Half the time, I just assume someone is on Prozac unless they tell me otherwise.

Actually, when David started working at the station it was at a real tough time in his life. He and his wife of twenty-some years had split up in some semipublic calamitous divorce back in Philadelphia. I didn't know the particulars, but he was apparently so shattered that he quit his radio job and spent the next eighteen months driving around the country, trying to regroup emotionally. He had a stepson in Arizona with whom he was very close, so he headed out west, to just *be* for a while. But after two Februarys in the desert he discovered he missed winters, he missed cities and he apparently missed radio.

When Samantha left, I'd been really terrified about having a new partner, but not nearly as terrified as I was of doing the show alone. I've always been a Tonto to someone's Lone Ranger and, all alone as Lone, I was lame and I was scared. So I was thrilled when our program director handed me some of David's tapes and said, "Take them home and tell me what you think."

What I thought was that he was funny and smart. Good thing, too. They'd apparently already hired him. God, I love management.

The good part, though, was that we really did hit it off, both on and off the air. The morning after Richard's letter arrived, I came in as usual at 8:15 a.m. and David had already bought me a black decaf from Starbucks. He was going through the *Tribune* for fodder for the show, and was in the midst of clipping something from the editorial page. We had a system. I clipped the *New York Times, Sun-Times* and *USA Today*. And he clipped the *Trib, The Wall Street Journal* and all the local sports sections. By ten o'clock when we went on the air, we had more material than our three hours would allow, given that the bulk of our show was call-ins from listeners.

"Hey," I said, tossing my battered leather purse down on our lumpy, stained couch. We had a much bigger office than we had paychecks—something both of us would have liked to reverse—but we didn't get to make the call. "Thanks for the coffee."

"My pleasure, Ms. Kate," he said with his tilt grin, looking over the top of the new reading glasses he'd gotten last week. "Has the world been good to you so far?"

That was his usual morning greeting and I kind of liked it. "Yeah, it's been good. Albeit a bit jolting in the past twenty-four hours. I didn't get a lot of sleep last night."

"Teenage disturbances?" He'd done enough stepfathering to know how regularly these boiled up.

"Nope. All's quiet on the adolescent front. It was this that threw me off." I pulled the letter out of my purse and handed it to him. David had long, graceful fingers—piano man hands. I told him that once and he smiled because apparently he really could play. But he'd sold his piano when he left Philadelphia, and hadn't sat down and noodled around on a keyboard in nearly three years.

He unfolded the letter and read it. "Richard? Is that your first husband?"

"Yup."

"The one who walked out?"

"The very same."

"Jesus. What a letter. So what is the proposition?"

"David, are you kidding? I haven't called him! For Pete's sake, I got the letter last night! Fifteen years of silence and you think eight lines on a piece of paper is going to send me rushing to the phone?"

"Well, you are going to call him, right?"

"Are you kidding? This is a horrible guy. A self-involved, undeveloped, beyond irresponsible horrible guy. Why should I call him?"

He regarded me as if I'd just grown horns. "For starters, how about because he's dying?"

"I don't do opera, David. I don't go rushing to the deathbed of some moral toad, bestow a kiss on him and expect him to emerge a prince."

"That's a fairy tale, not an opera."

"You know what I mean. I don't believe in transformations. And I don't give a rip about remorse. Remorse doesn't buy Danny back a daddy. Remorse is just some way for Richard to feel good about himself, you know, all masturbatory and self-gratifying. I don't need Richard to be remorseful. At this point I don't need Richard for anything."

"How do you know what you need and don't need until you hear what he says?"

David got up and closed our door because, apparently, I was shouting. "Look," he said, sitting on the edge of my desk in his well-worn jeans and navy polo shirt. David ran and worked out so he looked mighty nice in a polo shirt. "Obviously I can't tell you what to do, particularly because you didn't ask me. And I wasn't around during all those years that you raised your son alone. It's just that this seems like a very hard call *not* to make, and I'd be astounded if, after some reflection, you didn't make it. There's too much journalistic curiosity in you to pass up what could be a compelling story. You don't strike me as a woman who is great living with loose ends."

"What does that mean?"

"It means I think you are a thorough and inquisitive woman.

You're not a woman who just shrugs her shoulders and says, 'whatever.'"

"Whatever," I said, making sure to shrug my shoulders.

"Very funny, Kate," he said, giving my shoulder a squeeze. "Call him. If you don't like what you hear, you can always hang up."

So there I was with a one/one tie on whether to call Richard. Tim was a no, David was a yes, and for three days I was a real mess.

Part of the mess was compounded by Danny. This parenting thing has its challenges and black-haired, teal-eyed Danny had been a darling little guy for his first 14.9 years. Then, one day, over two years ago, it was as if he descended into the basement and his evil twin had come up and decided to stay.

I have taken it rather hard. I mean, I know it's age appropriate to be mouthy, sullen and attitude-laden, but that does not make it one whit easier to deal with. Particularly when all the mouth, sullenness and attitude are directed exclusively toward you, the one resident parent. Tim had said years before that for every teenage boy raised by a single mother there was always a moment when he would finally whip out his ultimate weapon, the old killer comment: *I hate you. I'm going to live with Dad.*

But for Danny and me that wasn't an option. He could hate me, but he didn't get Richard as a parental backup, and I didn't get Richard offering me a parental break. Unless that was what he had up his sleeve. And even if it was, why would I let Richard reinsert himself into the mix after a decade and a half of willful absence?

Nope, Danny and I were stuck with each other, for better or for worse. It was just that this fifteen-to-eighteen-year-old zone was heavy on the worse. *Everything* was an issue—curfew, drinking, the phone, grades, driving, mowing the lawn, wet clothes in the dryer. We were at each other constantly. Not that there weren't the occasional warm and fuzzy détentes, but they were few and far between and it made me sad.

Of course, sometimes just looking at him I'd melt in that goofy mom way we're all capable of. Danny had spent his first twelve years looking almost like a carbon copy of Richard, which I never let make me crazy. But in the past few years, his hair had gotten straighter, his chin had developed one of those Michael Douglas dimples, and while he still resembled Richard, he seemed to look a lot more chiseled, a lot more actor-y. Granted, *I* thought he was gorgeous, and several of the girls in his class confirmed my suspicions. The phone rang plenty from people named Amanda and Heather and Jen, but for the past six months he seemed to spend most of his time with a serious, plain-looking girl named Jamie. She wore glasses and a lot of washed-out-looking colors. She also seemed unusually prone to sighing, as if she carried the weight of the world on her shoulders. It was a bit unclear what the attraction was, but for the past few months they'd been almost inseparable. Comradely inseparable, not sexy inseparable.

Over the next few days I thought about Danny a lot—in terms of where he was headed and what he'd missed out on. It wasn't simply that he hadn't had an on-premises dad for most of his life, but there had been so many creature comforts that I hadn't been able to give him for a lot of years. Certainly during the first six, before I married Tim, most of his toys and clothes were hand-me-downs from friends. Finances were considerably easier once Tim and I married, but he wasn't making a huge salary at DePaul either. Then, after the divorce, it inevitably got tight again. Tim was great about supporting Sarah Rose, but Danny wasn't his financial responsibility, and it was odd trying to run a household where one kid was decently provided for by her dad and the other was completely cut off by his.

Of course the real financial killer for Danny was coming up—college. I'd put a little money away, but he wanted to go to art school and unless he won some sort of fellowship, he'd be taking on huge student loans. Not the end of the world, but when a kid's biological daddy is three thousand miles away, apparently sitting on a pile of money, the idea of that kid having to take on a huge debt can gnaw at a biological mommy. Especially one with two jobs, nagging credit card debt and no savings to speak of.

And that was the problem with this damn letter from Richard. If it hadn't shown up, I wouldn't have even dragged his abstract bank account into my psyche. I had spent years with him deleted from my brain cells ninety-nine percent of the time, and suddenly nine written lines appeared, and my stomach was roiling. That was giving him too much power.

"On the other hand, not calling him back gives him power, too," said Karen, when she got back from her biking trip two nights later and we finally connected by phone.

"How so?" I asked, as I nestled into my favorite place—the left side of my bed. My current bedroom was the closest I'd ever gotten to the bedroom of my dreams—well my low-rent dreams, anyway. One of the station's advertisers was Bed, Bath and Beyond, and a few years ago we'd been allowed to go there and get a few things at cost. My motif was Tasteful Cream. I'd been able to get a caramel cream area rug, taupy cream drapes, ivory cream sheets and vanilla cream throw pillows.

"Because if you don't call him," Karen said, "you'll always wonder."

"No I won't."

"Kate, this is me, remember? The woman who is eleven minutes older than you, who looks just like you and who shared a room with you for eighteen years. Yes, you'll wonder. And you'll stew. And it will just be easier on both of us if you call him. Come on. *'I'm dying, I'm rich, I've got an interesting proposition.'* What do you think it will be?"

"Probably a receptionist job at some business he owns."

"No, it will be more than that."

"Yeah, right. A receptionist job *and* dental…"

"No," she sighed from her place two miles to the south. "I mean it. How can you not call? You're trained as a reporter. You can't stand unanswered questions."

"I can if the answers are being provided by Richard."

But Karen was right. It took me a few more days to decide, but I woke up one morning and I just knew. "Okay, Mr. Richard Farley," I said as I stripped for my shower. "You're dying, you're rich, and you've got some kind of offer to make me. Fine. I'll call you. Collect."

3

Chapter Three

"Who may I say is calling, please?"

So many choices, so little time... "His first wife?" "The mother of his son?" "The woman he stiffed in Chicago?"

In the end I went the dignified route and said, "Kate Lerner." It was the same reason I decided not to call collect—too small-minded. And even if I wasn't above *being* small-minded, the least I could do was *act* as if I was.

God knows I *was* acting absentmindedly. All morning during the show, I kept cutting people off before their calls were finished. I'd punch them out on the call board before we'd said a proper goodbye. At one point David turned to me during a news break and asked, "Want me to take over the board, Kate?"

We work in a tiny glassed-in studio that faces Michigan Avenue—South Michigan Avenue, not the fancy part. It's a bit like being a monkey at the zoo. So whether you're scratching your belly or guzzling some water, it's completely viewable from the street. And I really didn't feel like getting up and switching places with David in front of the few people who happened to be looking into our window. "No, thanks." I smiled at him.

David had on a shirt and tie which was not his usual look. I wondered if he had a lunch date. Not that he seemed to be much of a dater. In the ten months he'd been at the station, he hadn't shown up at any station functions with a woman in tow. He had told me he was working on an idea for a novel, so maybe that was taking up the bulk of his free time.

"I'm sorry, David, I'm just feeling real distracted. I've decided to call my ex-husband when I get home today. Neither of the kids will be back until dinner, so at least they won't see me lose it in the event his proposition is completely off the wall."

Not only was I glad the kids weren't going to see me right *after* I spoke to Richard, I was also glad they didn't see me right *before* I placed the call. Because seconds before I went upstairs to phone him, I found myself at the bathroom mirror combing my hair and putting on lipstick. For a phone call. There was no explanation for this. It was just another version of the Divorce Court Cosmetics phenom. I'd noticed this bizarre practice the day Tim and I were legally split. Before a woman walks out of the ladies' room in the divorce court building, she inevitably combs her hair, puts on more blush, so she can look good for the guy she doesn't want to be married to anymore. Making up for breaking up, as it were. Of course at least those guys they are making up for are right there on the premises. Not three thousand miles away.

Nonetheless, there I was—lips perfectly glossed, perched cross-legged on my creamy white bed, waiting to hear the voice of a man I hadn't spoken to in fifteen years.

"Kate." No hello, no nervous clearing of the throat—just a simple declarative one-syllable sentence.

"Yes?" I couldn't bring myself to quite say his name.

"Thanks for returning the call."

"I'm not *returning* it. You asked me to *make* it."

"Well, I suppose that's right." He cleared his throat. "I'm sure you were rather surprised to get my letter. And needless to say, I—"

"Richard," I plunged in, "this is making me really nervous. I don't know if I can stay on the phone too long without throwing up or something. Do you think you could just tell me what you need to tell me."

"For chrissakes, Kate, cut me some slack here. This isn't easy for me either."

"I know." I swallowed, "Uh, listen, I'm sorry you're dying." Not my finest Emily Post moment.

"Yeah, well, this kind of cancer does that to you."

"What kind?"

"A blood kind. You wouldn't have heard of it. It's extremely rare. I'm in an experimental program that ostensibly buys me some time."

"A blood kind? Do I have to worry about this for Danny?"

"Not according to my specialist. I asked. It's rare and it's random. Listen, Kate, I have something I want to propose to you, and I can come down to Chicago any day in the next two weeks that would work for you to talk about it."

"Come down to Chicago?" My hands began shaking, my mouth went dry. The bedroom window was open and I could see that there was a whole glorious world out there full of trees, and kids, and dogs, and bikes, but for the moment it felt as if the bulk of the tangible world was stuck in my throat. I carried the phone into my bathroom so I could get a glass of water. "Richard, we don't have to *see* each other. That's why Mr. Bell invented telephones. So people could talk and not ever have to be in the same room. It's perfect for a situation like ours."

"Kate, what I'm going to propose to you is big. People don't make offers this big over the phone. They sit and face each other like two adults."

"Facing each other like two adults hasn't exactly been your forte for fifteen years, has it?"

"Look, if you need to get your shots in, get them in. But I don't have a lot of time to waste. You know my time line. If you don't want to hear what I have to say, okay. If you want to hear it, I will come down and present it to you, live and in color in the next two weeks. You just name the day."

I don't know who took possession of my body at that moment. I don't know what her motives were, or where she came from. All I know is that within one millisecond I answered, "Next Tuesday."

"Fine, I'll meet you at six o'clock for dinner. I know that's early, but it's the latest I can meet you because I'm going to have to make the last plane out at 8:15 and…let me check my airline schedule book…it looks like I can get into Chicago by 4:30 that afternoon from L.A."

"L.A.? You're a busy man."

"Yeah. Leave a message at this number when you decide where I should meet you, okay?"

"Fine. Uh, Richard, it's been a lot of years. Am I going to know you?"

"I imagine. I didn't make the cut for the witness protection program. I'm just about the same. What about you?"

"The same—Catherine Zeta-Jones with a zippy personality."
He laughed. God, why on earth was I trying to amuse this man?

Via Emilia was a small, unpretentious restaurant in Lincoln
Park. High ceilings, lots of light, great art. I'd asked for a booth—
which I never do since the backs of the banquettes always hit me
wrong—just because I didn't want to be in the middle of a room
when I heard Richard's proposal and have people all around me
watch me explode, or burst into tears, or push my chair back in
a rage and stalk out. This way, if he suggested something horrible,
I could decorously slide right out of the booth and disappear.

Of course, when it came to what he might propose, I'd run
a trillion scenarios through my head....

He wanted to take Danny out of school, bring him up to Canada, and bond with him for six months. But then, Richard hadn't
even asked about Danny on the phone. And why would he think
Danny would want him back in his life after all these years, particularly if death was going to yank him out of his life again a few
months later? Plus, I had no idea if Richard had a whole bunch
of other kids from any subsequent marriages. And if he did have
kids, why would he risk getting them all bent out of shape right
before he died, by bringing a half brother into their lives?

Then I thought maybe he wanted to start a trust fund for Danny, and just needed to meet with me to iron out the details. Boy,
that would solve a lot of problems. But the likelihood of that happening struck me as slim to none. I just didn't see a selfish, immoral man like Richard being transformed by imminent death
into Mr. Generosity. That happened in books and movies, but in
real life, the one where it gets confirmed over and over that people basically never change, it didn't seem even close to probable.

Then I wondered if Richard's "interesting proposition" might be strictly business. After all, business must have been one of the things that Richard found interesting or he wouldn't have made all that money. Whatever business it was, maybe he wanted to offer Danny and/or me some sort of percentage. But then the second family question inserted itself. How could he offer us something like that, without blowing possible family number two completely out of the water?

For every scenario I crafted, there was always a *yeah, but.*

Not to mention the *yeah, but* at Via Emilia. Richard was supposed to be there at six. *Yeah, but* he wasn't. He was twenty minutes late.

"*Señora,* perhaps while you are waiting you want to order a little wine and antipasto?" asked the portly waiter, clearly concerned that the *señora* might be in the process of being stood up. I smiled as much as I could for a woman who hadn't slept the night before, whose stomach was churning, and who that afternoon had gone to Filenes and spent fifty-eight dollars that she didn't have on a stunning, impress-the-ex-husband beige linen blazer.

"Sure," I said, "a chianti and an order of bruschetta."

"*Benissimo,*" he said, clearly pleased that at least if I was stood up, it looked like I'd at least stick around and drink so he could eke out some sort of tip.

The twenty minutes late thing kind of scared me. For starters, with the notable exception of missing Danny's birth, Richard had always been an extremely prompt person. It was also troubling because the very thought of this man actually being a no-show once again in my life was a potential bloodboiler. But even without the Richard part, mostly I was troubled because I am terrible at sitting alone at restaurants. Some people pull it off with great nonchalance, some even with grace. Me, I sit by myself and if someone doesn't show up within three minutes, I feel as if there is a huge marquee over my head. It has an arrow pointing down to me and in big red letters it flashes PATHETIC. PATHETIC. PATHETIC.

Over the years, of course, I've learned to carry a magazine with me so I can sit and read if the person I'm meeting is late, or if I've forgotten to do that, I succumb to this pitiful maneuver with my checkbook. I bring it out and I act as if I finally have time in my extremely busy and important life to catch up on the annoying details of checkbook balancing, or, and this is particularly desperate, I tear off a piece of paper from the checkbook and act like I am writing down very profound, very crucial, deep thoughts. Sort of a Kate as Proust thing. It's pretentious, but it gets me through the moment.

By the time six-thirty rolled around, I'd exhausted all my checkbook moves. The restaurant was beginning to fill up with people heading to the theaters in the area, insuring that if and when Richard ever did get there, we'd have a nice din as background to our incredibly awkward meeting. At one point, two thirty-ish blondes across from me were laughing hysterically over some photos one of them brought and, in handing them back, the other one knocked a glass of wine over the table. My waiter went scurrying over, mopped it up and then returned to my table, handing me a phone. "*Señora,* it's for you."

It had to be Richard. Sarah Rose and Danny were with Tim, and impatient as Karen was to find out what Richard's proposition was, I knew she wouldn't call me at the restaurant.

"Kate, there's been a mix-up."

"Where are you?"

"At a restaurant called Via Emilio on Lincoln Avenue, about two miles north of you."

It was unbelievable. I'd left him a message to come to Via Emilia on Lincoln Avenue. Right street. Wrong vowel. He'd apparently figured it out first.

"Oh, God, no. Can you hop a cab down here?"

"No, not really. There isn't time. If I come down to you or you come up to me, it'll give us only about eight minutes to talk because I have to leave for the airport at seven."

"So now what do we do?"

"I think we do it the way you originally wanted to do it—on the phone."

All I could think of was the fifty-eight dollars I'd spent on the blazer. That, and the fact that I think people who talk on cell phones in restaurants are completely despicable.

"Richard, if we have to do this on the phone, let's wait so we aren't like some split-screen scene in a movie with all these people in both restaurants watching. Can we do it tomorrow when you get back?"

"No. Tomorrow I'm going on a four-day family camping trip."

He'd said it. He'd said "family." It sucked the air out of my lungs.

"Kate, let's just do this now. I'll sit at my table, where I've been waiting for you, and you sit at your table, where you've been waiting for me, and we'll have this conversation. It's the best we can do."

That's exactly what happened. I ordered a bowl of pasta and another glass of wine in my restaurant. And Richard, sitting at his table two miles to the north, ate his dinner and drank his wine in his restaurant.

"Kate," he opened, "what I'm about to offer you is not out of guilt, though I'm sure you think I should be racked with it. It's more out of, Christ, I don't know, some need to die with as many of my problems resolved as possible."

"Problems? Is that the category Danny and I fall into for you?" I asked cupping my hand on the phone to avoid being overheard. "I thought we'd done a pretty good job of not being a problem for you, Richard. No support checks demanded. No visitations required. No nagging former wife coming up there after you with a cop in tow. I thought we were pretty well-behaved all these years. Or are you saying your conscience bothered you?"

"Listen, you know me well enough to know that I operate with a rather convenient disconnect from the traditional definition of conscience. I'm not proud of that, but I can acknowledge it. No, it's different from a conscience. For me, our split-up has always felt problematic, unresolved. Frankly, when you kicked me out, I did not want to leave you. I still loved you. I think if I hadn't still had feelings for you, I wouldn't have pulled the stupid stunt I pulled and disappeared."

I took a long sip of wine. "Excuse me? Let me get this right. You still *loved* me so that's why you slept with the hair spray woman, and when we divorced, that's why you disappeared on us and never sent us a cent? Does that mean if you hadn't loved me, then you'd have been faithful? And you'd have stuck around, and supported and been a father to Danny? Who, by the way, you haven't asked a single question about."

The waiter set down a bowl of steaming pasta. But it wasn't steaming nearly as much as I was, listening to Richard's convoluted logic.

"Christ, Kate. Of course I have questions. But how much I ask about Danny, and how much you answer, probably depends considerably on your response to my proposal."

"Well, why don't you just put it out there and then we can get this over with," I said, plunging my fork into the spaghetti and twirling it into a tomato-slicked spiral. Not that I was exactly capable of eating it. Especially after I heard what Richard had to say.

"Okay. Here it is," he proceeded. "I owe you a shitload of money—fifteen years of back child support and five years of spousal support is a pretty substantial chunk of change. Particularly if you factor in interest."

I didn't say a word. I just kept twirling my uneaten pasta.

"So I want you to go and figure that out—the full amount I owe you, including the compounded interest. Sit down with a calculator and come up with the figure. I'll give it to you."

I was stunned. "Give it to me? In one lump sum, just like that?"

"In one lump sum, just like that."

"Amazing," I said, shaking my head. "I just have to tell you the amount and you give it to me? That's it?"

"That's almost it. There's something else you have to do."

Here it was. Here was the big catch. I wondered if he wanted me to kill someone for him, or steal documents for him, or what the...

"I want you to come to Rome with me for a week."

This was not happening. This was some sort of twisted-up, dying guy, bad, bad joke.

"I'm serious, Kate. I will give you all the money I owe you, plus...a seven-hundred-and-fifty-thousand-dollar signing bonus, if you will come to Italy with me for one week."

My insides disappeared.

"You always wanted to go there and I always promised I'd take you. Have you been there yet?"

The restaurant was swirling around me. I held on to the edge of the table with my free hand while the other held the phone and I whispered into it, "No, Richard, I haven't. I've been kind of busy raising a son and a daughter and working a couple of jobs."

"Right. But will you come to Italy with me?"

"No. Of course not. I can't go on a trip with you. Why would you even think that?"

"Why not?"

I drained my wineglass. "Two reasons—I don't much like you and you have a wife."

"Where did you come up with that?"

"You just said you were going on a 'family' camping trip."

"The 'family' is my brother-in-law and his two kids. I haven't been married to my wife for seven years. But I'm still involved with her brother. Mostly because he needs me. I'm the one who built up the family business, and neither he nor my ex-wife has any interest in running it. They just want their checks."

"Oh."

"Anyway, that's the 'family.' There's no wife involved. And I've checked up on you. I happen to know there's no current husband."

"Checked up? God, Richard, you are creeping me out. This whole thing is—it's too decadent. Too scary."

"I'm sorry you feel that way. Because it is a real offer, Kate. I am dead—no pun intended—serious. Listen, I have to grab a cab and get out to the airport. But you can call me with your answer when…"

"No."

"No you won't call me?"

"No. The answer is *no*."

"Don't answer yet, Kate. Do the numbers. Roll it around a little in that complex mind of yours. Ask yourself all the questions you'll need to ask yourself. Ask me any others."

"No, it's just too perverse and too dark to think about."

"I can't hear you. The battery must be gone. I'll call you when I get back." Then all I heard was *click*.

"Another glass of wine, *señora*," the waiter asked as he came by to pick up the phone.

Another glass of wine? You betcha.

4

Chapter Four

I couldn't drink the wine. I was too rattled. So instead, I paid my bill, and decided to walk over to Karen's house which was just fifteen minutes west of the restaurant.

The house was the entirety of her divorce settlement from Bradley Aaron, her attractive, boring, fool-around husband of eight years. Bradley was a wheeler-dealer—and none of us were ever sure that the deals he wheeled were all that kosher. But Karen had fallen hard for him right out of college, even though he told her up front he didn't think he was a daddy kind of a guy. Karen had a bit of trouble with that and, like all new brides, she'd made the classic erroneous assumption that she could change him. When it became clear that Bradley had no intention of becoming even moderately paternal, she switched tactics. She began to appeal to him on the basis of his vanity—a rather vast zone—by telling him that all his gorgeous genes were going to waste. A generous statement considering that

Brad was not gorgeous. At best he looked no better than a mail-order version of Tom Hanks.

Their former marital residence, however, *was* gorgeous, or at least it would be if and when Karen ever fixed it up. It was a small vintage home that had a sweet turn-of-the-century parlor, with the original marble fireplace and worn, but lovely herringbone wood floors. Karen ran her meeting-planning business from that room and her dining room, and mainly lived out of the three rooms upstairs. I always thought she should have lived down there and run the business from upstairs, since all that historical good taste always looked so out of synch with the fax machines and computers and file cabinets that filled it. The one piece of period-appropriate furniture in the parlor was a huge oak desk that had belonged to our great-grandfather. That was precisely where I found her when I let myself in.

"Didn't you hear me ringing?" I asked.

"No," she said, taking off her headset. "I was listening to a tape of a speaker for this meeting I'm doing next winter. The client is really cheap though, so finding a keynote person has been a nightmare. To get anybody decent I may have to give up part of my fee."

"Don't do that, Karen. You can't afford it." Karen, too, struggled with money. She always had. But after being an aspiring actress, a photographer's rep and a caterer's assistant, she has finally found something she excels at. Her business is only three years old, but she's clearly a natural at it. She just needs to build her client list.

"So what happened?" she asked, coming around from the back of the desk, looping her arm through mine and taking me to the one uncluttered zone in the room, an old tweed couch from our parents' den.

I collapsed down on it. "I feel like I've spent the last hour in a subdivision of the *Twilight Zone*."

"I don't believe this," she gasped when I recounted the evening and then tried to describe the indescribable finale of Richard suggesting we take off for Italy. "What did you say?"

"I said no, of course. But he acted like he didn't hear me."

"No? Didn't you even think about it? Aren't you going to?"

"Are you kidding, Karen? This is demented! A man I can't stand offers me money—money he already owes me—plus a whole lot more money, to go off with him for a week! It's obscene."

"Well, so what? It's not like you've never slept with him."

"Slept with him? Oh, my God, Karen. I hardly think he's expecting me to sleep with him. That would be like a bad movie."

"Actually, it would be like a pretty good movie," she said, getting up to go to the office fridge for a Coke. "Remember *Indecent Proposal*? I just saw it on TV last night."

"Of course I remember *Indecent Proposal*," I snapped. "That was a completely different situation. It was a total *stranger* who asked the woman to sleep with him. She didn't even know him. I *know* Richard. I've spent the past fifteen years *detesting* Richard. Sleeping with a stranger has to be a whole lot easier than sleeping with someone you *hate*. A stranger doesn't count. Someone you hate is repugnant."

"Excuse me?" she singsonged. "Are you the same Kate Lerner who used to call me of a morning to tell me that Richard was a positively despicable human being? Only to call me the following morning sounding like a kitten who had spent the night bathing in half-and-half? God, Kate, you slept with Richard plenty of times when you thought you hated him. In fact you even said that you sometimes thought the two of you used rage just as an excuse to bring up the boiling point of your sex lives. Remember?"

"Maybe we did, I don't remember. But I do know there's a difference between *thinking* you hate someone and *knowing* you do. And now I—"

"Oh, come on, Kate! You told me as recently as a year ago, when we drank that incredible bottle of champagne Mom sent us for our birthday that the most incredible sex of your life had been with Richard. And you almost sounded nostalgic when you said it."

"How do you remember how I sounded? We were drunk."

"Well you can fight with me all you want about this, I still think this is something of an *Indecent Proposal* kind of moment."

"Oh for Pete's sake, Karen. The man the girl had to sleep with in *Indecent Proposal* was Robert Redford! Big decision. Like someone is going to say 'no' to Robert Redford? There isn't a woman in the world who wouldn't do it for free with Robert Redford! He doesn't even have to throw in the million dollars. No, this is *not* the same at all. This is warped and horrible, and I hate that Richard even reentered my life for two phone calls to put it in front of me. It makes me feel slimy just having heard it."

"Are you finished?" Karen asked, calmly and maybe a bit more solicitously than I liked. "Because I understand where you are coming from. I also understand that if you could just momentarily step down from the moral high ground that you're standing on, and stand back to take a look at some of the ramifications of Richard's offer, it might be a smart thing to do."

"A smart thing to do? Are you crazy?"

"No, a smart thing to just *consider* going."

"Karen, I think I'm going to throw up. I can't believe you are sitting there calmly, suggesting that I go off for a week with a man I detest, and then take a huge check for it. I mean what does that make me?"

"Maybe stupid. Maybe unethical. Maybe a good business-woman. I don't know what it makes you. But I hate to think that you're not even going to consider it. Take a look at what it could mean to you and the kids financially."

I started to cry. I don't know why, but the whole evening had been so jarring that I just had to cry. Karen put her arms around me and began to push my hair back so it didn't get all soaked with my stupid tears and gave me a few minutes to simply let it all out.

Then, after bringing me a Kleenex, and handing me a glass of ice water, she again sat next to me, took my hands in hers, and said, "Just hear me out. Let's just think out loud for a minute, okay?"

"Okay." I sniffed like some horribly clogged person in a Ny-Quil commercial.

"For starters, you do not have a whole lot of insurance money left for all the operations Sarah is still going to need, right?"

"Right..."

"What are the exact numbers, Kate? I know you're always worried about them. How much of your policy on Sarah has already been used up?"

"About two thirds on a two million dollar policy," I said softly, hating to face the figures.

"And how many more operations does Sarah have to go?"

"About five more," I said even more softly, hating to think of Sarah's ordeal.

"And since you're not poor enough to go on Medicaid, doesn't that mean at some point you and Tim will have huge out-of-pocket expenses for Sarah once her insurance tops out?"

"Yes."

"And haven't you told me that it isn't just the money for Sarah's operations now? That because of all these grafts and being in these burn studies, that as an adult she may never get decent, reasonably priced health insurance? That it's likely to be exorbitantly priced or possibly even not available to her?"

"Yes," I said, looking down at my hands, which she still was holding on to.

"So Sarah's being set to handle all her lifetime medical bills strikes me as one pretty good reason to consider—just consider, Kate—Richard's offer. Not that there aren't other reasons. Your house is falling apart, your editing work has been giving you horrible headaches and you have not put a whole bunch of money away for Danny's college education, right?"

"Right. But I'm hoping he'll win a scholarship to art school. Otherwise, he'll just have to take on some loans. It won't kill him."

"It won't be easy for him to pay them off either if he's planning to make his living as an artist."

"I know. It won't be easy. But Danny's a resourceful kid. He'll figure it out."

"I hope so, hon, you know I do," she said, letting go of my hands and pushing back her thick coppery curls. "But even so, in addition to Sarah and the house and the headaches and college, there's another reason you might want to seriously consider Richard's offer."

"What's that?"

"You. And your future. Right now you're currently earning your living in a very unstable business. So far you've been lucky—your little station hasn't gone Christian, or motivational, or Spanish. But you know damn well a station like yours can be swallowed up in a nanosecond by a conglomerate and forced to change formats, and then what? Half the stations in Chicago only want people who play music and do fart jokes between songs, the other half is all sports or all black, and unless you've got a secret side that I don't know about, you don't fit in any of those categories."

I didn't say anything.

"Kate, pay attention. Listen to me. The kind of money Richard is talking about could mean a vast and really important difference to you and your kids."

"Karen, you're really scaring me with this. You're sounding as if you think this is a viable concept. It's not."

"It could be viable, Kate."

"Sure, it could be. If I got a lobotomy or something."

"Oh, hon," she said cupping my chin in her hand. "I just know you need to think about it. That's all, Kate. Just think about it."

"There's nothing to think about. I hate Richard."

"Fine, then don't think about Richard. Think about yourself. Think about the life you could have, where you weren't working two jobs, and weren't angsting over how to get Danny through college, and Sarah through all the upcoming surgeries, and your furnace through the next winter.... I don't know, Kate, think about a life that felt a little bit less uphill than the one you have now. Okay?"

* * *

My bedroom was never dark enough. Even at night the light from the streetlamps filtered through my shutters. The phone rang. Once. Twice. I nearly knocked it off the nightstand reaching for it.

"Are you sleeping?" asked Karen.

"That depends what time it is. What time is it?" I mumbled.

"It's 5:30 in the morning. I figured you had a crummy night anyway."

"I had *no* night anyway," I said looking at the early morning version of the room I'd paced for three hours in the dark of night. I must have walked miles.

Slivers of daylight bordered my window shade, reminding me I was going to have to go to work and act normal only twelve hours after participating in one of the more abnormal evenings of my life. An evening in which my ex-husband made me a pretty perverse proposition and then my twin sister spent two hours more or less urging me to seriously consider it.

I'd never felt further from Karen than I did during that conversation. We were in such different places. So different, it was almost painful.

Like most identical twins, Karen and I had been inordinately interwoven with each other our whole lives. And while we weren't quirky enough to develop our own secret language when we were little, the way some twins do, we weren't interested in playing with other kids until we started kindergarten. Nonetheless, from the very beginning, our parents didn't want us to perceive each other as mirror images of ourselves. So they always made sure we didn't dress alike, wear our hair alike or get the same model bikes and roller skates.

It was a healthy move. To this day, Karen and I still get the heebie-jeebies whenever we see a pair of women, especially older women, in the same little outfit, with the same little 'do, toddling along together in duplicate geriatric cuteness. Last summer Karen used to see one set of twins all the time when she biked along the lake in the early morning. Almost seventy, they were in the same shorts, same T-shirts and they even had the same kind of dog. But the kicker was the day she called me and said, "You won't believe it. Today when I passed them they were in the water—synchronized swimming!"

"Karen," I said, staggering out of bed with the phone still in my hand, "let me call you back in five minutes. My brain is shut down right now, but if I can get some coffee in me I should be able to talk."

"Great. I've had an incredible idea about Richard's offer."

"This isn't going to be a repeat of last night is it? Because I don't want to have that conversation again."

"This definitely is not a repeat. Actually, I think this is a solution."

"What do you mean, a solution?"

"Call me."

I didn't call back for fifteen minutes. First I put up a pot of Café Du Monde coffee that David had brought me when he came back from New Orleans, and then I stepped into a steaming hot shower for ten minutes to cleanse my body, soul and brain cells. Wrapping myself in my old white terry cloth robe, I grabbed my coffee, and stepped out onto the back stoop to survey my early June garden. The iris was in bloom as was the columbine and the beginnings of my ligularia. Every year I messed with the placement of these, digging them up and trying to find a better home for them in the yard so they could finally live up to their full potential and just out and out flourish.

The morning was a lot more glorious than I was. I looked better than haggard, but I still looked like hell. Plopping down on the top porch step, I began to towel dry my hair. Normally I do the upside-down blow-drying thing, but even a good hair day was not going to help me look presentable on this morning. When it was nearly dry I went in to bring out the portable phone and call Karen.

"You said five minutes. I wondered if you'd fallen back asleep."

"I may never sleep again," I said melodramatically

"Yes you will. Especially when you hear my solution."

"Karen. There is no *solution*. The only *solution* is a loud and clear 'no.' We both know that."

"We don't know anything like that. At least I don't. I think there's a way to deal with Richard's proposition that is really and truly smart. Will you listen at least?"

"Sure," I said, taking a huge breath and steeling myself for what she was going to say. The breath I took wasn't huge enough.

"*I'll* go to Italy with Richard."

No noise came out of my throat.

"I'm serious, Kate. I think this is a perfect way to do this. Listen, you deserve this pile of money he's offering. It's so much money. It could change the lives of everyone in your family. You know that's true."

"What do you mean, *you'll* go to Italy?" I said, setting down my coffee mug because my hand was shaking too hard to balance it.

"I mean I'll do that thing they always do in the soap operas that always seems so implausible. I'll pretend I'm you. Richard hasn't seen either of us in fifteen years. So he has no idea what we look like. Even if I weighed fifteen pounds more than you right now, he'd have no way of telling us apart. We don't have any major birthmarks or anything. And he has no idea that you nearly sliced your thumb off five years ago either. So my not having that big scar you have won't be an issue at all."

"Karen, this is really crazy."

"No, it's not. Just listen. I've thought of everything. Like all the memories the two of you might have together. Not that Richard strikes me as a major 'remember when' kind of a guy, but I remember tons of your stories about him, and anything he tosses my way that I don't remember from you, I'll just say is because of all the time that's gone by."

"You're terrifying me. It's like you've been possessed by some cheesy Hollywood producer. Karen, this is real life. You're talking about real people. You're talking about impersonating me and spending a week with someone you don't much like either!"

"Yeah, but I don't hate him like you do. And putting his ethics aside, which is pretty easy since he never had any, I always thought Richard had a really interesting mind. I wouldn't hate spending a week with him if it was going to net you over a million dollars. And you're probably right, I don't think he's going to be interested in sex at all. The guy is sick, Kate. I doubt very seriously that lust is anywhere on his radar screen right about now. And even if it is, I'm a big girl. I can talk him out of it. Listen, I'm looking at this as something that could be incredibly fun."

"Fun?"

"Absolutely. This gives us such a sweet piece of power over Richard. I mean here he is, masterminding this scheme, pulling people's strings, being the same controlling son of a bitch he always was, except for one thing. We're nailing him. He isn't get-ting to leverage you one more time at all. It's all so win-win. He thinks he's the boss. We know we're the boss. He gets what he wants. You get the money without giving him what he wants. And I get to go to Italy. So, Kate? What do you think?"

5

Chapter Five

There is no way to have a decent day, when your day begins with a question like that.

But given that that was how *my* day started, it was just real hard to march along like a regular working mom with three hours of radio, two kids, one dentist appointment and a five o'clock parent-teacher conference over at the high school.

Which happened to be the way my day looked on paper. The conference was scheduled two days before when Danny's English teacher called and said it was time for "a little chat." It didn't sound like it was going to be lovely. Finals were two weeks away and according to Ms. Henry, Danny was about six weeks behind on his assignments. I think this was her 9-1-1 call to let me know how close my kid was to having his very own junior year redux.

Karen made me promise not to decide anything for five days. "Just don't dismiss my idea out of hand," she said before hanging up. "When we're down in Florida for Mom's birthday this weekend, we'll take a long walk on the beach and then you can tell me your decision."

"With Mom there? Are you kidding?"

"No. Not with Mom there," she laughed, as aware as I was that Muriel the Mah-jongg Queen was hardly the kind of gal who'd want to ponder the ethical quandary I was wrestling with. For Muriel, paper or plastic was about all she wanted to decide in any given day. The woman *loved* being retired. She wanted no stress in her life. Life with Daddy had done her in, and when he had his massive heart attack and died on the golf course six years ago, she'd grieved, and then she'd packed up his white shoes and bad outfits and had decided that the rest of her life was going to be happy, happy, happy all the time. She took off all the plastic covers Daddy always insisted be kept on the furniture; she had herself a little glass of sherry every night; she left the radio on to lite music all day so she could sing and dance whenever she wanted (she'd always fancied herself quite the undiscovered showgirl); and she never let another jar of Daddy's ubiquitous pickled herring in the house again. Nope, our mom was doing just great and would not have appreciated in the least hearing about the potentially amoral plot her darling daughters were taking under advisement.

At least I was pretty sure it was amoral. I could have checked that out with my ex-husband the ethics professor, who made his living discussing the morality meter of different societies, but I decided not to run any of this by Tim. I knew that just because Tim was a philosopher didn't mean he could respond to this philosophically. He could only respond to all this personally. In fact, when he asked me if I'd ever called Richard back, I just answered, "Nope. I followed your advice and steered clear of the whole thing."

And with that, began the first of too many lies.

No matter what I decided to do, I wasn't going to have a squeaky-clean record on this one, because I'd already decided not to tell Tim the truth. If he'd heard Richard's proposition, not to mention Karen's counterproposal, he'd have gone off the deep end. Tim had been such a great co-detester of Richard for so many years and, in spite of my not being the vulnerable type, he still had all these residual damsel-protection instincts that I really didn't have the energy to deal with.

Especially after I came home from the cozy parent-teacher conference that Tim missed anyway because he was teaching a class. As expected, the news had not been good. Danny really was up the creek if he didn't get his act together pronto, and Ms. Henry made it clear that she felt nothing less than a serious dose of parental intervention would make that happen.

"The problem is—" I smiled at her across the battered wood desk in her classroom "—that I've always tried to be something of a laissez-faire parent."

"I understand," she said, tapping her little French manicure on the desktop and continually tossing back her expensively frosted hair. "But Danny is in serious trouble. He's not on top of his work at all. He seems totally distracted."

Of course he's distracted, I thought. He has a teacher who's about two hours older than he is, and looks like she could be Gwyneth Paltrow's understudy. When I went to school our teachers had kinky gray hair and wore print shirtwaist dresses with sensible shoes. The only beautiful teacher I remember having was in second grade. Miss Miltenburger. She lived in a rooming house at the end of our block and Karen and I used to sit on her front steps and wait for her to come home. Once she even sat down on the steps with us, and let us each hold one of her hands and peel away at her "Love That Red" nail polish. Today I'm sure that would be construed as some sort of deviant behavior, but for two girls with a huge crush on their teacher, it was a peak life experience—given that we'd only done seven years of life.

But Ms. Henry wasn't offering Danny any such personal thrills. "I just want him to catch up and then get his big final paper in," she said, getting up from the desk and crossing over to one of the huge windows to adjust the blinds so the late-afternoon sun didn't spill in. "Do you know if he's even started his research?"

The question made me feel like I belonged in Remedial Mom School. I truly had no clue that there was this big final paper. But I also was not about to admit that to the twenty-eight-year-old hair-tossing educator. I'd promised myself years ago that I was not going to micromanage every major assignment a child of mine got. I remember the exact moment I made the promise—Danny's fourth grade open house. Because when Mr. Klein told all the mommies and daddies crammed into those teensy-tiny desks that there would be a five-page paper on the Underground Railroad at the end of the year, a huge communal sweat broke out in the room. You could feel the parental panic start to mount. Hands flew up with questions from all the clammy-faced mommies and daddies:

"Should it be done on the computer?"

"Will it have to have bibliographies?"

"Are you going to require footnotes?" It became palpably clear who the real Civil War scholars would be.

So the only way I could respond to Ms. Henry's inquiry was to do a little maternal butt-covering. "I'm sure Danny's done some of the preliminary work." Then I went home to find out how big a lie I'd constructed.

* * *

Danny's room was not attractive. Not that one expected a seventeen-year-old male to be a proud advocate of Crate and Barrel sensibilities, but Danny's room was well below the already putrescent standards of his particular age group. I know this for a fact, because six months before, the *Tribune* had run a contest called "Chicago's Top Ten Teenage Bedroom Pits." Danny's friend Jamie had submitted a photo of Danny's room, and the sorry fact was that my firstborn came in third runner-up. For a brief moment I was actually insulted that Danny didn't come in first. My rationale being, if you're going to be the worst, be the best of the worst.

Now admittedly, I'm not exactly tidy, but I *am* always clean. In our house, no dish, or glass, or item of clothing ever remains longer than two hours on a floor or table without being washed, hung up or returned to its proper place. The same cannot be said for Danny's room. So in addition to week-old—possibly month-old—biodegradable food remnants, there are mungy socks and towels, ripped up magazines and papers, piles of fetid tennis shoes, CDs and tapes everywhere, and all this lurks under a sort of Christo-like draping of the room in purple and black tie-dyed sheeting. It is clearly not the room of a Hardy Boy.

So I didn't exactly have high hygiene expectations when I knocked on his semi-open bedroom door. If it was closed, he was in there alone. Partly open, meant someone was over—and for the last half year that meant Jamie. I'd never once found them on the bed together, or even on the futon together. But together they always were.

"Hi, you guys," I said as I walked in.

"Hey. How'd it go with Jennifer?" he asked, looking up from

the book bag contents he'd just dumped out. Jamie pushed some books off his futon in case I wanted to sit down next to her.

"Jennifer?"

"That's what we call Ms. Henry sometimes. Because that hair-tossing thing she always does seems so lame on a grown-up. It makes her like such a Jennifer, you know?"

I smiled. Maybe I wasn't going to have to deal with his evil twin today. But still, this was very dicey territory. "Listen, Danny, I really need to talk to you."

"I can leave now, Mrs. Lerner, if you'd rather talk to Danny alone," Jamie said.

"No, it's cool." He motioned to Jamie to stay where she was. "Anything you say to me, I'll be telling Jamie anyway. Just give me the Jennifer report."

"Well, honey, she asked me to start riding herd on you about all these late assignments. According to her, you are extremely close to repeating your junior year."

"That's bull," he said in a significantly less concerned fashion than I liked. "Worst-case scenario—and she knows it—is that I do summer school and make up the class. What kind of crap was she feeding you?" he asked grabbing one of his notebooks and starting to laconically draw a woman's head.

I watched his hands. They were so comfortable, so at peace having a pen or Magic Marker in them. It had always been that way. Danny had gone through more sixty-four crayon Crayola boxes in any given school year than any kid in history. When he was little, he not only made me elaborately colored birthday cards, but he'd make his own wrapping paper; he'd do signs so there would be a treasure hunt for the present; and one year he drew me a really stunning eight-foot garden mural so I could put it up in the office and always feel I had flowers...I couldn't vouch for his mind all the time, but for sure his hands were seldom idle.

"Honey, I don't want to get into an argument over whether it's going to come down to summer school or a repeated year, okay? You've never had an academic problem in your life. Now all of a sudden I'm getting an eleventh hour call from this woman. It was like going to a meeting about a kid I didn't know."

He stiffened when I said that, and went over to his desk to pop in a CD. I did not want to have this conversation with Nine Inch Nails in the background, but I figured, pick your battles, girl. It's his room. You're picking the subject, let him pick the soundtrack.

"Danny, listen. I'm concerned. I assume—I hope—you're concerned. She gave me a list of the assignments that you're missing," I said handing it to him. "Some of them are really short. I know that you can get all of them done in the next few days. She's giving you until Friday to do them, which is basically pretty decent of her. The only one that's really a problem I guess is this final paper thing. She said it counts for forty percent of your grade."

"Yeah, I know, but we've been really busy at the insurance company. They've asked me to put in extra hours and I just haven't gotten my head together for this. I'll get it done," he sighed and sat down on the floor looking off into some zone of abstract teen ennui. Meantime, Jamie had said nothing, nor moved a muscle.

"Well, have you started on it? What exactly is the assignment? Ms. Henry said it was something about an interview with a family member who could be alive or dead. I didn't exactly get it."

Danny wrapped his arms around his knees, and trying to

reign in his exasperation with me and my meddling, said, "We're supposed to interview someone from our family, as if it were some A&E *Biography* or something. So if they are alive, you interview them, and other people that know them. If you decide to do someone who is dead, then you pretend you're interviewing them, and either use real people or you can make up people who might have known them."

I went over to the CD player to minimize the decibel level a bit. "Really? That sounds like it could be kind of an intriguing project, whichever way you decide to go. Have you given any thought to who you're going to do? Grandma would be interesting. She could give you a trillion stories," I said, thinking how I'd *love* to hear Muriel on Muriel in a Danny-driven Q. and A.

"Yeah," he said, unwrapping a toothpick and sticking it in his mouth faux-thug style. "Actually I have. I've been thinking it might be really interesting to interview my dad."

Everything in life is timing.

"Your dad? So you mean you'd do a made-up Q. and A. with him?"

"I guess I have to make it up. Unless you've got his phone number."

This was getting a little surreal.

"Just kidding, Mom. Man! The look on your face when I said that! He still really pisses you off, huh?"

"Oh, Danny," I sighed, hoping my insides would steady long enough to do a solid reprise of the speech I'd been making for years. "You know how I feel about all that. How horrible it was to just have him disappear on us. And how even his mother wouldn't tell me where he went because she never approved of me and for some reason was not into the grandma thing. Not because of you, but because of the kind of woman she was. Which I suppose explains the kind of son she had. So yes, I was hugely ticked off. For a long time. But Tim changed that. And time changed that. And I don't know, it's almost like the whole sequence of events and feelings aren't that accessible anymore. For the most part it's like they're on an old computer I don't use, and I'm not all that interested in booting them up again. I don't see the upside."

He mulled that for a minute and then said, "Yeah? Not me. Sometimes I think I have really strong, almost violent feelings about this guy. They are nowhere near being on an old hard drive. I can connect with them in a second. I just don't talk about them."

"Come on, Danny, that's not exactly true," Jamie piped up for the first time. "You've been talking about them ever since I was telling you what I'm doing my paper on."

"And what's that, Jamie?" I asked, somewhat relieved that at least some of the time the two of them talked about schoolwork.

"Well you know I'm adopted, right, Ms. Lerner?"

"Mmm-hmm."

"Well, I decided to do an imaginary interview with my real mom. It's actually been kind of fun. Sort of freeing or something. Anyway, Danny and I were actually just running down the list of questions I would pretend to ask her."

"Do you mind if I ask you what they are?"

Jamie adjusted her position to sit cross-legged, and gave one of her rare smiles to Danny before saying, "I don't know, the usual, I guess, for anyone in my situation… 'Why did you give me away?' 'Do you regret it?' 'Do you ever think of me?' Stuff like that."

"And what about you, Danny? If you do this imaginary interview with your father, do you know what you would ask him?"

Danny crushed the Coke can he had been holding. "Yeah. The same ones as Jamie, I guess. Plus one more. I'd also ask him how the hell he sleeps at night."

I was stunned. In the whole seventeen years I'd known this human, I hadn't heard that kind of rancor on this particular subject. "Oh, honey," I said, reaching out to touch his shoulder, which he yanked away, "I spent years asking the same question over and over, wishing I could hear an answer. But then I realized there is no answer. No answer that would be satisfying. Because even if he's tossed and turned and been guilt-ridden the whole of these seventeen years, it doesn't change anything. He still walked off."

"True. But you know what? Doing this paper on him. It just makes me feel like I can kind of get back at him."

"Danny," Jamie said, shaking her head, "you never listen to me. It's over. You can't 'get back' at him."

"Yeah, I know. Not with a term paper anyway. But what about real life? If there was some real-life revenge? Man, that would really be excellent."

6

Chapter Six

No question—I was blown away by the newly fueled toxicity of Danny's feelings about Richard. For years he'd insisted that Richard was a nonissue for him. And while I didn't completely buy that, I was unprepared for the fervor of his outburst that afternoon in his room. I barely thought of anything else for the next two days while I got my clothes together for the weekend at Mom's and got the refrigerator stocked for Tim and the kids at home.

Tim said he'd move into my place for the weekend since Danny's work was done on the family computer in our kitchen and this was not the moment for him to be home alone—maybe doing his work, maybe not. It felt creepy to envision Danny hammering away at the kitchen table on his fake Q. and A. with Richard while Tim was doing dishes five feet away. Two guys in the same room separately and silently hating a guy that one of them had never met and the other one couldn't remember. Tim wishing the guy would drop off the face of the planet and Danny wishing the guy would show up on our porch so he could screw him over in the worst possible way. A way that Karen and I now actually had the means to accomplish.

This was getting a little scary. It was particularly scary when I finally kissed Danny and Sarah Rose goodbye at the door and realized that the next time I saw them, I'd have decided what I was going to do regarding Richard's and Karen's proposals.

Karen was not with me on the flight down to Miami. She'd gone to Atlanta Thursday to pitch Coca-Cola about some event, and the plan was to meet at the Miami airport and rent a car to Boca. Muriel didn't do airports. "They make me too nervous and all the directions are in Spanish," she said the last time we flew down.

"Mom, the directions are in English too." We laughed. "Right on top."

"I know, but it's like I have Spanish eyes. They go right to the Spanish and by the time I move up to the English, it's too late— I'm already past the sign. Take a cab or rent a car, darling. I'll be here at the door with a nice glass of sherry for you. Unless, of course, Mr. Right comes along. Then we'll put out the Do Not Disturb sign and you girls can just fend for yourselves."

This was a sample of what Karen and I called Boca Widow Humor. All the ladies there seemed to go in for it. The fundamentals of Boca Widow Humor were based on these three facts: 1) the ratio of vertical men to vertical women in Florida did not favor the girls; 2) given that fact, most of the girls feigned a supercharged geriatric horniness, even though their dearly departed husbands (including our dad, I bet) would have undoubtedly testified to the contrary; 3) while the widows claimed constantly that they yearned for one of these aforementioned vertical men, most of them really only wanted a person who could see well enough to drive them around at night.

When I went to the Hertz counter there was a message for me from Karen saying that she would be three hours late and that I should go on to Mom's without her. She'd take a cab later. It was four o'clock when I arrived at the turquoise and gold lobby of the Mara-Belle Condos. Muriel buzzed me up and, as good as her word, handed me a glass of some dreadful sherry.

"It's a little early for me, Mom," I said hugging her carefully so I wouldn't disturb her hair. For her entire adult life my mother has had a standing beauty parlor appointment on Fridays at ten. No matter where we lived—Cleveland when she and Daddy first married, Chicago after we were born and now Florida—Muriel has had her "standing." The current 'do was a fantastical helmet of vigilantly lacquered, thin, wispy hairs all dyed a defiantly nonexistent red.

"Do you like it?" she inquired coquettishly. "I just went from 'Golden Russet' to this. A little birthday present for myself."

"It's great, Mom," I said at the same time I saw that she'd dyed her eyebrows the same weird color.

She must have seen me staring, because she said a bit apologetically, "They didn't charge extra for the brows. They just said it made the look complete. What do you think?"

"It's very, uh…complete. And I'm very glad to see you." I hugged her a bit more and hated that she felt smaller and smaller to me every time I saw her. Muriel had always been slim, but when she and Dad had first moved here, she'd put on a bunch of weight the one year she'd worked for Avon. "It's the coffee and cakes with my customers that are killing me," she said. We think she is possibly the first and only Jewish Avon lady ever. We also think she did it because she got it mixed up with Mary Kay and what she really wanted was the pink Cadillac.

The two of us sat around for a couple of hours noshing on Triscuits and cheese, until Karen buzzed up from downstairs around seven. "We've already missed the early bird," Mom said going to the door to buzz Karen in, "but we should be able to get in for dinner almost anywhere without a wait, now that it's June."

After Karen went through the hugs and hair-commenting ritual with Mom, she came over to me, gave me a kiss and winked, "And how are *you* doing, hon?"

"Just great," I said fake-lightly.

"Later," she whispered. And I couldn't get the evening over with fast enough. Not that I don't love my mom; I'm crazy about her. But I really needed—particularly after the discussion with Danny this week—some time alone with Karen. It didn't come until eleven-thirty when Muriel went in to wrap her 'do in tissue and then "go to bed with"—her phrase not mine—Jay Leno.

Karen and I retreated to the guest bedroom and shut the door. We peeled off our clothes and plopped down in our underwear on our separate blue and white toile bedspreads. Muriel had been very big on blue and white in the eighties. We think she did it to torment Daddy, because he was a very tan corduroy sort of a man. But the second he died, she relegated all the blue and white to the guest room, and went back to neutrals and tans in her room. There are many ways to show a husband who is boss. Even a dead husband.

On top of each of our beds were three or four newspaper articles that Muriel had cut out in the past week. Muriel was an inveterate Clipper Mom. From the moment we were eight years old, she began cutting articles out of the paper and leaving them for us. No matter that we were now forty-three. No matter that Karen and I each read several papers a day. Nope, the two of us *still* received a packet or two every week filled with helpful little articles like "How to Protect Your 401K" and "Should You Sell Now?" Apparently Muriel is convinced not only that the *Sun-Times* and *Tribune* don't have viable business sections, but she's pretty darn sure that the *Palm Beach Jewish News* really does have the inside skinny on money management.

"So," said Karen, dropping her unread packet to the floor about two seconds after I did, "and how are you *really* doing?"

"I've been a wreck since your call Wednesday morning. And then that same afternoon I had this hugely troubling discussion with Danny...."

' "Tell me about it."

So while she got down on the white carpet to do her nightly hundred crunches I brought her up to speed.

"Amazing," she puffed, somewhere around crunch number eighty, when I told her about Danny's outburst over Richard. "Life is so weird."

"No kidding. At six in the morning you're presenting me with this nefarious scheme to completely dupe Richard and eleven hours later my only son is breathing white-hot fire about how someday he'd love to get revenge on the very same man."

"You didn't say anything to him did you?" she asked, finishing her last set of sit-ups and then lying prone for a minute to catch her breath.

"Of course not! I'm confused, not crazy. I don't want Danny to have even the slightest notion how potentially sordid all the grown-ups he's related to might be."

"What do you mean 'might be'? We haven't done anything."

"Oh, for Pete's sake, Karen, we haven't done anything, but look what we're *talking about* doing. We're talking about being paid to spend a week with someone, like some girl gigolo, and then duping that someone about who he's actually spending the week with, like some counterfeit girl gigolo—this is huge stuff."

"It is," she said more somberly, opening her cosmetic case and setting up the lotions and potions on the bathroom counter. Karen was significantly more into maintenance than I was. So far there wasn't much of a difference between us, but no doubt in ten years, she'd start to get the big payoff. I'll have the first neck crepes, and I'll have the first liver spots, and by the time we're seventy we'll look more like some creepy Dorian Gray tableau than like twins. People will say behind my back—"Oh my God, Kate looks like hell, but that Karen looks just fabulous." And the truth is, I won't care. Because for all these years, I'll have gotten to go to bed at least fifteen minutes earlier than Karen who has to go through the nightly ritual of her endless toilette.

"No, I'd never risk telling Danny. He is so righteous all the time," I said. "He thinks he wants revenge on Richard, but if you and I pulled this switch on Richard, and he found out, Danny would do a complete one-eighty. He has very stringent standards regarding what is, and what is not, proper behavior for a mom. Remember the pot incident?"

"No. What pot incident?" she said globbing some cream all over her face. "You don't smoke pot anymore."

"I know. I wasn't *smoking*. I was being asked about smoking. It was when Danny was in third grade. He came into the living room one night when Tim and I were reading, and said, 'Mom? Have you ever smoked pot?' And of course there I was, sitting next to the ethics professor—in addition to being a big believer at the time in full disclosure—and so I said, 'Yes, honey, I've smoked pot.'"

"Why don't I remember this story? What happened?"

"Danny threw a complete Rumplestiltskin temper tantrum, wailing about how incredibly stupid pot smoking was. In fact, I remember his exact words. He said, 'Mom, only two things could have happened, and they were both horrible. Either you'd have really hated pot, and felt sick, or you'd have really liked it, and been hooked.'"

"Jeez. Clarence Darrow would have been proud."

"Yeah," I said, going into the bathroom to get a glass of water, "but Clarence Darrow didn't have to live with the supercilious little twit for the next month. He barely spoke to me. It was a memorable lesson in the mom candor arena."

"So even though he's feeling for the first time ever that he wants to connect with his dad and confront his dad, you're definitely *not* telling him about his dad's whereabouts? Not to mention his dad's offer, or my counterproposal?" She wiped the glop off her face with a Kleenex.

"No way," I said, incredulous that she might even think that was an option. "Richard hasn't asked for, and does not deserve, access to Danny. There's too much potential hurt that Richard could still cause him. Such as dying on him, or just disappointing him along the way. Whatever feelings Danny seems to be wrestling with now, I honestly believe he will work through. For years he went along not terribly interested in the whereabouts of his dad, and now at seventeen, he's not only interested, but furious. I think that's appropriate, but it doesn't mean I have to produce the object of his nonaffections."

Karen thought about that for a minute, came around behind me while I stood in front of the bathroom mirror and gave me a huge hug around my shoulders. "I think you're right," she said. "I think turning Danny over to Richard would be reckless. Look at the two of us. We're both wary about dealing with him, and we're thirty years older than Danny. Which brings us to the big question. Are you still considering walking away from his whole proposition or is one of us going to Italy with him?"

The moment had arrived. "One of us is going to Italy with him."

"And who, may I ask is that?"

"I think you," I said, taking a big breath, and looking into the mirror at our comingled reflections. They really *were* remarkably interchangeable. "I can't believe I'm saying this, but I am going to take you up on your offer. Unless you've changed your mind."

"Are you kidding? Of course I haven't changed my mind. I'm completely serious," she said, taking my hands and turning me around so we faced each other. "Kate, this is a once in a lifetime opportunity for you."

"I know," I said softly, terrified that this really was on its way to becoming something real.

"Listen, this is an okay thing to do. We can get you rich, we can get me over to one of my favorite countries in the world, and I kind of hate to keep pointing this out, but we can get Mr. Farley royally nailed."

"I know, *I know,* I said taking one last look in the mirror at the woman I used to be. Or maybe it was the first look in the mirror at the woman I'd just become. Then I headed back into the guest room.

Karen followed me, and said, "Oh, I'm so glad we're going to be able to do this. What made you decide to say yes?"

"Everything you said," I answered softly. "The difference this will make for Sarah as she goes through life. The fact that she will never be a prisoner of her medical bills. She'll have enough to go through as an adolescent, and later as an adult with those scars, but this is something I can fix for her and that feels like a lot. The same with Danny. To be able to give him a life where he can give free rein to his passion for drawing. Obviously, it's not the same as having had a great dad around, but again, this is something I can do for him. You know how much Richard owes Danny?"

"No, how much?"

"Four hundred and thirty-eight thousand dollars!"

"You're joking!"

"I'm not. I'm not even figuring in the five years of alimony he owed me. I don't want that. But Richard owes Danny a half million dollars. And that's what he's going to get. Sarah Rose gets the rest of the money."

"And what about you?"

"What about me?"

"Aren't you going to use any of the money for you? For your future?"

"My future will be fine if theirs is okay. I'm not saying I'm going to put you through this so I can walk around in rags, but I really don't see this as being about me. I can earn a living. And if I get fired one day, I'll figure it out."

"Oh, Kate, for Pete's sake," Karen said slamming her hand down on the bed. "Do you think a person needs to be destitute to consider accepting a windfall like this? Or maybe it would be more justified if you had a tragic disease and this money was the only thing that could buy you the miracle cure down in Mexico? Come on! You're entitled not to be financially stretched! You're entitled to give your kids some kind of break! And you certainly are entitled to even take some of that money for yourself. To have some sort of financial backup to do whatever you want to do with your life in case at some point you get sick of being Ms. Congeniality in front of a microphone every day. Don't you ever think about that? About what you might want to do next?"

"Sure I do." I turned toward her and propped my head on my hand.

"What is it?" Karen stretched out and propped her head up in her hand, too.

"Well," I said, smiling, because I knew this sounded a bit weird, "I think it has to do with flowers and solitude and mornings. I mean, obviously it's ten years away if it has to do with solitude, since Sarah is only seven. But I can envision the whole thing."

"What's it like?"

"I see myself on some porch steps, drinking coffee, early in the morning, and looking out over the mountains. I don't have neighbors, I'm all alone and gloriously happy to be that way. And somewhere in there, I think I have my own nursery."

"And that's it?"

"No, I'm wearing a plaid flannel shirt. When I think of the next thing in my life, it always involves plaid shirts."

"Coffee, mornings and plaid shirts—it sounds like a Folger's commercial."

"A Folger's commercial with greenhouses."

She laughed. "That's so great! I'm going off to Italy for a week with your ex-husband under an assumed name so you can wind up in a Folger's commercial with greenhouses? I love it!"

"You do?"

"I honestly do. It makes me happy to hear you talk like that," she said planting a kiss on my forehead.

"I'm glad. But what about you?"

"What about my next thing? I'm just getting good at this one."

"No, not your next thing. What do you get out of all this? You can't think I'm going to let you do this—impersonate me for a week with a man we both do not like one bit, if you're not going to let me share some of this with you. Tell me what you want."

"Kate, I'm not doing this for a cut of the money. You know that."

"Of course I do, but still…I want to be able to *do* something for you. It's important. You have to let me."

"Fine," she said, standing up and pulling her cheeks way back with her hands. "You can buy me my first face-lift."

"Don't start with me," I laughed, even though I was creeped out by her Norma Desmond look.

"Fine, I won't start with you. Except on the details of our little scheme here. Let's start talking specifics," she said, grabbing her Filofax from her bag and then opening it to a fresh page. "You know, I've planned a lot of meetings these past three years, but this one's definitely going to be the most challenging."

Chapter Seven

We must have been up until three or four in the morning, going over and over the what-ifs....

What if, for instance, Richard wanted Karen to drive part of the time? Karen had never learned to drive stick shift like I had. My college boyfriend had an old red MGB and with inordinate patience and courage had taught me how to master the intricacies of manual transmissions. Ever since, I'd always driven a stick car because I loved the control it gave me, but not Karen—Karen had always gone for automatic. And the problem was, a huge number of the cars in Europe are manual. What would Karen do then if Richard wanted her to take over any driving duties?

"I don't think he'll do that, Kate. He's such a control freak. But, if he does, I'll just tell him that I've forgotten how." She leaned back on her pillow and crossed her arms over her stomach. We had changed into our sleeping gear by then—I was in an oversize T-shirt with the station logo, and Karen was in

some cute little eyelet pajama number. I think she had an open
account at Victoria's Secret.

"You don't *forget* how to drive stick. It's like forgetting how
to ride a bike. It doesn't happen."

"Well, how about this? I'll wear an ace bandage on the trip
and say I have carpal tunnel syndrome and I can't work the
gearshift. That ought to work."

"I can't believe your mind," I said shaking my head with as-
tonishment and admiration. "It's so fast and so devious. It's a
great solution, but don't you think it will be a drag wearing an
Ace bandage every day?"

"Not as much of a drag as it would be to be busted by Richard, if he figured out I wasn't you."

"Then what are we going to do about fish?" I asked. "He knows
I've always loved fish and that you detest it. Remember when
he and I were dating and he threw that lobster boil and you
wouldn't eat any of it? Not ordering fish at some point on the
trip could be a dead giveaway. Do you think you could just order it somewhere to deflect him?"

"I'll just tell Richard that I've developed an allergy to most
fish in my old age. He'll buy it. A lot can happen to a person in
fifteen years. Look at our boobs."

That I did not want to discuss. Karen and I had been blessed
with very perky breasts all the way into our twenties, and then
a completely weird thing happened. As I started to lose mine,
due to what I presumed was pregnancy and nursing, Karen's too
started to point a bit less heavenward than she would have liked.
"What do you think has happened," she wailed one day when we
were standing in front of a mirror at my house and she was showing me the two reasons she could no longer go braless in a

T-shirt. To this day we have always wondered if this wasn't some twin phenom—sympathetic sagging or something—though there didn't seem to be any research on it in all the twin studies we'd ever read.

We were still pondering contingencies when Muriel's hall clock chimed three in the morning outside our door. "Oh, God, Karen," I said sitting up in bed and hugging my knees. "Maybe this is just too much to take on. It's like there are all these trillions of details that could screw up the whole plan. Every time I think we've knocked one off, there is always another one."

"It will work out just fine," she said, holding her hand out in front of her to inspect her nearly perfect nails. "I'm sure. I can't wait to get back to Italy. I haven't been there for three years."

"Oh, no! Passports!" I jumped out of bed. "What about your passport? We're screwed. Richard could see those stamps on it. He'll see you've been there."

"Kate, he's not going to see *my* passport. He's going to see *your* passport. Remember? I'm going as you. In order to pull that off, I'm going to have to have your passport. Plus your credit cards, and driver's license, and insurance card, and..."

"Oh, God, Karen. Insurance? What if the plane goes down? Seriously, what if you crash and then Danny and Sarah Rose think they're orphans and I have to spend the rest of my life pretending that I'm their aunt? Oh, my God, we've been crazy. We can't do this!"

At this point Karen started really laughing. "You've been watching too many bad TV movies. Listen to me. You're not pretending you're me over here, and you're not going to tell the kids you're going to Italy anyway. You just have to be off the air and out of town in case Richard gets suspicious of our plan and checks up on you. Tell them you are going to Wisconsin or something and then go there. You'll want to be where they can reach you, right?"

"Right."

"So if the plane goes down, just tell them their Aunt Karen died…which, I might add, would be true and I'd prefer you sounded a bit more grief-stricken about it. I mean, if the plane goes down you *will* be short one fabulous sister. Granted, in addition to your paralyzing grief, you have to explain to the U.S. government that the woman on the flight manifesto was actually your crazy twin sister who stole your passport. Don't worry—feel free to defame me to the Feds. I'll be dead anyway."

By the time we heard ourselves talking like that, it was obvious we were in need of sleep. I snapped off the light, threw Muriel's horrible foam pillow on the floor, and I think by the time it landed, I was out cold. I probably could have slept until noon, had that not been the hour that Karen and I were hosting Muriel's seventy-fifth birthday luncheon at Le Ceil Azure.

Muriel swore Le Ceil Azure had the best French food in "all of *South* Florida." This was not exactly a huge accolade since, according to her, the best French food in "*all* of Florida," was at Chefs de France in Disney World. She also assured us that the fact that Le Ceil Azure was in a strip mall was not to be seen as a deterrent. "We have lovely strip malls here," she proclaimed. No point in arguing with Muriel that the terms "lovely" and "strip malls" were mutually exclusive. This was where she wanted to hold the soiree.

Of course, it wasn't exactly a soiree, given that the invitation was for noon. But "the driving situation," as Muriel called it, tended to limit the evening activities for Muriel and the twelve other invitees who were collectively referred to as "the girls."

"You know it's very difficult for women my age," she said to us over instant coffee that morning as we were getting ready for the party. "We can't drive anywhere at night, but we look like hell in the cold light of day. The best present you could give a woman my age is her own personal lighting director."

"I think Barbara Walters and Barbra Streisand have already taken the best ones," I said.

"Come on, Mom. You know you look great," Karen added, graciously ignoring Mom's current hair tragedy.

Then, changing the subject, I asked, "Mom, do you still have that 'nightgowns of the future' drawer?" Muriel had been purchasing gossamer nightgowns on sale for the past five years, just in case she met the right man to take them off for. They were all wrapped in tissue and still had the tags on.

"Well, yes, dear, I do."

"So why don't you stop saving them? When are you ever going to wear them?"

"Oh, I thought they'd look nice when I check into the funny farm. You know, with some nylon knee-highs and a pair of rubber boots."

"Mom, I'm serious. It's very weird to be saving new clothes if you're not waiting for the first day of school."

"Kate, leave me to my quirks. And I'll leave you to yours."

Oh, God, I thought, she should only know my latest one.

Muriel loved her luncheon. There she sat, surrounded by all her other hair spray-helmeted girls, decked out in pastel pant suits, gobs of makeup and jewelry for days. The morning drizzle had finally stopped but, nonetheless, as each woman walked into the restaurant she was still wearing the signature 'do-preservation device of their generation—the ubiquitous plastic rain bonnet.

"God," Karen whispered to me as we smiled and kissed each perfectly blushed cheek, "what do you think will be our version of the plastic rain bonnet?"

"What do you mean?" I asked after kissing and murmuring the perfunctory "you look fabulous" to Beryl Metzger and Bunni Liberman, Muriel's two best friends.

"I mean what *objet* do you think we'll all be carrying around that will have Sarah Rose and her friends in stitches like we are when we see these stupid plastic bonnets?"

"I have no idea, hon. But I'll let you know as soon as Sarah Rose is fifteen or so and she gets bitchy enough to torment me with it."

"God, I can hardly wait," sighed Karen.

As it turned out, I could hardly wait for the luncheon to be over. Partly because the white wine made me sleepy, and also because the main topic of discussion turned out to be a "shrimp tree" at a granddaughter's wedding one of them had attended the weekend before. "Shrimp trees" seemed to have considerable cachet in this crowd, and within minutes several of "the girls" were going down Shrimp Tree Memory Lane, recalling some of the more resplendent examples they'd encountered at the myriad weddings and bar mitzvahs they all seem to attend.

I tried to catch Karen's eye during this, but she and Bunni had stepped away for a few minutes and then reentered the room carrying a huge box. It was wrapped in silver with a floppy gold bow and was set right in front of a somewhat giddy Muriel while a dissonant "Happy Birthday" was sung to her.

But she went from giddy to euphoric when she opened the box and pulled out the contents—a glorious custom-made quilt.

Three months before Bunni had sent every woman at the lunch, including Karen and me, a twelve-inch square of pale yellow silk, and told us to embroider or sew or paint something on it that represented a moment we'd had with Muriel. Then she asked for all the squares back by early April, and had taken each one of them, fourteen in all, and sewn them into this extraordinary quilt.

Karen and I had put our two squares together and done a mini-mural of mom-daughter highlights over the years: the frizzy failure of our first perms, the second-prize glory of my Ping-Pong ball solar system at the Fourth Grade Science Fair, the shoulder pads Karen ripped out of one of Muriel's best dresses and then used for falsies and finally the mink stole Muriel said we could use for dress up, so we didn't think there'd be any problem if we cut the stole in half. All "the girls" seemed to have really gotten into it. Sylvia Fine did an all-sequin boat from the Caribbean cruise the two of them had taken in February; Myra Weinstein had glued several mah-jongg tiles onto her square; Rona Fleisch, a friend of Mom's since high school, did a before and after of the two of them getting their nose jobs...the whole quilt was a remarkable work of art and love.

That night Karen, Muriel and I spent several hours curled up under it, watching old family movies on the living room couch. Muriel and Daddy had documented everything—Girl Scout camp, our first formals, the sweet sixteen party, our gimpy cocker spaniel Rocky, Daddy's new golf clubs, Muriel's famous yellow '65 Chevy convertible—we hadn't vegged out on nostalgia like that in years. It was a treat.

But it was odd, too. Because it made me wonder what the videos might be like at my seventy-fifth birthday. The beginning would be an edited compilation of all these movies we were currently watching in which I was a kid, followed by a cameo appearance of Richard as a starter husband and biological dad to Danny, then years of Danny's birthday parties with bunches of kids and one mom and one aunt, then the welcome, albeit short-lived, addition of Tim as resident dad, followed by the arrival of the wondrous Sarah Rose, and then…no videos for the two years following her accident, and then a short segment on our trip to Door County, Wisconsin, last summer, and then what next? What would our video lives look like in the future, in the years after the…the what? What did we call this insane upcoming week in Italy? The trip? The deal? The sellout?

Oh, God, I thought as I fell asleep that night, please don't let this be a sellout.

Whatever I was going to call it, the main thing I knew as I drove to the airport the next day, was that there were a lot of details to put in place in the next couple of weeks. Basically, I had to figure out three key things. One, how I wanted to construct the payoff from Richard. Two, where I would really go while Karen impersonated me with Richard in Italy. And three, exactly what I would tell Tim and the kids was the reason for my sudden departure.

Which meant once again, I was on my way to more lies.

8

Chapter Eight

Oddly enough, the next one turned out to be a cyber-lie.

I didn't log on to the computer until nearly midnight. When I came home from Miami around ten Sunday evening, Danny was on the phone in his room, Sarah was sound asleep in hers and Tim was lying on the couch doing the *New York Times* crossword puzzle.

Seeing how *déjà*-domestic the whole scene was, I laughed and said, "God, if I didn't know better, I'd say we were still married."

"If we were still married," he smiled, getting off the couch to kiss my cheek, "I'd probably already be asleep and snoring."

I set down my suitcase, and collapsed in my favorite green armchair. A huge vase of delphinium, and Queen Anne's lace, and bachelor buttons was on the coffee table in an old milk jar. It looked lovely.

"Where are those from?"

"Sarah and I went to the Farmers' Market down in Lincoln Park.

It was fun, but pricey. I think it's the only place in the city where you can spend more for melons than you can at Whole Foods."

"True, but you're paying for ambience—you know—the illusion of country wholesomeness plunked right down in the middle of all those overpriced, highly taxed, gentrified streets. You're basically buying the movie set, not the melons."

Tim and I talked for twenty minutes or so while he filled me in on the details of the weekend. Sarah had had a sleepover with her friend Annie Jordan, and Danny apparently had spent nearly every waking hour, which in his case means starting at noon, at the computer working on his big report.

When he finally got off the phone and came into the kitchen a half hour after Tim left, I was putting the juice box in Sarah's lunch for the next day.

"Hi, honey, I missed you."

"You too," he said absently looking at the computer screen.

"You need the computer?" I inquired, dying to ask how his paper was going, but not wanting to crowd him.

"No, I'm whipped," he said, grabbing an apple out of the refrigerator while I still had the door open. "You can use it if you want. How was Gram's party?"

I gave him the Cliffs Notes version and ten minutes later he said, "I'm going to crash."

I kissed him good-night—a gesture he thought he'd outgrown, but I refused to relinquish—and then sat down at my computer to get my e-mail. There was this split-second when I considered going into Danny's folder on the screen to read what he'd written so far in his profile of Richard, but even I, taker of tarnished money/deceiver of ex-husband, couldn't quite stoop that low.

So I decided to cyber-lie to my best friend instead.

Here was my e-mail from Samantha…

Hey babe,

Thought of you this afternoon when a gaggle of seventy-something women came into the restaurant for somebody's birthday. I swear, there are no blue-haired ladies left in the world. At least not here in California. How'd it go with Muriel and all the Botox Babes? Tell me the two biggest highlights of your last forty-eight hours.

Tell her the two biggest highlights?

I couldn't. I couldn't start typing that I was about to accept this bizarre offer from Richard who, second to Tim—and now apparently Danny—almost no one hated as much as Samantha. And then telling her about Karen's scheme would only make things worse. Sam had always thought that Karen had *way* too much influence over me. I've always wondered if all best friends of twins might not feel that way.

Thus, my e-mail back to her was a little short on candor.

Two biggest highlights? First was watching Muriel's face when she opened up the quilt I told you about. She adored it. Second biggest highlight? Hilarious Mom Story Karen told me about a friend of hers whose mother had heart failure and was taken into intensive care last week in the hospital. Her friend raced over to the ICU in the middle of the night to stay with her mom, and when the mom came to later the next day, the first words out of her mouth to her daughter had nothing to do with her recent life-and-death drama. Nope, her first words were, "You could use some lipstick, Susan." Isn't that perfect? Beyond that, not much else. Remind me never to live in Florida. Every day there is a bad hair day. And now I'm off to bed. Backatcha tomorrow.

So chalk up that e-mail as yet another lie. Granted, it was lying by omission, but then that's what most of the world's big-time liars have always done. I mean, what did Brutus do but omit mentioning to Caesar that it was probably not that good an idea to show up in the Senate on the fifteenth? Likewise with Oedipus. Someone just forgot to tell him that his wife was really his mother. So *my* lying by omission—at least next to theirs—was hardly world-class, but it still made me feel crummy.

Plus, I never doubted for a minute that I'd eventually come clean with Samantha. But not until this whole thing was a fait accompli. I really needed that accompli part attached. That way it would be too late for Sam to talk me out of it. Not to mention, it would also be too late for *me* to talk me out of it. Because now that I was back home in my own kitchen, surrounded by all the banal realities of my daily life, the magnitude of this whole thing began to gnaw at me again. The layers of duplicity that were going to be required were really beginning to scare me. No wonder I looked like hell when I showed up at the station the next morning.

"I'd ask if the world's been good to you so far, partner, but the answer's all over your face," said David looking up from his desk and taking in the newly acquired dark circles under my eyes. "I'm hoping it's just because your plane got in late last night."

"Actually the plane landed on time," I said, setting my purse on the floor and getting out my yellow highlighter so I could go through the wire copy our producer, Cody, had pulled. "I just don't seem to have a close personal relationship these days with the elusive commodity of sleep."

"Well, as my old shrink would say, that seems situationally appropriate," he replied.

"*You* went to a shrink?" I asked. "You've always struck me as kind of a Marlboro Man."

"Why would you say that? I'm not a 'yup-nope' guy. If I were, I wouldn't be in radio."

I watched his face closely when I answered because I hadn't intended to hurt him. "David, I didn't mean in a 'yup-nope' way. I just meant in a self-sufficient way. You just seem to be someone who has always managed his own pain or stress."

His smile was almost cryptic. "That's because you haven't known me during times of pain or stress. You've been the professional beneficiary of knowing David The Just-About-Healed. We can talk about it sometime if you want."

"Okay," I said, wondering if David was finally feeling safe enough to really *connect*. Not that I was looking for trouble. Especially not now. But it would be nice to have a real friendship, something more than the on- and off-air cordiality happening between us. David struck me as really good people.

We happened to have an amazing show that morning. Amazing in terms of topic, but particularly amazing in terms of timing. The topic was deceit.

"Hi, Janice," said David. "What's up?" Of course he already knew what was up because Cody had screened the call, and on our computer screen it said, "Line 2: Janice, 41, just got busted by mother."

"Hi, David. Hi, Kate," said the disembodied caller voice. "I have a horrible situation going on and I want some input from you guys."

"We're at your disposal," I said, eternally amazed that strangers were always so willing to lay out their lives on the radio. Not to mention ask for advice from the likes of us.

"Well, here's the thing," sighed Janice. "My mother is this horrible control freak. Whenever we have Christmas, it has to be at *her* house, on *her* schedule, with *her* menu. And the kids have to open their presents in this certain order, and it's not very joyous at all. We're not even allowed to have any wine and she makes us dress formally. It's horrible. So anyway, last Christmas, my sisters and brothers and I decided to have one Christmas with Mom on Christmas Eve, but then have a real one, a fun one, on Christmas Day without her. We didn't do this to hurt her, but we couldn't stand it anymore...."

Janice went on to describe how all the siblings each told their mom that they were going to their in-laws' houses on Christmas Day, but how they actually all went over to her house that day and had this fabulous time. They all hid their cars, and every hour one of the five siblings would call their mother—ostensibly from some in-laws' house—to wish her a merry Christmas.

David and I exchanged looks of incredulity.

"She didn't even seem unhappy," Janice continued. "She'd had the regulation Christmas she wanted the night before, and then *we* got what *we* wanted the next day. All of us felt a little guilty, but we also felt entitled. We were even planning to do it again this year, except now I don't know what we'll do...."

"Why? What happened?" I asked.

"She was over here yesterday, and while I was putting away my groceries, she went into the photo album and saw the pictures from our secret Christmas."

Of course the lines lit up. Half the people were furious with Janice for what she did to her mom. The other half wished they had the nerve to do that to their mom. We had a great show based on that one call.

Back in the office, David tossed his headset on the couch, and said, "Man there's a lot of deception on this planet."

I went over to the window to adjust our Venetian blinds. "Is that a judgment or an observation?"

"An observation, Kate. I'm a forty-six-year-old man. I've lived some. I know that complications and deceits aren't just things that happen to people who call talk radio shows. There are a million moral swamps out there, waiting to suck people in. I've been pulled into some, I'm sure you have, too."

It was too good an opening. Too good an opening from too impartial an observer. I needed someone to talk to. Not just Karen. But someone outside the loop to use as a sounding board before I called Canada and signed on with the devil. David would be the perfect person for me to bring this all to. He had no feelings about Richard. He had no feelings about Karen. And he had no feelings about me. Maybe not no feelings, but no vested interest in me.

"David, I want to take you to lunch."

"Great. When?" he asked as he started to attack the huge stack of our mail.

"Now. We're going to Chinatown. I could use a really lucky fortune cookie."

9

Chapter Nine

Wong Yee's was not on Wentworth Avenue, the main drag of Chinatown. It was tucked way back in an alley and it was a gem. Possibly the only restaurant in the area with no garish reds and golds, no fake flowers and no telephone book-size menus, Wong Yee's was done all in grays and whites and they more or less told you what was for lunch. That alone was reason enough for me to have always loved it, because I hate the deciding part at Chinese restaurants. It always seems as if they are basically serving six main dishes, but on one version they leave out the bamboo shoots so they give it a new name and number, and then the next one they put the bamboo shoots back in plus toss in some black mushrooms and it takes on yet another name and number and, no matter how you order it, it has one thing in it you hate, and one thing not in it that would make it perfect.

Madame Wong Yee—at least I always assumed that was her name, given that she seemed so wife-of-the-boss-like, smiled a cautious smile and seated us up front near a window so we could have a romantic view of the alley.

"Have you been down to Chinatown before?" I asked, noticing how odd it was to be face-to-face with him at a table instead of next to him at the console like I usually am when we're on the air. It made me realize I knew David's profile even better than I knew his face, which was something of a waste considering what a great face it was. But then again, considering what a great face it was, radio was something of a waste, too.

"Yeah, my wife and I came down here years ago when we met up with some friends in Chicago," he said, unfolding his napkin and looking out the window so he could avoid eye contact when he talked about his wife. This was still a tender subject for him, and even though I'd always considered myself interviewer extraordinaire, it didn't seem right to push. He'd be out there with it when he was ready.

Within minutes Madame Wong Yee came over and placed two dishes in front of us. "Dragon pancake," she announced.

"Thank you," said David. And then without indulging in any social preliminaries, he asked, "Do you want to tell me what's going on?"

"How do you know something is?"

"Kate, you ask me to lunch—which in all these months of our working together has happened about twice, you say squat in the car, all morning your face has been the color of a flour tortilla and a week ago you show me this letter from this slimeball ex-husband who claims he can make you a stupendous offer, and then you tell me you are going to call him... I don't know, call me crazy, but why do I think all that is interrelated?"

"Because it is," I sighed. "It's definitely interrelated."

"Then tell me," David said, deftly cutting a pancake piece with his chopsticks and plopping it in his mouth. "What's the big offer?"

I pushed my plate toward him because I suddenly had zero appetite. "Richard offered to pay me every cent he's ever owed me for Danny all these years, plus interest, and give me an extra $750,000, if I would go away with him to Italy for one week."

"Jesus," he whispered. "That is one hell of a deal."

"What do you mean, one hell of a deal? One hell of a good deal? One hell of a bad deal? One hell of an obscene deal?"

"One hell of an unusual deal," he said setting down his chopsticks.

"You don't think it's a little twisted? Being hired to go off and spend a week with your ex-husband? My sister thinks there's an outside chance he might even assume I'd sleep with him if I accept. What would you think of me if I went?"

"Kate, I'm not a good person to ask about this."

"Why? You've been divorced."

"But I've never been a woman. As awful as this sounds, I'm pretty sure this is more of a moral dilemma for a woman than a man. This may not be true for all men, but if a woman told the average guy, 'My ex-husband is going to hand me more than a million dollars to go away with him and maybe even sleep with him again,' most men would say, 'Wow. What are you going to do with the money?'"

"You're kidding me," I said, stunned.

"No. I'm not. Kate, we tend to be a pretty pragmatic gender. And as far as the sex thing goes, the sorry truth is, for most men, it's just sex."

"Are you saying that if you saw your ex-wife, you'd automatically consider sleeping with her?"

"I'd like to think I wouldn't." He started doing that jiggle-the-leg thing under the table that guys do when they get uncomfortable. "Jennie really hurt me. But I don't know that I wouldn't sleep with her again. It would depend on the circumstances, I guess. Stranded together on a desert island? Definitely. Finding ourselves at a big cocktail party? Unlikely. Finding ourselves in some nostalgic mood at my stepson's wedding? Who knows? I know that doesn't make me seem noble, but life is complicated. Humans are even more so. An ex is *still* someone you were once attracted to and someone you once loved. So even if you aren't particularly fond of her now…"

"God, that's amazing."

"Yeah, I suppose it is. So, what are you going to do?" he asked accepting course two from Madame Wong Yee.

"Shanghai snapper," she pronounced, whacking the head off with her chopstick, and filleting it in no time at all.

"Well, at this moment I do have a plan, but I'm still wavering about whether or not I am constitutionally capable of executing it." And then I told David about the Kate/Karen switch—the whole convoluted, duplicitous scheme. Watching his face as I cited the layers and layers of lies required to pull this off, it was impossible to tell what he was thinking.

"Do you think I'm human pond scum?" I asked dipping my fish in the killer spice sauce it came with. "I hate being a person with secrets."

"Everyone has secrets. Deceitful things they have done for complicated reasons."

"What about you? Have you ever done anything as deceitful as this? And in the unhappy event that you ever got caught, have you ever done anything as potentially damaging as this?"

"Yes," he said softly, setting his chopsticks down on the plain white plate. "Other than my ex-wife and my sister, nobody has ever known about this. But when I was in my twenties, I deceived my best friend. Even worse, he's now my brother-in-law."

"What happened?"

David started fiddling with the brown leather strap on his watch—hooking it and unhooking it. Obviously, the story still pained him. "My friend Steve and my younger sister Robin had been going together about two years," he sighed. "He was crazy about her, and she was crazy about him too, except that she managed to get herself involved for a couple months during her senior year in college with a good-looking exchange student from Brazil. Steve and I had already graduated and she met this other guy at the school newspaper or something.

"Anyway, my sister came to me at the end of fall quarter and told me she was pregnant. She was panicked about it because she honestly didn't know whose baby it was—Steve's—who she was commuting to see every weekend—or this exchange student's—who she already had broken off with the month before. Robin knew if she told Steve she was pregnant he'd want to get married right away and while she really wanted to marry him, she was terrified that the baby they might raise together might not be his. She didn't want to live the whole rest of her life with that lie. There was also this troubling biological fact that Steve and Robin are really, really fair-skinned, and this exchange student was very, very dark. All she could think of was what it would be like if she delivered some swarthy little baby."

"So what happened?"

"I paid for her to have an abortion. I took her to Boston and stayed with her for three days after the operation. We lied to

Steve about having to go to some family birthday party, and about six weeks later the two of them got engaged."

"Are they married now?"

"Yeah," he sighed, "but they're wrestling with a terrible sadness. They've been trying to have kids for the past eleven years with no success. They've done tests, surgery, in vitro, all sorts of stuff. The docs even say that at this point nothing is wrong with either of them, but it just isn't happening. Every time Steve talks about it, and I see the raw pain on his face, I wonder if we took away the one child the two of them could have had. And every time I look at Robin I know she's convinced she's being punished for having cheated on Steve. So I understand where you are coming from. To this day I believe we did it for the right reasons, but I hate that there is this huge lie between Steve and me, and between Steve and Robin. And yet, I bet if you went to any family dinner party in this country it would be the same. There wouldn't be one that didn't have some complex, well-meaning, complete mendacity at its center. Shakespeare and Tennessee Williams don't have a monopoly on family intrigue."

"Oh, God, David, why don't they tell you it's going to be like this?"

"Because then, dear partner lady, none of us would ever want to graduate eighth grade and leave the playground."

I smiled resignedly.

"So," he continued, cupping the tea we'd just been handed, "that's my story. What's yours? When are you going to respond to your ex-husband's offer?"

"Not yet. I have to figure out where I'll disappear to if Karen is masquerading as me in Italy. I mean, obviously I can't be on

the air with you that week if Richard thinks I'm in Italy with him.
I definitely have to go somewhere."

"Why couldn't you just stay at your sister's place?"

"I thought of that, but it's too weird. If someone in her neighborhood saw me and talked to me as if I was her, it would just
duplicate the duplicity. Or what if I ran into Tim? No, I think it
makes more sense to take off for some remote place. I'm going
to have to pretend I'm going to some Women in Broadcasting
seminar or something, I guess. Oh God, this makes me feel horrible...."

David watched me writhe in my resurgence of ambiguity and
then said quietly, "If you want, you could use my cabin in the
Blue Ridge Mountains. You don't have to answer now, but please,
at least consider it."

We hardly talked on the way back to the station. When I
dropped off David, he turned to me before getting out and said,
"Listen, Kate, my offer for the cabin is serious. You know that."

"David, I don't know… If you give me the cabin, it makes me
feel like you're becoming some sort of accomplice in this."

"Accomplice? Kate, you are not committing a murder. No one
is going to be hurt by this. This is an extreme act because it's an
extreme situation. If you do this, you need to understand that
it does not make you a moral reprobate. Life is messy." And then
he cupped my chin and kissed me on my forehead.

It's not that I wasn't aware that some line had just been
crossed. But I had too much on my mind to dissect the kiss. And
anyway, I was sure he meant it to be platonic.

10

Chapter Ten

Two days later I called up my trusty divorce lawyer, Jack Meegan. Jack had been the official undoer of both my ill-fated unions, and I liked him and trusted him enormously. He was smart, he was as ethical as being a divorce lawyer allowed a person to be and most important of all, he was also an accountant.

Before I called Richard back, I needed Jack to help me structure the method of payment I wanted from him. Given that the man had a track record of being a consummate shit when it came to honoring deals, I didn't want to give him any opportunity to pull the rug out from under me when it came to the payout. Granted, I was going to be pulling the rug out from under him by sending Karen, but I was uncomfortable telling Jack that. Years ago Jack and Karen had gone out for a few months, and she had sort of broken his heart. I knew he wouldn't want to think about her going off with Richard. So I had to log in that omission as yet another lie. I was probably up to twenty by then. Some of them already executed. Others soon to be.

I met with Jack the next afternoon in his LaSalle Street office. He'd always been in the same building, but every time I went to see him, his offices were bigger and on higher floors. Five years ago when Tim and I split up, Jack was in a four-room space down on the sixth floor. This time I was stepping off on the twenty-second, and the whole floor now went under the name of Meegan, Frank, Lewis and Rosen.

"Jack Meegan, please," I said to the striking Asian receptionist behind the Plexiglas desk. "I'm Kate Lerner. I have a two o'clock appointment with him."

After confirming with his secretary that Jack was expecting me, I was escorted down labyrinthine halls lined on one side by expensive bad art and on the other side by glass brick walls. Finally we arrived at Jack's vast gray-carpeted inner sanctum. Oak bookcases lined two walls floor-to-ceiling, and the other two walls were floor-to-ceiling glass overlooking the city to the north and east.

Jack was a little Toulouse-Lautrec kind of guy. Everything about him was short, stubby and intense. He came from behind his desk and I noticed he seemed to have more hair than the last time I'd seen him. I hated thinking that it was probably a piece. Why don't men understand the inherent pathos of a toupee? Karen once went for a consultation with a plastic surgeon and the minute she saw he wore one she knew she'd never let him near her. I completely agreed. I mean, why would you turn the future of your face over to someone who thought a toupee was a good aesthetic decision?

"Kate," Jack said, smiling. "It's been so long. I hope you're not here about another divorce. A prenup is fine, but another divorce would make me very unhappy."

I smiled. "Not to worry, Jack. Anyway, I probably couldn't afford you anymore. Look at this place! It's like a movie set."

"That's what I told my sister-in-law. She decorated it," he sighed, indicating a burgundy leather couch for me to sit in. "As far as I'm concerned, it's too much like some barrister program on PBS. But don't worry, you won't have to finance it. You know my rule, Kate, I don't raise my rates with old clients. You get me for the same eighty-five dollars an hour that you got me for fifteen years ago. The new clients pick up the slack. So what can I do for you?"

"About eighty-five dollars worth of pondering." And then I told him about Richard's proposal, why I was going to accept it, and that I wanted him to structure the payout.

"Hmm," he said, stroking his salt-and-pepper beard which I hoped wasn't fake hair, too. "That's an extraordinary proposition, Kate."

It was hard to get a read on what he meant by "extraordinary." But Jack seemed nonjudgmental enough. After all, he was in the divorce business, so he had no doubt encountered every squirrelly deal ever thought up by mankind. "Let me gather my thoughts here a moment so we can guarantee your being paid," he said, pacing back and forth in front of the windows. Then he sat down at his desk and started scribbling for about ten minutes.

"Here," he said, handing me a piece of yellow legal paper. "I'm going to explain everything I've written on this sheet." I took the legal paper, amazed that a man like Jack still didn't have a computer in the room.

"You're going to tell Richard to deposit the money into an escrow account in your name. The amount we are talking about is $438,000, plus $750,000, right?"

"Right."

"Okay, that totals $1,118,000. I'll draw up an agreement for Richard to sign. It will stipulate the following things. One, within ten days, he is to pay $1,118,000 into an escrow account that I will set up for you. Two, he will agree that all the money in the account is to be paid out to you on the day that you return to Chicago, after your spending a week in Italy with him. Three, he will agree to your taking a photo of you two together every day with the front page of a newspaper."

"Why? Richard hates having his picture taken. What is that for?"

"It will be incontrovertible proof that you have met the terms of the agreement. Four, should any dispute arise, he must agree in advance to have that dispute arbitrated through the American Arbitration Association. And five, I also want to put in a God Forbid clause."

"What's that?" I asked, astounded at minds like Jack's that thought of taking snapshots with the newspapers.

"The God Forbid Clause says that God Forbid, should the plane go down, that all the money in this account be put into a trust that we will set up in advance for your two kids. You have to figure out if you feel all the money should go to the son you had with Richard or if you want to split it between both of your children...."

I didn't want to tell Jack that we didn't really need the God Forbid clause because if the plane went down, my children wouldn't be without a mother, they'd be without an aunt.

I stopped by that very aunt's on the way home from Jack's to bring her up to speed on the contract he was putting together.

"Wow," Karen sighed, handing me an iced coffee in her kitchen. "Escrows, newspapers, photos—Jack always did have a great mind, didn't he? I guess it's beginning to look like we really are going to do this. All you need to do is to arrange for Tim to take the kids, and then tell Richard you can go."

"Yeah, that's *all*," I said softly.

Karen came over and put her arms around me. "It's going to be all right, Kate. Someday we will look back on this, after it's processed and integrated into our lives, and be very glad that we took advantage of an incredible offer in an incredible way. I'm sure of it."

That night I asked Tim if he would take Sarah Rose and Danny while I attended a Women In Broadcasting seminar in Blowing Rock, North Carolina. "No problem," he said, "I'll just have the kids move in for the whole week."

Sarah Rose was always glad to spend some extended time with Tim, but Danny wasn't one bit happy that I wasn't leaving him all on his own at our house.

"God, Mom. I'm seventeen. I don't need a baby-sitter."

"Tim is hardly a baby-sitter, Danny. I just feel better knowing you guys are with a responsible adult."

"I know how to be responsible. Why don't you trust me?"

"It's not about trust," I said, fully aware that this was hardly a topic that afforded me any high moral ground at that moment.

"Yes it is. It's always about trust. Just the way it was after the taco incident. Remember how frustrated you were that I wouldn't trust you for so long?"

"Oh, Danny," I said with exasperation. "Are you ever going to stop dragging up the taco incident?"

The taco incident had taken place when Danny was nine. It

had been a subzero winter night. I'd planned to make tacos for dinner and at the last minute realized I didn't have any lettuce to shred. Driving to the store in that weather was out of the question, particularly since I did have a few leaves of fresh spinach in the refrigerator. Danny hated spinach, but I tried to get it by him anyway. I chopped it up, sprinkled it on his taco, and the minute he bit in, he made a face.

"Is this spinach or something, Mom?"

"No, honey. You hate spinach. It's just lettuce. Like usual."

He ate it, and I thought I'd gotten away with it. I was wrong. The next morning when he went to throw his cereal box into the garbage, he looked into the bin and pulled out the clear plastic bag that said fresh spinach.

He was furious. He was also devastated. "You lied. Moms shouldn't lie," he cried, sloppy tears of rage sliding down his cheeks. "Moms should always tell the truth."

I reached out my hand for him, but he pulled away. "Oh, honey, you know moms try to tell the truth. Almost always. But for some things like Santa Claus and the Tooth Fairy we don't."

"Santa Claus is different," he huffed.

"Well, I don't know. Maybe it is. But there are other times. Like when a dog has to be put to sleep at the vet's and a mom might say the dog went to the farm. You know people do that."

"Yeah," he continued to snivel, "but that's just to make the kid feel better. Telling me that spinach is lettuce isn't going to make me feel better. It's just a dumb lie."

And he didn't let me off the hook for years. But I wasn't about to let him leverage me with the taco incident into letting him stay alone while I was gone. "You can be here alone until ten every night, so you can work on your paper at the computer. But after that, I want you at Tim's."

"Fine," he mumbled desultorily.

The next unpleasant conversation I would have was with Danny's father. It was time to call Richard and tell him that I *was* accepting his offer.

"Yeah?" he barked when he answered the phone.

"It's Kate."

"Hold on a minute. I'll get off the speaker. Glad you caught me. I'm leaving for Calgary in a few minutes."

"Richard, if you don't mind my asking, what exactly do you do?" I was in my kitchen putting together a peanut butter and jelly for my lunch. I'd forgotten to eat earlier. I remembered when Richard and I were first married, he couldn't believe that anyone over eleven years old was eating p.b.j.s, but I've never shaken the habit.

"What do I do?" he snorted. "Fly on airplanes a lot and buy and sell businesses. Listen, I'm in a rush here, Kate. Where are we on my offer?"

I put the sandwich down and hung on to the kitchen counter for dear life. My mouth opened up and these words came out, "I think I accept."

"You *think* you accept or you *do* accept?"

"I *do* accept," I said, wondering whether he was as surprised to hear my answer as I still was. "Do you want to know the amount that you owe Danny?"

"Kate, I'm in business. I can ballpark the amount. For child support alone, it's somewhere between four hundred and four hundred and fifty thousand, depending on what rate of interest you figured."

"Six percent."

"Then that's about four hundred and forty thousand, right?"

"$438,000. Plus the additional $750,000. I don't want any of the back alimony."

"I'm sure Gloria Steinem would be proud," he cracked.

I ignored him. "And I've already talked to someone about how to structure the payment."

"You don't need to talk to anyone but me, Kate. *I'm* the one making the payment."

"I know. And that's why I thought it was best to have a payment agreement structured in advance."

"For chrissakes, Kate, I'm not going to renege on you. I'm planning to pay you!"

"Uh-huh. But when, for instance, are you planning to pay me?"

"When the deal is completed."

"That's what I thought," I sighed. "Listen, the thing is, Richard, and I'm sure you can understand this given your track record, I can't have it set up like that. Sorry to be such a cynic, but I have to know that the money is deposited in my name before I set foot on Italian soil."

Then I proceeded to outline the plan that Jack had put in place. There was a lot of quiet on the other side of the phone. Particularly when I told him the part about the daily photos of us with the newspaper.

"Kate. For chrissakes, that's one hell of an insult."

"Insult? God, you really are a piece of work. You vanish on Danny and me fifteen years ago, not a single phone call, not a single cent, and then suddenly you have the right to be insulted? It—"

The front door slammed. "Mooooommy. I'm hooooome." It was Sarah Rose.

"Be right there, honey," I called.

"Richard——" I lowered my voice into the phone "——I've got to go. But that's the deal. It's the only way I can go. So do you want to think about it? Or do you want to pass?"

"Neither. We'll do it your way," he snarled. I couldn't tell if he sounded so ticked because he thought the payout plan was so infuriating, or because it was basically very sound but *he* just hadn't been the one to think it up.

Chapter Eleven

A few nights later I was headed up to David's house in Ravenswood for dinner. He had a bunch of books and maps on North Carolina and wanted to brief me about the quirks of his cabin in Blowing Rock.

David's house was in one of those typical, leafy, stoop-studded neighborhoods that pepper Chicago. Stucco homes were next to brick homes next to clapboard homes and on a perfect seventy-degree evening like this one everyone was stoop-sitting or porch-lounging. David, however, was doing neither when I pulled up. Instead, he was handing over some dug-up rust-colored day lilies from his front yard to his neighbor.

The neighbor, a great-looking brunette in a ponytail and tight jeans, was either seventeen or one of those forty-year-olds they use in the Oil of Olay ads. I couldn't tell until I got closer.

"Kate, come over," David hailed. "I want you to meet Nancy. She's been a listener of yours ever since you and Samantha were on." That took care of the age question. Our listeners were definitely not high school juniors.

"Hey, Nancy," I said, extending my hand, "nice to meet you."

"Oh, God," she gushed, setting the day lilies down and showing me up close and personal what the right moisturizer can do for a midlife woman, "I just can't believe I'm meeting you. I've been listening to you for years."

This was always the uncomfortable part. It didn't happen often, but there is something so derailing about meeting someone in real life who relates to you like you're some sort of, I don't know, low-rent celeb. I mean they don't see you as low-rent, even on a small station like ours. But I see me as low-rent.

The three of us spent about ten minutes chatting and then David said, "Nance, Kate and I have to go in. My coals ought to be just about right and I've got some trout that I'm grilling for our dinner."

We said our goodbyes and I followed David up the stairs into his house. It was a total surprise. I expected lots of books and comfy sofas and a scattering of general guy detritus—pipes maybe, a lame attempt to rearrange old marital knickknacks, a gargantuan TV and stereo equipment. Wrong. When you stepped inside this all-American bungalow it was as if you'd set foot in Kyoto. The whole place was white and gray and very spare.

The only art in the room was a stunning antique screen covering most of one wall and then a recessed, built-in gallery with spots shining down on a collection of glossy black vases and pots. A low green-black lacquer table in the middle of the room was completely bare except for a tall ocher vase containing a dramatic arrangement of tall grasses.

"My God, David," I said trying to take it all in. "This is gorgeous! And so incongruous! It's such a shock."

"I know." He grinned, clearly pleased that I loved it. "It was incongruous to me too, as I began to do the remodeling and furnishing. When I bought this place I had no idea that I was about to turn it into this. But I had done a lot of reading about Japan during my eighteen months off and suddenly, instead of just repainting this place and moving my old stuff in, it seemed like the right time to create a physical version of something that had been mentally lurking in my head."

"It's quite extraordinary," I said, going toward the vases to see if they felt as satiny as they looked.

"I know. It's at odds with most people's expectations. But it has felt exactly right for now in my life."

"In what way?"

"Because it's such a spare, uncomplicated room. The rest of the house is regular—come and see. There are no shrines or moss gardens—though I'm tempted."

"I didn't know you gardened," I said, having observed that the front was a pretty standard Chicago yard of day lilies, impatiens and geraniums.

"Only in the back so far," he said, guiding me out to one of the loveliest little cottage gardens I'd seen in years. It was filled with hollyhocks, cosmos, nasturtium and stock.

"Yeah, I've been having a great time with it," he gestured to the pile of gardening books on the back porch. "Actually what I really like is that nothing goes together. I'm English out back, Japanese in the living room, American through most of the rest of the house—it's like being my own Epcot Center."

I laughed. In a way it was terrific. And very guylike. I mean he didn't need a theme. He just wanted what he wanted when he wanted it. I was just sure if David had been part of a couple, the distaff part would never have gone for the United Nations School of Decorating. But for him, it really was perfect. And so was the meal he cooked—grilled trout, asparagus vinaigrette and some room-temperature herbed new potatoes.

After dinner he brought out all his North Carolina books and maps and spread them out on the low lacquer table in the living room. "Come here," he gestured, "so we can get started going over some of the cabin's idiosyncrasies and mapping out your stay."

We sat there for forty-five minutes while David went over the cabin's how-to's, and walked me through a packet of photocopied tourist info. "Listen, whatever you do, get to Mast General Store and make the drive to Lake Lure. Even if the weather is crappy, it's great fun to be up in the mountains. I've told my neighbors, Ray and Susan, that you'll be there. Ray watches over the place for me when I'm gone and Susan is a sweetheart. Actually they said they'd be happy to take you with them when they go out dancing. They're devoted two-steppers and spend weekends following the bands in different country bars. It's generally great barbecue and even better music."

"God, I'd love to, but I don't think I can dance like that. Sometimes I see it on the country music cable station when I'm channel surfing—everybody moving in a circle all swaying and synchronized, but I don't think I could learn it."

David grinned. "Sure you can. I can teach you. Get up."

"Here? You're going to put country music on in the middle of this Shoji temple room?"

"You bet I am," he said, heading to his compact little stereo, then signaling me to stand up.

"Are you telling me you lead a secret life of a gardening, two-stepping Japanophile?"

"Actually," he said placing his hand on my waist and holding me at a graceful distance, "I'm a gardening, two-stepping, Japanophile, potter. All those vases are mine."

"Smelling salts, please," I whispered, pretending to faint.

"Not so fast," he said as Clint Black began singing. "You're not getting out of your lesson that easy. Now come on. One-two-three, back, back-close, one-two-three, back, back-close…"

We danced for maybe twenty minutes. David was a wonderful teacher and surprisingly (why did I keep getting surprised?) a terrific dancer.

When we sat down on his back porch swing to cool off over some iced tea, I said, "I loved that! It was so therapeutic."

"Therapeutic how?" he asked, scratching his head.

"Because it completely took my mind off this whole Richard in Italy thing. That's been the hardest part of these past couple weeks. I mean I'm walking around looking like a normal mom, but my inner life is running on a completely different track. You know, sending my sister off to impersonate me with my ex-husband, hiding out in the mountains, questioning if any of this is worth it to collect all this money…it's almost all I think about. And I hate that. I hate that it just looks like I'm chatting on the radio and eating pizza with my kids, but inside I'm on this dark second track. But the dancing part now was really good. I mean it looked like I was dancing, my mind was on the dancing and I really was dancing. God, I hate being on two tracks. That's what Samantha always said was the worst part about having an affair."

David's black eyes flashed intently. "Did she have a lot of affairs?" he asked with more interest than I'd have expected.

"Not a lot. But she had two long-term ones. One was for nine years. The guy was married of course and never once said he was going to leave, but every year he would arrange to take a week in February and a week in September with Samantha. And it nearly killed her. She spent forty-eight percent of her life waiting for the trip to come, another forty-eight percent bemoaning that it was over, and maybe two percent living it. Not that she didn't live it, but I always knew when we went to dinner or to a movie that she was only partly with me. The other part of her was thinking about Jordan. It was all such a waste."

"Is it over?" he asked as I spotted the first lightning bug of the season.

"Yeah," I sighed. "Finally she ended it. I remember exactly what she said to me, too, when she did. She said, 'Having affairs for some married men is a *way* of life—having affairs for single women is a *waste* of life.' I told her she had just invented a bumper sticker. Did you ever have an affair?"

David got up from the swing and looked out over the yard. The moon was fuzzy yellow and the crickets were just tuning up. "No. But my wife did."

"She did?"

"Yeah. I was married for twenty years and my wife was having an affair for the last six of them."

I said nothing. He turned back to me and if it wasn't exactly pain in his eyes, there still was something that told me this was a dicey conversational path. "She had it with a guy she worked with. She was a lawyer in a big firm in Philadelphia. He was a client. And when I found out—not because I was so damn smart, but because she finally told me—it was as if my stomach had been ripped out. Not my heart. My stomach. And for the exact reason you're talking about. That double track deal. I flashed back on all the moments we had been together during those six years, on ski trips, at parties, camping, making love— all those times when it looked like Jeannie and I were really connecting and in truth she was thinking about this other guy the whole time. It devalued our whole marriage."

"What happened?"

"I was devastated. And I was a real schmuck when we drew up our divorce decree."

"It's hard to imagine your being a schmuck, but then I have Richard setting my standards…"

"I wasn't a schmuck in a screw-you way. I was a schmuck in the getting screwed over way."

"How?"

"Well, in exchange for her relinquishing her half of the house to me—a house I'd always loved and she'd always hated—I agreed not to tell anyone about the affair. She was terrified she'd lose her job and be disbarred if it got out that she'd been involved with a client."

"Was it hard not to tell?"

"You bet. I was hurt. And pissed. Worst of all, the name of the radio show I was hosting then was *Truth Time*. It was an overnight show, we got great ratings, but the premise was that in the wee small hours people can no longer escape their demons and it's easier to come clean. So there I was running *Truth Time* having agreed to suppress a story that could have gotten my ex-wife disbarred. It was ultimately why I took off from radio for that year and a half. I hated the duplicity."

"God, we're not even bad people and our lives are so riddled with subterfuge."

"Yup," he sighed, getting up from the porch.

I thought for a minute. "You know what I want, David? I want to make a pact with you. I mean I'm thinking of the deceits you've told me that have come down in your life, and I'm thinking of all the deceits I'm setting up with this Italy trip, and I think I'd like to make a deal with you."

"What's the deal?"

"I'd like to propose that we structure our relationship to be a deceit-free zone. To date I think we already have that, unless there's something I've done at work that bugs you and you haven't told me."

"Nope. Not that I can think of," he said, draining his glass of tea.

"Well good. It's just that if you think about it, deceit-free relationships are so hard to find. I don't quite have it with Samantha, I certainly don't have it with my kids, I guess I haven't completely had it with Karen."

"That surprises me."

"I know. But I didn't tell her until she finally divorced her husband that I had always, always thought he was a jerk. But she and I are related and he was going to be in my family. So that's different. But you and I are not related, we don't have a long history, we aren't in love—all the subcategories that usually foster duplicitous behavior at some point. What do you say we just try to see if we can pull it off?"

He stroked his chin for a moment. Why hadn't I ever noticed he had one of those movie star dent things in it like Danny had? "A deceit-free relationship?" he mulled. "I don't know, it might already be too late."

"Why? Have you lied to me?"

"Just once."

"When?" I asked, my back already stiffening in anticipation of some huge falsehood.

"Tonight. You know when I was teaching you the two-step and I said you were doing great?"

"Yeah?"

"You're not. You dance great but you're trying to lead. You've got to be more yielding."

"Yielding?"

"Yeah, come here." He took my hand and led me back into the house so I'd dance with him again. "We'll work on it a bit more, then I won't be a liar, and you'll be the best dancing Northerner in Blowing Rock."

And I bet I would have been.

Only I never got there.

Chapter Twelve

"Hey, Mom," said Danny when I walked in from David's at eleven, "you're supposed to call Aunt Karen. Right away."

"Why? Is something wrong?"

"She's at the hospital," he said, putting a frozen pita pocket into the microwave.

"The hospital?" I gasped. Oh, God. For a millisecond I had visions of Karen lying there like some *splat!* on the highway And then I realized that *splats!* can't make phone calls to their nephews. "What happened?"

"She broke her leg. Rollerblading. She's in the emergency room at St. Joe's and she said for you to call right away or just come over."

Saint Joseph's was only ten minutes away and by the time I got there, Karen was already the proud recipient of one cast and two crutches. Granted, hospital lighting could turn Meg Ryan into Medusa, but I don't think I've ever seen Karen look that grim—all gray, clammy and bruised on one side.

"God, I am so glad to see you," she said, gathering her crutches up from the ripped green vinyl hospital couch so I could sit down. She was still in her zippy pink neon shorts and tank top. Who knew where her kneepads, helmet, skates and other equipment were. "This has been a really shitty two hours."

I leaned over to hug her, scared that I might hurt some purpling part of her and asked, "What happened?"

We hung on to each other for a bit and then she pulled away saying, "I have a double fracture. I must have hit a pebble or something on the lake path and *wham!* I flipped up in the air and came tumbling down. I guess when I landed, I blacked out." She raised her hand to her hair, which was still matted down with a little blood on one side.

"Just think if I hadn't been wearing my trusty helmet," she said. "I probably would have had Jell-O for brains."

"I think you had them anyway. Why in the world were you out rollerblading? This afternoon you were complaining to me that you had too much work to finish before you left for…" I stopped. For the first time it hit me. Italy! Karen couldn't go to Italy.

"Oh, my God!" I jumped up from the couch with my hand over my mouth. "Italy!"

"Kate, what's the matter?" She grabbed my hand in two of hers and said, "It's going to be okay. I'll get to Italy. We can still pull this off."

"Oh, hon," I said, easing back on the couch so I didn't jangle her leg, "Look at you! You can't travel now. No way are we going to send you to Italy. You've got a broken leg. Thank God it's only that, but face it, our whole master plan is dead in the water. Completely dead."

I took a deep breath and let it out. "Maybe this is fate. Maybe this is some big fate intervention thing stopping me from making the mistake of my life."

"No it's not." She smiled with more élan than I could ever pull off in an emergency room. "Don't go cosmic on me Kate. This is not fate. It's a delay. All you have to do is call Richard and ask him to postpone the trip a bit. The doc said I should be fine in four weeks. I'll be in a walking cast by then."

"Karen, don't be crazy," I exclaimed as a young man came through the door bleeding under an ice pack over his eye. "This trip is not something we can put off for four weeks!"

"Why not?"

"Because I've already told Tim that I'm going to this broadcasting seminar, so what am I going to say? That it's been postponed for four weeks? Nope, this isn't meant to be. It just won't work."

"Kate, just hang on…"

"No, this is clear as day. Actually, I'm relieved. I'll tell Tim I'm not leaving and tell Richard I'm not coming. Then I'll take the week off and take care of you." I held my arm out for Karen to hold on to me so I could settle her in the regulation wheelchair, and said, "Come on, hon, let's get you home."

"No. I am not going anywhere until we hammer this out," she said stubbornly, refusing to get up from the couch.

"Karen," I said slamming my purse down next to her, "there's nothing to hammer out. We are not *postponing* this trip. It is over. It is completely, definitively off."

"Why does it have to be off?" she asked. "Kate, Danny deserves that money. So does Sarah Rose and so do you. It's a once in a lifetime shot at some guaranteed security. It's crazy not to take advantage of it. So, if the trip *has* to be taken next week, then it will be."

"How?You can't go!"

"I know. But *you* can."

I collapsed back down on the couch. "Me? Are you crazy?"

"No, if you think about it, it's a lot less complicated."

"For *you* maybe. It's not less complicated for me."

"Yes it is. It is for both of us. It's one less lie. At least it really will be you."

"One less lie and one more huge impossibility. Karen, I'm not going to Italy with Richard."

"Why not?" she asked stretching her good leg out in front of her so she could slide into one of the flip-flops I'd brought over from my closet.

"Because of *Richard*. I'd have to be in cabs with Richard. And in restaurants with Richard. And according to you, I'd be spending my time fending off Richard. The whole thing would be too disgusting. The only reason I agreed to all this was that we could get Danny's money, but I wouldn't actually have to *be* with Richard. I'm done with this whole thing. I'm going to get the car. Do you want me to spend the night at your place?"

"No. All I want is for you to *consider* going to Italy. I hate to see you turn your back on the huge opportunities that money will bring for you and your kids."

"Listen, Karen, even if I *was* willing to go, how would I explain it to Tim and the kids? I've already told them I'll be at a seminar in North Carolina. Don't you think it would be a bit transparent to tell them that the seminar suddenly got switched to Rome?"

"Well," she said as she plunked herself down in the wheelchair that the hospital insisted she take to the front exit, "you could just invent a whole new fabrication. Rather than relocate the seminar, maybe you could say that American Airlines had just signed on as an advertiser at the station, and that they were flying selected hosts from six Chicago stations to Rome for five days as part of their new Chicago-Rome promotion. And that the station manager wanted *you* to have the trip."

Where did she get that kind of brain? And of course she didn't relent even when I brought the car around and got her settled in the front seat. "Ouch!" Karen winced, pushing back the seat so she could extend her plastered leg. And then without missing a beat she said, "Please, think about this, Kate. There is just no reason for you not to go. The money is in the escrow account, your kids are squared away for the week and you're scheduled to be off the air. You don't even have to worry about clothes. I have everything in cleaning bags in my front closet all set to go."

"I'm sure you do." I smiled in spite of myself. Karen was notoriously well organized—make that obsessive—when it came to outfit planning. Since our sophomore year in high school my sister had religiously logged her outfits into a daily journal in the bizarre belief that outfit repetition was right up there with murder and coveting thy neighbor's ass. I, on the other hand, would buy and stock two or three of the same clothing item if I liked it, because I didn't want to ever have to think about what I was wearing. Working in radio and editing manuscripts doesn't require you to be stunning on a daily basis, and I've always considered it one of the pluses of my jobs. So the truth was, if I'd been going to Blowing Rock, North Carolina, whatever was clean and hanging in my closet would have worked fine. But Rome? For sure my closet couldn't have come up with even three decent options.

"Well, thanks for the offer," I said, buckling my seat belt. "It's

nice to know if I ever decide to go to Rome that six impeccable black-and-taupe outfits await me in cleaner's bags."

"How did you know everything was black and taupe?"

I leaned over to kiss her. "Just the first forty-three years of
being your twin."

13

Chapter Thirteen

I hit the alarm button three times, but the ringing didn't stop. Finally I figured it out. It was the phone. My bedroom was still dark, so I was sure it was some middle-of-the-night emergency from Karen. I wondered if she'd fallen. She was so damn insistent that she could manage the stairs.

"Kate, it's Richard."

"What time is it?"

"It's noon here. I'm in London. Sorry to wake you up, but there's been a change of plans. I need to push the trip up by a few days so I can get back to our side of the Atlantic by July 3. I know this is last minute, but could you rework your schedule by three days so we can meet in Rome earlier in the week?"

Oh, thank you, Lord. This was the perfect excuse I needed to tell him the trip was off. Instead of having to come up with some twisted story so I could back out, I could just say, no I couldn't manage the three days and maybe we should just drop the whole thing. I flicked on my nightstand light and saw it was only 5:00 a.m. I'd never broken a date quite that early in the morning, but...

"And one thing before I forget," he said. "You'll probably be on your own most afternoons. I'm in the middle of a big buy-out deal with a company in upstate New York and I have to be available from about three until eight most days doing business with the States. I've gotten us two adjoining suites so you won't be bothered by all the calls and faxes."

Oh. My. God.

What an announcement. Two suites. Amazing! How wonderfully, platonically amazing. Two suites changed if not everything, certainly a lot. If nothing else, it meant I wouldn't have to be with Richard all the time. Secondly, it meant that it was very unlikely Richard was planning to be in some romantic, let-me-make-it-all-up-to-you mode. It sounded much more as if it was business as usual except that there was an ex-wife along. I didn't know that for sure, of course, but it definitely sounded like that.

I needed time to think. Because an astonishing thing was taking place. Somehow I was actually considering the very thing Karen suggested—that I go to Rome with Richard myself. But I needed to know something first.

"Richard, tell me something. Just what exactly are you expecting from me on this trip?"

"For chrissakes, Kate. I just told you I was getting you a suite of your own. So if it's sex you're worried about..."

"I'm not *worried*. I just want to know what you're expecting."

His silence was not reassuring. Then he cleared his throat and in a low voice said, "I am somewhat stunned to hear myself saying this, hackneyed as both the concept and word are, but I think what I am looking for is 'closure.' At some level I'd just like to feel like less of a shit."

"You are unbelievable. You think leveraging me into a trip before paying Danny what you owe him makes you less of a shit?"

"Look, Kate, I'm not going to argue with you. You asked me what I'm expecting. I'm expecting nothing more from you than that you show up. How you feel about it is your business. How I feel about it is mine. I'm not looking to rekindle anything or convince you of anything. All I want is to give you this money and, for some reason, to spend a few days in your company. Dying guys don't have to justify anything, and dying rich guys have to even less."

And of course he was right. *I* was the only one having to justify taking this trip. And in spite of knowing that Danny was owed this money, and Sarah Rose would surely need this money, I still wasn't positive I could handle going.

"Listen, Richard, I don't know what I can do about changing the dates," I said, stalling for time to reflect on all this. "Give me a day or two to see what I can come with, and I'll call you back, okay?"

"No problem," he said. "I hope you can arrange it."

I didn't say "me too." I just hung up, went directly into the bathroom, and stood under a steaming hot shower for the ten minutes it took each morning to feel completely human. Swaddling myself in the fat Egyptian terry cloth robe Karen had gotten me for our birthday, I padded back into the bedroom and pulled out one of the big red leather photo albums I kept on my bookshelf. It was marked Kids: 1991-2000, and even though I hadn't looked in it for the better part of a year, I always liked to have these albums close by. As anal retentive as Karen was about her clothes, I was the same about my pictures. There wasn't a

Christmas or a birthday party or a trip that wasn't fully documented and mounted in an album within one week of the event.
Whenever any of us were sick, we always piled all the albums
on the patient's bed to be pored over. It seemed to be foolproof
family medicine—whether you were three or forty-three.

Actually, Sarah Rose was four in most of the shots in this album. And while the majority of time we steered clear of photo-
graphing her right side, every now and then a snapshot would
show up that made it painfully clear what a lot of plastic surgery
lay ahead for her. There were two or three shots of her at a Grant
Park stage when a bunch of Disney characters came into town
and she'd begged to have her picture taken with Sleeping Beauty.
Sleeping Beauty must have been sleeping that day, because it
would have taken nothing but a compassionate twirl to Sarah's
other side and the photo would have been completely altered. But
no such luck. Instead, the raised topography of Sarah's scars was
highlighted by the sunshine and exacerbated by the contrast to
the silky porcelain beauty of the Disney character. I remember
when we first got the photo back, my first thought was to toss it
out, but something kept me from doing that. Getting her picture
taken with Sleeping Beauty was the whole reason Sarah Rose had
wanted to go to the Disney show, and it wasn't fair to edit her
memories for her. Besides, she was only thrilled with the picture.
In the first few weeks after we'd had it developed she'd asked for
a blowup of the picture to keep in her room. So if she could live
that comfortably at four with her scars, that photo always re-
minded me I was going to have to learn to live with them, too.

Danny's pictures from those years were less dramatic to an
outsider's eyes, but not to me. I could still wince looking at a
couple of them. There was one at the beginning of the album

when he was five years old, just before Tim and I were married. Money was particularly tight and Danny and I had had one of those classic Nike tennis shoe battles that plenty of parents were waging—and losing—with their kids. Only I didn't lose. There was no way I was spending $70 on a pair of tennis shoes for a five-year-old. I took him kicking and screaming to a discount store for a pair of knock-off shoes he detested and absolutely refused to wear the next day to his own birthday party. So all of the photos of him at his fifth birthday party show him in bare feet. Feeling completely defiant, completely deprived. And in some ways he had been. Not in terms of the economic perks so much as the emotional ones he could have had if his dad had stuck around and been honorable.

When my alarm actually did go off I put the album away, and went into the kitchen to sit down at the computer. The sun, streaming through the blinds, created uneven buttery stripes across our old wood floor. I logged on and opened a new document. Why I Should Not Go/Why I Should Go. A half hour later this is what I came up with…

Why I Should Not Go:

1. I detest Richard and everything he stands for. Why should I accommodate him on anything?

2. I have lived a rich and full life without his money and I can continue to do so.

3. What does that make me in my own eyes if I go? And more importantly what would that make me in my kids' eyes if they ever found out?

4. I do not want to lie to my kids.

Why I Should Go:

1. Danny deserves that money.

2. If I invest all of the $750,000, in nine years it will double and that will hopefully cover every single operation Sarah will ever need or opt to have.

3. Other than having breakfast and dinner with Richard, the only thing I will have to do with him is sightsee.

4. Unless he is lying to me yet again and he wants to have sex.

5. It sounds like he doesn't.

6. It's only six nights.

7. I'm a big girl and this is a big opportunity. All I have to do is go, get through it, come home and forget it.

That was the whole list of reasons. But the worst part was that once I put them down in black and white, none of the clarity I'd hoped for showed up. I still had no idea what I was going to do.

At least not until David put my entire dilemma out on the radio airwaves the next day.

Chapter Fourteen

"What's that?" inquired David when he walked into our office at 7:30. I'd beaten him there by five minutes for almost the first time ever—but then Richard's call had jump-started my morning.

A still steaming black coffee was sitting on his desk and on top of it, I'd set the keys to his cabin.

"It's coffee," I said, going to open the blinds. If we didn't shut them before leaving at night, every sunrise turned our office into a blazing hothouse. Over the years the navy couch had faded to dusty lavender, the hunter-green pillows had bleached to a tired lime and the once-orange desk chairs were now barely melon. Our office was a festival of seventies bridesmaids' colors.

"It isn't just coffee. It's coffee and the keys to my cabin," he said, holding the keys up to make sure they really were his.

"Kate, what's up? Why are you giving back the keys to my cabin? I thought everything was decided."

"It's not. Everything has changed and I don't know what I am going to do."

"Tell me what's going on," he said, taking a big gulp of his coffee and then giving me his full attention.

"What's going on is that I've been paralyzed by a sudden dose of bad news/good news."

"What bad news/good news?"

"Well, the bad news is Karen broke her leg and can't go to Rome, so if I want the deal to go through, I have to go to Rome my very own self. The good news is, at least we are out of the dicey impersonation game."

"So you've decided to go?"

"I still don't know. I am really torn. Part of me feels I should just put on my halo and walk away from this and the other part says, what would you rather have—a halo or a secure future for your children?"

"Tough question."

"The toughest."

"Suppose we put it to our listeners."

"What are you saying? I can't go on the air about this!"

"I'm not suggesting that. I just mean let's toss out the question to our listeners the way we do all the time—in completely hypothetical format."

"Are you kidding?"

"Of course not. They'll never know it's one of us. Remember when we asked what you do if you can't stand the child of your best friend? They didn't know that I was really talking about my college roommate's youngest daughter. And they didn't know it was your neighbor when we talked about people who always leave their dining room table permanently set and we got all those great calls from people who have been do-ing it for years. Come on, Kate. Let's see what Mr. or Ms. Av-erage America would do in your situation."

"Not Mr. Average America. You've already told me a man would have no problem taking off and maybe even going to bed with his ex-spouse—even without the money."

"Okay," he laughed. "Ms. America only. Are you ready to see what they'd do if they were in your place?"

"I suppose," I answered.

We walked into the studio and adjusted our headsets, while our producer Cody was already screening calls that would kick off the show. People seemed pretty hot under the communal col-lar that morning because of some just-mandated changes an-nounced in the local no-smoking regulations. The regulation no-smoking area in restaurants was being expanded from sixty percent to eighty-five.

We let the smokers vent for the first fifteen minutes of the show and then the topic moved over to the lottery. A huge Big Game winner had just been located and the usual "what would you do if you won the lottery" discussion ensued. I knew David would use it as a springboard to his little focus group plans, so I wasn't surprised at all when he segued into the topic. "Sup-pose you could get a windfall like the lottery, but to get it, you had to do something some people might think was really wrong."

"What do you mean, wrong?" I asked a bit defensively, won-dering whether at some level that was David's real take on my going to Rome.

"Not illegal or anything," he said, leaning back in his chair, but refusing to look at me. "But something some people might think was immoral."

"Like what," piped in our news guy Steve, a man addicted to ruminative discussions. He could spend hours in our office proposing "what if" situations.

"Like, let's see..." David pretended to conjecture. "Suppose your ex-husband, who owed you a bunch of money, offered to pay it all to you in one lump sum if you would go away with him for a week. Would you do it?"

"An ex that you like, or one that you don't like?" I asked hoping to crystallize the real quandary.

"An ex you can't stand. An ex you might even hate," said David, this time looking me directly in the eye. "Yup, here's the question, would you go away for a week with your very detested ex for a bunch of money? And just to make it more interesting, let's add this—what if sex with him was possibly part of the deal? Give us a call at 555-7200," David continued, pushing the control button so we could break for a few minutes of spots.

The phones lit up instantly. All five lines were flashing before we were even thirty seconds into our first commercial. David leaned back in his chair, nodded at the control board, and grinned. "Guess we found ourselves something of a conversational hot button. Just in case you thought your dilemma was too bizarre for people to relate to."

The calls were astonishing. The first woman said flat out, "No way would I travel, much less sleep, with my ex-husband for money."

The next caller was a woman named Melissa.

"Hey, Melissa," said David, "so, do you have an ex-spouse that fits the 'I can't stand him' category?"

"Actually, I have two," said the woman.

"And if either of them were to say to you, 'I'll give you cash money if you will come away with me for a week,' what would you say?"

"Well, to the first one I'd say, 'how much cash money?'"

"And to the second one?"

"I'd say the same thing, but I'd also want to know where we were going."

"Why is that?" I interjected.

"Because I really do hate the second one, so even if it was a lot of money, if it was just to someplace like Dubuque for a week, I might have to reconsider."

"So let's say it's London," I added. "Detested ex-husband number one or detested ex-husband number two is offering you a week in London. How much money would it take for you to spend a whole week with one of these guys in London? 'Cause you're saying you'd do it, right?"

"Right. I would. Let's see, a week? Well, with Gordon, my first husband, it would take maybe $50,000, but with Jeffrey, my second husband, it would take more."

"Why?"

"Because I really do hate him."

"How much more?"

"I don't know, maybe another $150,000. That's what it would take. $200,000."

"Well, as long as we have you on the line, let's go to part two of our inquiry. For the $200,000 would you be willing to have sex?" asked David, ever the provocateur.

"Sex?" gasped Melissa.

"Yes, sex, Melissa," said David. "Do you think either one of your ex-husbands might expect that his offer included sex?"

There was a momentary silence. "Well…Gordon probably

would, but I don't know about Jeffrey. I'm not really sure what they'd expect, but if either of them did, I'd have to say I'd tack on an extra $100,000 for that."

"So let me get this right, Melissa. Unlike our first caller, you would definitely go off for a week, even sleep with, either one of your two ex-husbands, both of whom you hate."

"Correct," she said unapologetically. "I mean, I don't know if it's 'correct' or not, but yes, I'm pretty sure I would do it."

The rest of the calls were just as amazing. Maybe two more people called in and said, "no way" to the hypothetical (for them, anyway) proposition, but the bulk of the calls revealed that very old, very shopworn truth: everybody has a price. For some it was two million, for one woman it was $20,000, there was no universal amount. The only thing universal about it was that if the amount was significant enough to change the lives of the woman and her family then, much as she'd like to be a martyr, she'd ultimately go for the deal.

I was blown away.

David and I signed off at one o'clock and as we walked down the hall to our office, he said, "Feel like processing some of what we just heard?"

"I guess," I said, setting my headphones down on my desk.

"Great," he said, grabbing my arm. "Let's go. It's too nice to be inside. Let's grab one of those tables on the river walk."

Within minutes we were out the imposing Art Deco doors of our building and headed a few blocks north on Michigan Avenue.

Several years ago some developers decided to construct a mini boardwalk along the Chicago River in order to perch several lovely summer cafés along the water's edge. All you had to do was walk down thirty stairs from the gargantuan concrete sculptures on the Michigan Avenue Bridge and it was as if you'd descended into a charming, umbrellaed Mediterranean resort. White tables were scattered everywhere, pots of flowers hung from the trees, and it felt like a hit of St. Tropez in the heart of the Midwest. Tables always went fast, and by the time we got there, things were bustling.

It was one of Chicago's glisteny days. Our table was right on the edge of the glorious sage-green water. Everything reflected silver off everything else. If you worked for the tourism bureau on a day like this you might as well go home. Nothing you could do in the office could sell the city half as effectively as it was selling itself outside.

David unfolded his napkin and picked up a bread stick. "So what do you think?"

"I think it was astonishing to hear how many of those women would take their ex-husbands up on this offer. Weren't you surprised?"

"No, I wasn't," said David, pushing his sunglasses back on his head so I could at last see his eyes and not my own squinty reflection. "For all the high romance women claim to have, I find you to be a remarkably pragmatic gender."

"I guess so. Still, spending a week with Richard...I don't know, just being polite to him is going to feel so fake. I can't imagine it."

David motioned the waitress over to take our orders. When she left he said, "Of course you can imagine it. It will feel exactly like the long commercials we have to read sometimes for a product we think is stupid. Come on, Kate. You and I get paid to fake it."

"But only in sixty-second increments."

"Then maybe just look at this as a week-long commercial," he said, leaning forward on his tanned arms.

"Why are you sounding so cavalier about my going, David?"

I must have caught him up short, because he stiffened and said, "Wait a minute, Kate. How do I come off as cavalier? I've told you from the beginning that either way you decide, I am there to support you. I *care* what happens to you. And I'll tell you something that's tough for me to say. I've been guarded and at arm's length for almost three years. Not just from you, but from everybody. I didn't want to let too much in. But your directness and your candor are compelling qualities. Qualities I value. I like you. And I like feeling the feeling of genuinely liking you and being off automatic pilot. You want to know the truth? I'm not crazy about the idea of you going to Rome and meeting this guy. But for me to say that, given our current relationship, would be completely selfish and completely inappropriate. So trust me on this, I am not feeling one bit cavalier about you taking off to meet this guy. Not even close to it."

Relationships shift in odd ways at odd moments. Not only with candlelit dinners or cataclysmic fights, they can shift in broad daylight in a public place seconds before a waitress comes up to you and says, "So who had the club sandwich?"

She set mine down in front of me and I squinted at it, pretending to see if the bacon was crisp enough, but actually stealing a look at David to confirm if I could see any visible signs of the shift our relationship had just taken, or if it would just be something I would feel. But feel it I did. It was nice. It felt like a little bit of shelter. I was ready for that.

"Listen," he said cutting into his cheeseburger and then setting it down without taking a bite. "I can't tell you what to do.

There's a whole lot of money riding on this decision—money that plenty of people, as we heard this morning, would not be able to turn their backs on. But if you do go over there, and you need someone other than your sister to phone so you can re-ground yourself from the strange space you're stepping into, I want you to call me."

"Okay," I said, feeling touched and tentative.

"We're used to talking every day anyway, you know?"

"Yeah." I smiled. "I know."

What I didn't know was how it would feel to actually sit down and tell the kids I was going to Rome.

But given that I had two different children, of course it felt two different ways.

Sarah Rose seemed actually excited. "Mommy, is Italy far away—like past the North Pole? Will they give you pizza for breakfast every morning? Will you bring me some candy from another language?"

Danny's reaction was considerably less effusive. Ever since school had ended, he'd been working extra hours at the insurance agency and he came home crabby and listless every night. "Rome? I guess if you're stashing us at Tim's for a week, you might as well be somewhere really far away." He shrugged, pushing his plate away. The three of us were having our regular Wednesday Backwards Dinner. We called it Backwards Dinner, because it was all breakfast food. Five or six cereal boxes were always on the table along with fruit, bacon and my famous ched-dar/chive/chorizo scrambled eggs.

Sarah Rose looked confused by Danny's churlishness. "Mommy, even though I'm staying at Daddy's, can I still go to Isabelle's birthday party?" Isabelle Vinicio lived next door to us and was having a Chuck E. Cheese's birthday party the following weekend.

"Sure, honey," I said, pulling her over to my lap, missing her already. "Daddy or Danny will drive you there."

"Mom, no way am I going to Tim's. I've told you, I do not need a baby-sitter!"

"Danny, Tim is not a baby-sitter. He's your stepdad."

"*Was* my stepdad. You got divorced remember? Like you always do," he said, pushing back from the table, and noisily stacking the dishes.

"That was absolutely uncalled-for." I slid Sarah off my lap and stood up. "I'm going upstairs with Sarah now to give her a bath, and when I come back down, and you've done the dishes, we will finish this discussion."

It didn't go particularly better when the two of us reconvened a half hour later. Danny was merely disgruntled that I was going, but he remained livid about having to stay at Tim's. Nonetheless, it was not even a negotiable point as far as I was concerned.

And that was just the beginning of the logistical challenges I still had to orchestrate. Because when you are woman who is about to fly off to secretly meet an ex-husband you hate, there are indeed some serious logistical challenges.

Like…how in the world do you do it?

Well, for starters, you arrange with your program director to take your vacation a few days early, just as your detested ex-husband has requested.

Then you ask yourself, "What the hell am I doing?"

Then you tell your not-detested second ex-husband that,

oops, you are *not* going to a North Carolina seminar after all, you are going on a free trip to Rome and you give him the actual hotel number where you'll be staying.

Then you ask yourself, "What the hell am I doing?"

Then you open a courier envelope and take out a fully paid first-class ticket sent to you by your detested ex-husband.

Then you ask yourself, "What the hell am I doing?"

Then you pack up your suitcase, pull out your passport and kiss your cherished two kids (even the churlish one) goodbye.

Then you ask yourself, "What the hell am I doing?"

And then two hours later you do it. You get on a plane, and the ticket says Rome, and you hope with all your heart that this isn't the dumbest move of your entire life.

Chapter Fifteen

One of the things that I've always found comforting when I travel to foreign places is that the word "taxi" is the same in so many languages. That way you always know you can do at least one thing right—i.e., get a taxi—before you start screwing up. Of course in Italy, the *getting* of a taxi is not problematic—it's the *being* in one.

Because the taxi you are in is being driven by an Italian, who has a completely different set of driving rhythms and moves than Americans are used to. For instance, in Italy if there is a stop sign, your average Italian driver doesn't stop. To stop would be suicidal. It would guarantee being rear-ended. So there is an entire *stop / start / slide / almost crash / swerve / swear* ballet that goes on over there all the time. It's Dodgem with big people cars. Not that I didn't have respect for Italian driving skills, it's just that I didn't have quite enough deodorant left on to maintain my ladylike appearance during our harrowing drive from the airport into the city.

I was grungy and hot when I checked in to the Hassler's front lobby. Perched at the very top of the Spanish Steps, the Hassler is something of a Roman institution. What the Plaza is to New York, the Beverly Hills is to Los Angeles, that's what the Hassler is to Rome. It was Richard's kind of place—long on service, even longer on cachet. It would be important to Richard to say to someone, "Call me at the Hassler."

"Buon giorno, signora," said the porter as I tried to unstick my wrinkled blouse from my sweaty back while exiting the cab.

"Buon giorno," I parroted back, without adding the *"signor,"* for fear of sounding too much like I was back in my high school Italian class. This language stuff was always dicey. I remembered Karen's hilarious story about her first bilingual affair. She spent her junior year abroad and after eight months in France she fancied herself quite the first-rate French linguist. Just before coming home she went to the South of France for a month where she fell in love with a boy named Jean-Claude. He spoke no English and Karen, as linguistically arrogant as she was, was positive that she could handle all their relationship moments in his native language. And maybe she could have—if they hadn't gone to bed together. Because as they were making love the first time, her caring French boyfriend asked her the universally problematic, "Was it good for you" question. And while it was only so-so for her, she did what all women do at some time or another—she lied. She said in what she assumed to be impeccable French, "Yes, I just came."

And the French guy burst out laughing. Because the problem was, Karen didn't know that the way to say that in French was *"j'ai joui,"* which literally translated means "I have enjoyed." She instead decided to do a direct translation of French into English, which wound up saying *"je suis arrivé."* And in so doing, had basically said something along the lines of "the train has just arrived."

Nonetheless, it appeared that so far I hadn't insulted the Hassler's porter with my highly rusty Italian. Again he said, *"signora,"* and nodded for me to follow him inside. The yellow marbled lobby was blessedly air-conditioned and filled with smart-looking people in good outfits. It took no time at all to register, given that Richard had already taken care of that, and when the spiffy man whose name tag said Alessandro handed me the key, he also handed me an envelope. *"Un messaggio, signora."*

Richard didn't even use the hotel paper. It had to be his own stationery—an oversized, thick creamy card with R. L. Farley embossed along the side. It said "6:00 a.m." at the top and then the note read, "Kate, I'm going to Geneva for the day and should be back by early evening. Be ready for dinner at eight-thirty. We have a table at Agnoletti's two blocks down on Via Sistina. Enjoy your day. R."

What a break. One whole day out of six where I'd only be with him for two hours. It seemed like a good start.

Suite 819 was only perfect. A small paneled foyer led to a stunning pale yellow sitting room. A gray love seat faced a mirrored fireplace. Floor-to-ceiling bookshelves covered one entire wall while the other contained two sets of French doors opening onto a balcony. A third set of French doors opposite the fireplace opened into my bedroom, which was also pale yellow and had a beautiful Venetian glass mirror over the dressing table. The bed was covered in a creamy damask spread and faced yet another set of doors. These were oak-paneled and must have opened into Richard's part of the suite. But at the moment they were blessedly locked.

Everyone had left for the morning when I called Tim's and left a message that I'd arrived, so I hung up, unpacked and surveyed the clothes Karen had loaned me for the trip. The woman had actually drawn me a diagram of all the different ways I could mix and match the ensembles she'd put together. It was like having a customized version of one of those "Six Pieces, Forty-Seven Outfits" articles they always have in the magazines. And the truth was that Karen's mix-and-match diagrams were a huge help. Karen got all the accessorizing genes when we were born. I am emotionally exhausted after putting together a white T-shirt and khakis.

Not only was Karen a chronic cataloger of her wardrobe, but she also invoked the dreaded "one hundred times and then toss out" numbering system. That meant every time she wore an item of clothing, she logged in what number that particular wearing was. And after the one-hundredth wearing, that item, whether she still loved it or not—went directly into the Goodwill pile. Which, blessedly, I got to go through before she gave to Goodwill.

I showered, slipped on a black-and-taupe print sundress and went out to my balcony to get the lay of the land. Where to start in the Eternal City on virtually no sleep? Anywhere my map and my guidebook would take me. I'd decided that it was stupid to spend any psychic energy on pretending I wasn't a tourist when I most certainly was. Granted it's embarrassing to be a tourist anywhere. Not that travel isn't cool, but you reek of not knowing the ropes. My plan was to give in to that—hang the camera around my neck, and gawk when I felt like gawking.

Every city has a different kind of light. Paris's is a bruised pink, Chicago's is blue/white, Amsterdam's is an old pearly gray. But the light of Rome is a dusty, seasoned sienna and it makes everyone and everything look radiant from within. I must have walked the streets for two hours, taking in the smells, the clanging of lunch dishes being washed and put away to dry and even the muffled murmurs of siesta time going on behind the closed brown wooden shutters. The city felt like no other place I'd ever been at three-thirty in the afternoon. So conspicuously shut down, yet so conspicuously full of promise.

I staggered back to my hotel, closed my own shutters, and took a much-needed three-hour nap. For forty minutes anyway. Then I bolted awake, heart pounding, stomach roiling, mouth cottony dry. I knew exactly what was coming next—dinner with Richard.

And of course he was impeccably prompt.

16

Chapter Sixteen

He didn't even look shitty. How can a dying man not look a little shitty? Particularly a shitty dying man? There was no justice.

If anything, Richard looked better than I remembered. His hair had gone to salt-and-pepper, and if he'd lost any, it couldn't have been more than about twenty-seven strands. Lovely crow's-feet winged out from his light blue eyes, but beyond those, there wasn't a single wrinkle or pouchy jowl thing to indicate that he was about to be fifty—not to mention about to leave this earth. His clothes were exquisite with an attention to detail I hadn't quite remembered. Tie, sport coat and slacks were all in different, but completely blendable shades of taupe. The crisp white shirt he wore set off his tan—I guess if you've got one kind of cancer, you stop worrying about another—and the overall effect was like being confronted by a real-life mature guy ad from *GQ.*

"Kate." He smiled, extending his hand and touching me for the first time in fifteen years. "It's wonderful to see you."

I'd failed. I failed the hello test. It was the test that Muriel had explained to Karen and me years ago after having dinner with an old high school boyfriend. This man had moved to California, but every few years he would come through town and call her for lunch. She wasn't still in love with him or anything, but she always seemed pleased when he came to town. And then one day when Karen and I were about twenty, Muriel came home from seeing him and was a complete wreck. "I knew I shouldn't have met him outside in all that natural light," she groaned. "Every year we've gotten together for lunch he's always said, 'Mur, you *look* great.' This time he said, 'Mur, it's great *to see you*.' A knife, I'm telling you, a knife in your mother's heart."

And while Richard's "It's wonderful to see you" was hardly a knife in my heart, it did lead me to believe he'd had a more youthful version of me superimposed on his expectations. Oh, well, *c'est la biological vie*. I'd put on this little black jersey dress that Karen had marked "wear with the strappy black and red sandals and the chunky silver earrings and necklace in my jewelry bag." I was about as pulled together as I can get, but even with fresh makeup, I didn't look twenty-eight. And twenty-eight was exactly how old I'd been when Richard and I last stood face-to-face.

This time, however, Richard and I stood side by side as we descended to the lobby in the mahogany elevator. It was so strange. We made no pretense at any catch-up conversation. Instead, both of us looked straight ahead as if we were a long-term married couple who knew every quotidian detail of each other's lives and what could we possibly have to talk about on yet another elevator ride? *"Attenzionei, signori,"* said the operator as he let us out into the lobby.

The evening was warm and heavy. Even at this hour people

were still rushing home with their glossy shopping bags from the upscale stores on Via Borgognona and Via Condotti. Cell phones were glued to the ears of most of them and the air was filled with staccato snippets of fast-paced Italian conversation. They were probably only saying things like "I'll be home in twenty minutes," but to me it all sounded urgent and exotic. We walked up the steep narrow sidewalks of Via Sistina past fancy purse stores and art galleries and apartments to the front entrance of Agnoletti's. Like all restaurants in Rome, half of the place spilled out into the street underneath the requisite green awning. By the time we got there all the pink linened tables were jammed with animated diners. Richard had reserved an inside table in the back. "They're one of the few restaurants with air-conditioning," he said, nodding as he stepped back to let me walk in front of him and behind the maitre d'.

It *was* cooler inside and that was a relief. But the minute I sat down and realized I was about to spend two hours across a table from Richard, I felt a close personal affinity with alcoholics all over the world: I *craved* a drink.

Richard must have too, because within seconds he had called *"Senta! Ci porti una bottigila di barolo,"* to catch the waiter's attention and order some wine.

"Where'd you learn the Italian?" I asked, somewhat curious.

"I haven't really. But when I moved to Canada I became interested in opera, so I've picked up a few words."

I let "moved" to Canada go. No point in getting my dukes up if we were both hoping to get through this alive. Well, at least one of us was hoping to get through it alive. Plus the more interesting piece of information was that Richard had taken up opera. He'd always professed to hate it when I'd known him.

We talked a bit about Puccini, whom he apparently favored over everybody, and between the opera chat and the wine kicking in, it got better. Not lovely, not warm and fuzzy, but better. For starters Richard actually asked to see a picture of Danny. I had such mixed feelings about it. On one hand, how dare he ask to see his son? On the other, how dare he not?

I reached into my bag and pulled out my wallet. I've never been a mom who walked around with a mini album, but every year on the first day of school, I've taken a send-off picture of the kids. I handed Richard the one from last fall saying, "That's Danny heading off to junior year in high school, and that's his sister, Sarah Rose, on her way to second grade."

Richard was quiet for several minutes. I didn't know if it was because he was putting a face on this kid who had been not only an abstraction, but a huge piece of denial all these years, or if he spotted the burn scars on Sarah Rose's neck, and was deciding whether to ask about it.

"Remarkable," he said, setting the photo down by his silverware. "Mind if I leave it here while we eat?"

"Sure," I said hesitantly, finding the request both touching and infuriating. As was his next question.

"What kind of kid is he?" he asked absently while motioning our waiter over to give our order.

"You want the Cliffs Notes version of our child, Richard, or the unabridged? I mean, I can give you either," I said ripping off a chunk of coarse peasant bread.

"Jesus," he said, leaning back in his chair and setting his hands at the table's edge. "Let's do take two on this, okay? I'm not looking for any trouble here. I understand that you're still angry. I can't do anything about that. I can't change what happened fifteen years ago. But I'm going to die soon, and I think it's understandable that I'm interested in who this kid is. I'm not saying I'm entitled to information, but since I'm never going to know him, asking questions is the only way I can find out about him. We've got a couple days so I don't need everything up front, but I would like to hear more about him. Do you want some more wine?"

"Sure," I said, actually feeling a bit guilty that I'd snapped at him, which was a completely girl way to respond. It was the old "you've been a son of a bitch for fifteen years, but please forgive me for mentioning it" moment. Even so, it was clear we'd better stay off the topic of Danny for the evening. "Do you come here often?"

He smiled. "That sounds like a seventies pickup line, remember?"

Reluctantly I nodded. "Yeah, I guess it does. But I don't think anyone ever used it on me."

"I certainly didn't," he said, making room so the waiter could set down our plates of *prosciutto e melone.*

"Why would you have even used a pickup line on me? We already knew each other."

"But don't you remember what I said to make it clear that I was interested?"

"Richard, I don't want to go down memory lane here."

Ignoring me, he plowed forward. "It was after the floods in Kankakee. You were down there for three days, knee-deep in mud and muscling out half of the TV guys to file your stories. Remember the one you did on the orphaned pets? Anyway, you did a hell of a job. And you walked into my office at the station in these khaki shorts and a sleeveless shirt, gritty and muddy, and I was very proud of you. And very turned on. You looked like an Amazon warrior."

"I'm too short to be an Amazon warrior," I said, trying to deflect him from cheap nostalgia. But he plodded on.

"And when we were done talking, I said to you, 'Take off the rest of the day. Get yourself a beer or a shower.' Actually, I think I said, 'I'd be happy to provide either one.' Do you remember?"

Of course I remembered it. With horror. Double horror. Horror that twenty years ago a boss could say things like that to a woman employee, and horror that at the time I thought it was about the sexiest, most exciting thing I'd ever heard. So much for being twenty-six. I nodded that I remembered. And I remembered everything else that followed.

How we traipsed over to Riccardo's even though I was sweaty and grimy, how we proceeded to throw down two double martinis (again so much for being twenty-six), and how two hours later we were naked in Richard's shower kissing and soaping each other on our way to twelve incredible hours in bed and all the trouble that followed. Oh yes, I remembered.

"So what exactly were you doing in Geneva today?" I asked in a determined effort to pull Richard away from the hot memories zone and back into the land of the here and now. It worked. Until it was time for our espressos. Suddenly Richard reached for my hand. "Richard, don't," I said pulling it back.

"Kate I need to say something to you. I need to tell you how much it means to me that you're here. When a man gets to the end of his life, he starts to look back over it and review the parts that seem to be the most valuable. You were one of those parts. In all these years there was never another woman who came close to you—you dusted them all. You really were the only one. And that's why it seems so important to get things right."

Had the air conditioner stopped running? The sweat was running down my back. "Oh, please God, don't let this speech last one more second," I was praying. "Don't make these five days be filled with declarations of too-late love and too-useless regret," because I didn't want to hear any of it.

God was listening. Mercifully, Richard shut down the devotion machine as quickly as he had started it up. He leaned back in his chair and announced, "Well, enough of that. Let's see. Maybe we should talk about tomorrow. I think the best place to start is the Forum." It was so Richard. So tour director. So impervious to the and-what-would-*you*-like-to-see concept. And yet what did it matter? I was happy to see anything.

As long as it wasn't too much of Richard.

Chapter Seventeen

In truth, that first night was remarkably painless. Richard simply left me at my door and said, "Meet me in the lobby at eight tomorrow morning and we'll run down to Caffe Greco for coffee. I'll have the driver pick us up down there at eight-thirty. Good night, Kate." And then he squeezed my arm and turned to go to his room.

I stepped into mine and it had been transformed. The bed was turned down, the shutters that I had closed against the late-afternoon sun had been opened so the twinkling lights of the city surrounded me, and all the plastic cleaner bags that I had left strewn around the room had been neatly folded and placed on the top shelf of my closet.

I pulled off the little black dress, dropped a Cubs T-shirt over my head and dove for the phone. Rome was seven hours ahead of Chicago, so my hope was that Sarah Rose would be home already from day camp. She was, and before I could even ask how she was, she squealed, "Mommy, Mommy, what's it like in Italy? Is the pizza the same?"

"I don't know, honey. I haven't had any yet."

"Didn't you have dinner?" she asked, sounding concerned I might be hungry.

"Yes, but I didn't order pizza."

"You didn't order pizza?"The child was incredulous. "Mommy, you are really silly."

I laughed, but only stayed on the phone with her for a few minutes. She and Tim were just leaving to go sailing. Tim kept a sailboat up in Wilmette Harbor and they were heading up there for a picnic on the boat. I knew Danny wouldn't be home from his insurance company job yet, so I placed a call to Karen whose machine must have known I'd check in, because it answered, "If you are wondering why Her Royal Gimpiness isn't at home, it's because she's making her first sortie to the doctor to have her cast recast. If you are my sister, please report in tomorrow. If you are a robber, be duly warned that my fierce and loyal rott-weiler, Thor, is indeed still home and will have to kill you if you show up. Right, Thor?" And then there was a terrifying roar from the nonexistent Thor that Karen must have pulled off some other tape.

My last call was to David. But unlike the other two, which felt somewhat routine, this one felt a little different. My rela-tionships with Tim and the kids and Karen were very fixed, very constant. But that wasn't the case with David. We were clearly reformatting our relationship, moving from being just col-leagues to being personal friends. Or something. It was tricky stuff. I mean, in the past two weeks besides kissing my forehead and cooking for me, David had even danced with me. Dancing with someone these days is a big deal. I had never thought about that until two years ago when Samantha and I had a call on our show from a woman who told us that in the past ten years she had actually slept with more men than she had danced with.

"No one ever dances anymore," the woman had lamented. "In fact this is probably the first time in history when people are more likely to sleep together before they dance together. I can think of two times in particular when I was well into a relationship and then realized I had no idea how the man danced. And both times I panicked when I realized that maybe I had already been naked with a person who would turn out to be a huge clod on the dance floor. For me bad dancing is a deal point. I think it's important to sleep with someone before you marry him, but I think it's even more important that you dance with him before you sleep with him. You don't want to be stuck being in love with a lousy dancer."

Well, David had definitely passed the dancing part, I thought as I took the phone out on the little balcony overlooking the red tile roofs and mosaic basilicas, and sat down in the wrought-iron chair, to call him.

"Hello," he answered. A Carly Simon CD was on in the background.

"Hi. I am so glad you're home."

"Me too. I just got back from my run."

"How far do you go?" I asked while flashing on the fact that I may have already danced with David, but I had actually never seen his legs. Not that guys' legs tend to surprise you the way women's legs do. For the most part, the unseen guys' leg was not going to disappoint. You definitely could not say that about women's legs. Women's legs tended to go south on them somewhere around their twenty-third birthday. It was one of the great inequities.

"I usually run four miles or so. Did you have a good flight?"

"Mmm-hmm. Did you have a good show?"

"No. It sucked. I'm not used to operating alone anymore. You've turned me from a solo act into a real partner."

I smiled. I knew what he meant. Most people in radio want their very own solo show. I never have. Nor had Samantha. We both wanted our partner to be there all the time, to hang with, to bounce off, to disagree with. For a woman who fancied herself pretty individualistic in life, I was very collaborative in work. The show that I liked to give listeners was a show based on chemistry—not ego.

"Why did the show suck?" I asked.

"Kate, why are we talking about the show? Tell me about Rome. Not the sights, which I assume you haven't seen much of, but what it feels like to be there with this Richard."

"Why *this* Richard?" I asked, dodging the question because it was so hard to crystallize my answer.

"You mean instead of saying 'Richard' or 'your ex-husband'?"

"Yeah. It makes him sound like a specimen."

"Well," he said thoughtfully, "let me see. One, I don't know him, so 'Richard' seems inappropriately familiar. And two, I guess because it's a little defensive. It keeps some twinge at bay. A twinge that arguably I have no business having, but in the twenty-four hours since you left, it's a twinge I seem to have nonetheless."

What do you say when someone says something that makes you feel so good? Not good because David was jealous—because he wasn't saying that—but good because he wasn't neutral.

And that made me feel connected to him—newly and sweetly connected.

"Kate, are you there?"

"I'm here," I said, standing up so I could survey the rooftops that were lacquered by moonlight. "I am so glad to be talking to you."

And then I really began talking. I told David how bizarre and edgy I felt with Richard, how I wondered if I would ever process my rage about his leaving Danny and me, how the very sight of him triggered all these dark unhealthy emotions that I had presumed to be long gone, and how maybe I'd made a huge mistake in coming. He just let me rant on until I ran out of steam.

"David? How come you're not saying anything?"

"I can't, Kate," he sighed. "I can't say to you don't have your feelings, and don't worry, everything will be fine. I don't know any parallels to the situation you are in. I don't know your history—I know your facts but I don't know your inside emotional history with this guy. So who knows how you'll be? I'm thinking you'll do fine because of the thought you've put into your decision to go there and because of the person you are. But this is a real loaded situation."

"I know," I said quietly, wishing more than anything it was six days from now.

"But, Kate, listen to me. I am here—" he stopped a second "—man, I have not said or felt this in a long time, but I am here for you in whatever version you want—partners, friends, I don't know, you know what I'm saying?"

And I did. I knew what he was saying, and also what he *wasn't* saying. I felt it seven thousand miles away.

It felt good.

18

Chapter Eighteen

Count on Richard to pick the one place where you could spend more on a cup of coffee than anywhere else in Rome. Even though the espressos at Caffe Greco were still bargain-basement priced compared to Starbucks.

"This place has been around since the seventeenth century. Goethe, Dickens, Mark Twain, Oscar Wilde—all of them hung out here," said Richard as he expansively gestured around the red velvet room. You'd have thought he owned it. But then he'd always acted that way, no matter where he went.

The café was cool and dark, a welcome prerespite from what promised to be a scorching day. I had gotten up at five and stepped out onto my little balcony to take in the glorious morning smells of fresh bread baking in the ovens of a nearby *panificio*. Without showering I slipped on a pair of shorts and my Nikes and headed out of the lobby for a solo walk. The doorman on duty, clearly used to the grungy workout wardrobes of foreigners, suggested that I walk down to the Trevi Fountain.

"Ees easy. You just go down the Spanish Steps to Via dei Due Macelli and then over to Via del Tritone. La Fontina ees very crowded later in the day," he counseled, "but in the morning, is *perfetto. Molto calmo.* Is difficult in Roma to find the *calmo* sometimes."

I thought it was a good a suggestion. When I got there twenty minutes later, I thought it was a fabulous suggestion. Hidden way back on a side street, this gargantuan, ornate, completely-out-of-sync-with-its-surroundings-in-terms-of-scale-and-elegance fountain defies you to do anything but gasp. It isn't clean; it isn't graceful; it is simply complicated and imposing. And just as the doorman promised, I had it all to myself. No humans, no gelato vendors, no gasping buses could muffle the sounds of the cascading waters.

I took a deep breath and wondered whether to do what you're supposed to do at the Trevi Fountain—toss in a coin—to insure a return trip to Rome. But depending on what happened in these next few days in Rome, how did I know if I'd ever want to come back?

I hung on to my money.

Richard pulled 3,000 lira out of his wallet and left it on the marble-topped bar. *"Andiamo,"* he said, taking my elbow to steer me outside to the waiting car.

"Come on, Richard," I said, extricating my elbow. "So you speak fifty words of Italian. I'm an American. You are too. Let's stick to our native language."

"Jesus, Kate," he said almost smiling. "The old bullshit detector is still cranking, isn't it?"

I couldn't tell if that was a compliment or chastisement, so I just let it go and followed him to the waiting black sedan. Our driver's name was Fabrizio, and he was not only in charge of the driving, it turned out he was a certified guide for the city and environs. He couldn't have been more than thirty, with wavy brown hair, pale green eyes and a grin that made you know he spent a lot of hours engaged in the national pastime—mentally undressing every woman who crossed his path.

"*Buon giorno, Dottore.*" He nodded to Richard. In Italy, every man who wasn't a plumber seemed to be referred to as "*Dottore.*" It had to be a heartache for all the Ph.D.s.

"*Buon giorno.* This is Signora Lerner. She has never been to Rome before, so suppose we start with the Forum? *Va bene?*" Richard asked me, completely ignoring my request to drop the patronizing Italian. Of course, this was a man who could be patronizing in many languages, so I supposed the exact words weren't really the issue.

For the next ten minutes, while we snaked our way through the already glutted, alley-sized streets of the city, Fabrizio proceeded to recite the legend of Romulus and Remus, the twin baby boys suckled by the she-wolf, and raised at the foot of the Palatine hills, where Rome was allegedly born. It was a wonderful story and more wonderful still was our entry into the Forum which completely short-circuited the long lines of Germans, Japanese and Americans already lined up for the nine o'clock opening.

"*Venite con me,*" said Fabrizio. "Come. We get in a few minutes before eet opens." And we passed through another gate, while he nodded and paid a discreetly excessive amount of Richard's lira to one of the ticket-takers. And suddenly the three of us were alone, surrounded by two thousand years of open-air history.

Walking around the Forum is like walking through a crumbling Hollywood backlot. There is an initial sense that what you are surrounded by has to be fake, has to be an illusion. Probably because it is too powerful an idea at first to acknowledge that you are actually standing on the same terra firma where Julius Caesar once stood. Even if you haven't thought of Julius since the eighth grade.

And though it is initially hard to visualize the way this vast village of ruins actually worked, once you spend a couple of hours walking among the felled columns and ancient stones and hearing the descriptions of daily life from the fabulous Fabrizio, you began to feel the distinctly palpable resonance of what was once a raucous, vibrant world. Decadent baths, sacrificial virgins, haranguing orators, haggling merchants all were no longer abstract fragments of some arid history lesson. They seemed viable and feel-able when you were standing right there at the epicenter.

The awe I was feeling must have been registered on my face, because the whole time we spent in the Forum, I could feel Richard's eyes insistently glued to *me,* not our surroundings. He was like a parent who takes his child to the circus, but the show for him is watching the child watch the circus, not the circus itself. In someone else I might have found that proprietary attitude rather sweet, but in Richard I hated it. It felt so Richard as Benefactor-ish. Had he been able to get away with it, I had no doubt that he'd have wanted me to think he'd built the Forum for me.

"Wait till I show you the Colosseum," he said so grandiosely that he nearly morphed from Richard as Benefactor to Richard as Emperor.

It took us ten minutes to cross several bus-crammed boulevards to get to the ancient scaffolded arena. Once we were inside, Richard's cell phone began to ring and, of course, he not only took the call, he stayed on for twenty minutes. No matter that signs saying No Cell Phones were posted all over the place—rules didn't apply to Richard. And no matter that even without the warning signs, a normal person would just know that it's not good form to be yammering on a phone while visiting one of the treasures of the ancient world. But yammer Richard did, as Fabrizio and I wove our way through the curious arches and he described in detail the bloody athletic events that once went on right where we were standing.

Richard eventually caught up with us. "Sorry," he said perfunctorily, placing his hand on my shoulder.

I stiffened instantly. There were a lot of things I didn't want on my shoulder—a basket of heavy wet laundry was one of them. Bird poop was another. But at that moment Richard's hand was at the top of my list. I pulled away. Unperturbed, he lifted his hand to shade his eyes as he pretentiously clucked, "Look at all this. We come and surround ourselves in the past and yet we seem destined never to learn from history."

It was a typically hyperbolic statement from Richard. But also one that was hard to argue. How much had I learned from history? After all that had happened with this man, I still had flown across the ocean to spend a week with him—a week that felt longer and longer with each passing hour.

"*Signori,*" said Fabrizio, who could speak enough English to understand that his clients had just hit a scratchy moment, "ees too hot now to tourist. We eat a little something. I take you to a trattoria *molto bella.*"

And within minutes we were at a very beautiful little trattoria—simple, cool, with a lovely grapevine-covered patio. The second we walked in, a large, dark-haired woman pulled a rope on a big bell to signal a noisy welcome. *"Caro Fabrizio, vieni qui. Mi piacere vederti. Non ci vediamo da molto tempo. Come va?"*

"Non c'e male, Francesca," he said, kissing the woman on each cheek tenderly. *"E tu? Come stanno i bambini?"*

"Benissimi," she said. *"Sono dietro in giardino."*

"This is my cousin, Francesca," Fabrizio said to me. "Francesca, Dottore Farley *e* Signora Lerner."

"Piacere," said the woman extending a rough hand. *"Andiamo a tavola."* She led us to a longish wooden table covered with a big square of the kind of paper we used to finger paint on. In the center there was a water bottle filled with fresh stems of bougainvillea, and while we seated ourselves Francesca raced to bring us three glasses and a bottle of cold white wine. Richard pushed his glass away. "None for me. Last night was an exception, but I'm not supposed to drink with the meds I'm on."

Fabrizio poured Richard some water, and said, "Francesca and *la famiglia?* They leef upstairs. Theese trattoria ees very *famosa* here in Rome for the *rigatoni arrabbiati.* But it ees too hot to have it today."

I couldn't think about food. All I could think about was that this woman acted perfectly normally, but she lived right here within eyeshot of the Colosseum! "Fabrizio, are you saying they just *live* here?"

"Si, Signora."

"That's amazing! I mean that's like living next door to the Great Pyramid! What is that like when you're explaining to the Chinese restaurant where to deliver? 'Just go to the Colosseum, hang a right at the big arch and we're down the block a bit?'"

He threw his head back and laughed. "Ees not a problem. We don't have much China restaurant here. Some *vino, signora?*"

It was easily two hours before we left the table. Having Fabrizio there eased some of the tension, enough in fact that Richard didn't even seem to stiffen when I asked Fabrizio to take the first of our prerequisite photos with the daily newspaper in it.

Being served such an exquisite meal probably didn't hurt either. Francesca didn't even let us order. She just kept bringing out things. Grilled eggplant, bowls of olives, *insalata di mare, fusilli al pomodoro,* and finally a large grilled fish that she deftly slit, filleted and divided into three succulent servings. It was three-thirty in the afternoon when we left the trattoria and walked back into the sunlight.

"Kate," said Richard, looking at his watch, "I need to get back to the hotel. But I can take a cab, and then Fabrizio can take you to see more of the city. Unless you'd rather come back to the hotel with me?"

I was exhausted. But given the choice between a long afternoon back at the hotel with Richard a closed door away, and tromping around the Eternal City in a sultry ninety degrees, my decision was crystal clear.

I watched Richard hail his cab as I stepped into the back seat of Fabrizio's car. "And so, *signora,*" he said, "I take you now to the Piazza Bocca della Verita. Eet is a place with much power and mystery."

"Good idea."

"*Si.* You put your hand deep in the mouth of a beeg stone face.

But...eef you not be person who always tells the truth? Thees stone face— Boom! Eet bites off your hand!"

Maybe *not* such a good idea.

19

Chapter Nineteen

My hand remained decidedly attached to my wrist.

Not that I wasn't a bit anxious when I gingerly inserted it into the big mouth of the Bocca della Verita. But I was spared. Either the ancient gods were off duty that day, or the myth was a bigger lie than the transgressions of all us hand owners. In any case, Fabrizio did not have to administer Italian first aid to my American left hand.

Instead, he drove me in his blessedly air-conditioned car up to the Aventino—one of those famous seven hills of Rome. Villa after fancy, salmon-colored villa stood behind huge iron gates as we wound through the silent, heavily shaded streets for several minutes until we came upon a small piazza and he stopped.

"Come," said Fabrizio, circling the car to open my door. "We are at the Piazza dei Cavalieri di Malta."

"Is this a famous place? I don't think I've ever heard of it."

"Not so famous for the tourists. But...very special. Let me show you *una vista fantastica*."

He walked me to the gateway at the Priory of the Knights of Malta. Its green door faced directly out onto the square and there was a large, eye-level keyhole in the top half. "*Signora,* here. Look through this keyhole and tell me what you see."

What I saw was like a living breathing Dali tableau, perfect in its starkness and surrealism. The keyhole framed an endlessly long, narrow corridor formed by two rows of tall, pointy cypress trees, and dead center at the far, far end burst the glorious white dome of Saint Peter's Basilica.

"You like?" asked Fabrizio.

"I love."

"Maybe you bring Dottore Farley here near sunset tomorrow. He is your *fidanzato,* no?"

"You mean my fiancé?"

"*Si.*"

"No. He is not my fiancé. He is my..."

"*Si?*"

I couldn't bring myself to say "friend." Richard and I were most definitely not friends. "He is my ex-husband, Fabrizio. We used to be married a long time ago."

And Fabrizio, suddenly anxious to get to the car, said, "Oh, I see."

But of course he didn't. Just as the Bocca della Verita didn't. Just as the concierge at the hotel didn't. Just as every single person in the world—except David and Karen—didn't. None of them saw the real arrangement. None of them saw that my presence here had been handsomely paid for, and that I continued to be uneasy about what might be expected in return.

Apparently, David was too.

He and I got into a scratchy moment on the phone when I got back to the hotel around six. I'd caught him just before he headed out to a Saturday Cubs doubleheader.

"How's it been going?" he asked.

"Not great, not terrible," I answered. "I had an excellent day though, being an impressionable tourist."

"And what about the person you're touring with?"

"I don't know. For the most part he's been pretty much as expected. Very Richard."

He laughed halfheartedly. He was not sounding like the regular version of David. "Well, what about you?" I asked. "Is this the first time you've ever gone to Wrigley Field?"

"Nope. But it is the first time I'm going to be sitting in the bleachers."

"The bleachers?"

"Yeah. About six of us from the neighborhood are going to sit out there, drink beer and emit egregious belches."

"They don't let people into the bleachers who use the word 'egregious,'" I teased, wishing like crazy I was going to the game with him and not to dinner with Richard. "Don't you know there are definite rules in Chicago for being a bleacher bum?"

"Like what?"

"Like in addition to all the rowdy behavior, a true bleacher bum always strips his shirt off."

"Yeah?"

"Yeah. Soooo…"

"So what?"

"So what do you think? Are you going to be disrobing in front of others today?"

He was quiet for a minute. "I might ask you the same question."

I was completely blindsided.

"Kate. Oh, Jesus, I'm really sorry I said that. Really sorry."

I took a deep breath. "David, where did that come from?"

"I don't know," he sighed, obviously upset with himself. And then he added, "That's bullshit. I do know. It's like I said yesterday, now that you're there with this guy—and believe me, I know I have no right to say this—I'm having less of an easy time with it than I thought I'd have. Not the ethics of it. I swear to you, Kate, that isn't where I'm coming from. But I am having a harder time about your just being with this guy than I did when all this came up a few weeks ago. I guess I'm operating with a different set of feelings."

"Oh, God, David. Listen, I'm glad about the feelings. A little scared, but glad. But the timing is so weird. It just makes everything here that much more complicated. You know?"

"Boy, do I," he sighed. "We are definitely dealing with some shitty timing here. No question."

"Yeah, no question."

"Hey, Kate, it's going to be okay. We both need to remember that. But without question this whole thing is big-time verification of my old *life is messy* axiom."

"It sure is," I said, nodding my head in agreement.

Only I had no idea until later that evening how very messy it could get.

Chapter Twenty

Just as I stepped into the tub to soak off the sightseeing grime, the phone rang again. "God, I love hotels," I thought as I reached for the receiver mounted on the creamy tile wall. At home I could never track down my handset to bring it into the bathroom— one or the other of the kids would have stashed it somewhere. But fancy hotels had real phones anchored to real walls in their bathrooms and being able to reach through the lavender scented bubbles to the wall receiver made me feel very fancy indeed.

It was the concierge. "There is a delivery for you, *signora*. Can we bring it up now?"

I was hoping to soak for at least another twenty minutes. "Just leave it at the door, please. I'll get it shortly," I said, hanging up and desperately hoping that this delivery didn't mean that Richard was starting the high romance portion of our trip.

Richard had always been really big on flowers. And the problem was, the flowers had always been really big. Garishly big.

Embarrassingly big. Like Mafia funeral big. For a guy with impeccable taste in clothing he sure had a block when it came to
flowers. He'd send awful things, like huge bunches of gladiolas
and spider mums with hideous clumps of waxy foliage. I remember after an enormous fight following our first anniversary how
he'd sent me a gargantuan wreath of dyed blue and green car-
nations made up in the shape of a peace sign. I never figured out
if this gross botanical contrition had to do with his inherent ex-
hibitionism or his inherent predilection for excess. I only remember that the flowers he sent me always made me extremely
uncomfortable. So it was with some trepidation that half an hour
later I stepped out into the hall to see what had been left at the
door.

It *was* some kind of bouquet, but the box was surprisingly
small—more suited for a wrist corsage than a Mafia funeral
wreath. I felt somewhat relieved, until I opened it. Because inside was a horrible, ugly, withered, cactus, all spiked with black-
ish-gray needles. Next to it was a note:

Dear Richard...
    Pricks for a prick.
    You'll be ever so sorry to hear that the piece is almost
finished and my executive producer loves it. I still haven't
dug up the reason you're in Rome, but I will. Hopefully
before airtime.
    No longer yours,
    Rebecca

Two things became instantly clear. One, this package had been
misdelivered—it was for Richard, not for me. And two, apparently
I was not the only member of the Girls Who Hate Richard Club.

I wondered what had caused this woman to join up. But I had to wait for two hours to find out.

Earlier, Richard had left one of his personal stationery notes for me at the desk asking that I come to his room for a drink before dinner. I knocked on his door at eight-fifteen.

If I had thought my part of the suite was fabulous, his was downright royal. It had a frescoed foyer leading into a vast living room. The room was terraced on two sides, so you could step out and see across the Tiber from one and past the Vittorio Emanuele monument from the other. My view was lovely. His was spectacular.

The pale vermilion sky gave everything in the room a sophisticated feeling, but it would have been a pretty adult room even without dusky lighting. Lots of damask couches, overstuffed chairs and inlaid period furniture. On one side, there were double French doors opening onto a stately formal dining room and on the other, there was a heavy carved wooden door that opened onto the dimly lit master bedroom.

"Care to see the rest of it?" Richard asked gesturing toward the darkened room.

"No, that's okay," I said a bit too quickly. I sat down on the long fawn couch and reached into my tote. "Here, this was mistakenly delivered to me," I said, handing him the box. "Your name wasn't on it—it just had the suite number, so I opened it."

Watching Richard as he opened the box and then read the note was like observing a facial conjugation of the words "mad," "madder," "maddest." I don't know that I have ever seen anyone move through those emotions as visibly and as swiftly as he did. He morphed right in front of my eyes from reasonable to rabid.

"Bitch," he said, crumpling the note. Then he hurled the box down on the floor and furiously kicked it across the room.

"Richard, what is it?"

"Nothing." He turned on his heel toward the mahogany and cut crystal bar. "I'm getting a drink. The hell with my meds. Do you want something?"

"Maybe later," I said, not one bit satisfied with his nonanswer. He came back with a vodka martini for himself and some pinot grigio for me. "Just in case you change your mind," he said nearly slamming the glass of wine down on the table.

"Richard, I really don't want anything right now."

"Fine," he said, proceeding to drain half his martini, take a deep breath and inquire with completely fake insouciance, "so how was your afternoon?"

I wasn't playing. I wasn't talking basilicas and vistas in order to win the Good Manners Prize. Something big and relatively unattractive existed between Richard and this Rebecca woman, and I wasn't going to Scarlett O'Hara my way through our evening and think about it tomorrow. I wanted to know. Now.

"Richard, what's this about? Why is this woman mailing you cactuses and calling you a prick? Do you have some *Fatal Attraction* situation here?"

"I don't know what the hell I've got here," he said gulping down the rest of his drink, "other than a world-class crazy woman who is out for blood."

I watched him get up to pace up and down the parquet floor. "Why is she out for blood? Did you walk out on her too? The card did say, 'no longer yours.' Is this another ex-wife?"

His glare was unnerving. But at least he answered the question. "No, Kate, she's not another ex-wife. I topped out at two. You women got too expensive."

It was my turn to glare. "I hardly think that over all these years I qualify as an expensive ex-wife."

"Well, we're about to rectify that, aren't we, Kate?"

The conversation was feeling snipey. I didn't like it. I also didn't like that Richard went over to the bar to make himself a second martini. Liquor had never made him particularly genial.

"Are you supposed to be drinking like this?"

"Why don't you let me worry about that, Nurse Nightingale, okay?" he snarled.

That did it. I pushed away my untouched wineglass and got up from the couch. "You know what, Richard? Maybe we should just forget about tonight. You're obviously agitated and jittery about this woman, and you're obviously not going to be straight with me about what's going on, and that does not bode well for a relaxing evening. Maybe it would just be smarter for us to each order room service so you can calm down, and take care of whatever little business you have to take care of with this Rebecca."

Richard was shaking. He took out his handkerchief and wiped the back of his neck. I couldn't tell if he was sweating because of the drink or because of his rage. "Kate, just hold on. Just sit there for a second while I straighten out my thoughts, okay?" He walked to the terrace, opened the door and stood there a minute to regain his composure. Then he turned back to me saying, "You're right. Rebecca's note does have me agitated. She's a spiteful, driven, reckless woman and she's been making my life impossible for the past five months."

"How?" I said, perversely interested.

"Oh, shit," he said shaking his head, "I don't suppose telling you at this point will make any difference. Let me finish fixing this drink and I'll tell you what this bitch has been up to."

This time he didn't down the drink in two gulps. He sipped it. And he struggled. He struggled as he always had when pressed to tell the truth. Because the truth with Richard was frequently never pretty. It was hard to hear, and it was hard to face, and, as usual, it was also hard to fathom.

Chapter Twenty-One

Richard's voice was unsteady as he began. "Rebecca is a woman I was seeing for about a year," he said, folding and unfolding his hands. "She lived in Toronto and we had a nice long-distance thing going."

"How'd you meet her?"

"At a funeral."

I couldn't help smiling.

"What?" he barked.

"It's just that you think of romances starting at weddings, not funerals…"

"Right. I should have seen that as a sign."

"Since when did you become superstitious?"

"Since I got cancer," he said ruefully. "Cancer can have you reaching for odd explanations since none of the old ones seem to work anymore. In any case, Rebecca and I began seeing each other hot and heavy for the first few months. She's a correspondent for *Candid Canada,* something of a Canadian *Sixty Minutes,* and when we met she had just finished a profile on a man whose company I was trying to buy. "

"What's his name?'

"DeLouche. Henry DeLouche. He owned a chain of very successful discount computer stores. But he was holding me up for money. The bastard would not come down on his price. Rebecca was very helpful in getting him to do that."

"What does that mean?"

"It means in the tapes she shot for her interviews of DeLouche she had recorded some very valuable information, and she let me watch those tapes."

"What kind of information?"

"It doesn't matter. What matters is that it was information that wasn't relevant to her piece, but that DeLouche would not have wanted me to have."

"Richard! You've been a journalist! You know she shouldn't have given you that information."

"Yeah," he said, plucking two olives out of his empty glass, "but she was in love with me."

"And you weren't in love with her."

He smiled wryly. "I don't do 'in love' anymore, Kate. It doesn't seem to be part of my DNA. 'In heat' maybe. I was plenty 'in heat' with Rebecca. And like most women, she mistook that for love."

"Meaning…?"

"Meaning she started pressing me. Getting as many assignments as she could out in Vancouver. Crowding me. Buying tickets for plays and things so we'd always have plans in the future. Hovering around me like some widow-to-be when I first got diagnosed. You know I hate hovering. It was one of the things you and I had in common."

It was true. Richard and I had made a pact when we were married—just about the only one we kept—that if either of us was home with the flu or a cold, the other one would bring in the juice, bring in the phone, bring in the aspirin and then disappear. Loitering was not allowed. But we never talked about how we'd behave if the other one had a life-threatening illness.

"But weren't you terrified when you got diagnosed?"

"Sure I was. Hell, I still am."

"Then weren't you glad to have someone there?"

"I would have liked someone nearby. But Rebecca doesn't know from nearby. She was dripping tragedy all over me. She became solicitous and wifely and she went deaf when I asked her to back off. I finally had to tell the hospital to bar her from visiting one day when I went in for treatment. That did it. We had a big explosion and it was over.

"I walked away relieved, but the problem was, she walked away pissed. About two weeks later I started getting strange calls and some crackpot deliveries—rancid liver one time, a shattered mirror—and all of them came with these dumbass notes like this 'pricks for a prick' one." Again, he took out his handkerchief and wiped his neck.

"God…"

"None of it truly bothered me…"

"Right," I said, pointing to the opened box that he'd kicked across the floor. "I can see that it didn't."

"It didn't." His eyes flashed at me. "What bothered me was a month later when I found out that she was working on some big investigative piece on me for the fucking TV show."

"Why? Are you so newsworthy?"

"I don't think so, but she apparently does, or at least managed to convince her bosses that I was."

"How?"

"Packaging and bullshit. I'm one of three American expatriates she's investigating in a show called *Our Imported Scoundrels,* so she's trying to dig up every single piece of business and personal shit she can on me."

"Is there a——" I never finished the sentence.

All of a sudden, bells and whistles and sirens went off in my brain. All of a sudden it became Tiffany diamond clear why Richard Farley had reached across all these miles and all these years to try to rectify the personal and financial betrayal of his son and me. It had nothing to do with making things right so he could die with a clean conscience. It had nothing to do with the "you were the absolute best woman in my life" speech he'd given me the night before. It had to do with one thing and one thing only. He was terrified this Rebecca woman was going to find out what he'd done, and eleven seconds before he died, the man who thought he'd gotten away with running out on his wife and kid was going to be exposed on a national TV show.

I leaped up from the couch. My blood was curdling. "You son of a bitch."

"What?" he said, genuinely confused. "What the hell are you talking about?" He turned his back on me and walked a bit unsteadily over to the open terrace door.

"Turn and face me, Richard."

He did. His face was sweaty—all his features looked like they were melting into each other.

"God, Richard. How dumb do you think I am? Too dumb to

get it? Well I'm not! I get why you suddenly show up out of the blue to make up for your slimy behavior fifteen years ago. It has nothing to do with Danny, does it? And nothing to do with me, either. It doesn't even have to do with your dying. You're just covering your butt in case this woman finds out and exposes you for the bottom-feeder that you are."

"Kate, you're wrong," he said shakily, lowering himself into a chair.

"No, I'm not. And you know it. You know that if this woman does find out about it, you've already trumped her. Right? Because you can claim to have suffered some sort of deathbed remorse, paid me all this money and come off like a guy mired in retroactive decency. Very smooth. Of course no matter to you how I come off. Nice, Richard. You've actually come up with a new, creative way to save your backside and to renail me."

"Renail you?"

"Are you kidding? I'm a mother. I also have a radio show. How do you think it will look in print or on TV that yes, you repaid me all that money, but only if I went away with you for a week?"

"There's no way anyone has to find that out," he slurred. "It wouldn't help *my* case for that to get out, either."

"Oh, please. If this woman finds out one thing she'll find out the other. She's already trying to figure out why you're in Rome. If she's any kind of reporter, she'll find out who I am and that I'm here, too."

"So what if she finds out you're here too? All we have to say is that I brought you here in order *to propose* the deal, not that the deal *was contingent* on your coming here. No one is going to question your coming here to discuss the particulars any more than they're going to question your accepting the money. You aren't going to come off as a bad person. You've merely accepted what's rightfully yours."

"Then why didn't you just make that offer in the first place? Why didn't you just offer me the money flat out and leave this whole awful trip out of it?"

"Ah, Kate," he said, leaning back and undoing his collar button, "because then, what was in it for me? Good PR on my deathbed to be sure, but this way I could still have the good PR and yet assure my perverse soul that even you are capable of selling out."

I felt like I was going to throw up. "I'm leaving," I said, heading for the door.

"Our reservations aren't for another twenty minutes," he said, taking his cold glass and holding it against his forehead. His face was flushed.

"No, Richard, I'm leaving. Leaving this hotel, leaving Rome, leaving..."

"Kate," he said, clutching the arms of the chair and leaning toward me, "if you leave now, you won't get the money."

"I don't want the money. I thought I could take it, but I can't. I don't even want to be on the same planet as you and your money."

"Oh, for Christ's sake, Kate, stop posing as such a pillar of virtue."

"It's not hard to feel like one next to you."

"Kate, don't be stupid. You aren't going to be exposed."

"Oh, my God, Richard. It's not about that. It's not that I'm worried that some Canadian journalist is going to expose me. It's that I am sickened to the core that you have jerked me around one more time. That what looked like belated decency was just current damage control. And that you have exceeded even my worst expectations of reprehensibility. You're beyond despicable. I want nothing to do with you ever again. Nothing."

And I meant it.

Which makes it hard to explain why thirty minutes later my lips were glued to his.

Chapter Twenty-Two

I was shaking as I slammed out of Richard's room.

Maybe I was naive. Maybe I shouldn't have been flabbergasted that a man once capable of walking out on his wife and child could continue to operate—even in the face of death—in such a slimy, self-serving way. And yet I really was. Richard's initial claim to want to right the wrong to Danny seemed so logical to me. I mean, who wouldn't give thought to that at the end of their life? But no, it had nothing to do with any remnant of integrity, or fear of eternity, or anything even remotely lofty at all. It had to do with bullet-dodging. If this woman hadn't had the journalistic gun pointed at Richard Farley's privates, no way would he have sent me the letter of faux contrition. The letter in which he said, *"I know I was a schmuck…"*

Wrong tense, Richard. Wrong tense.

I was so rattled it took me two tries to get my key into the door.

As soon as I got inside, I bolted the door, and made sure that the bedroom door connecting our two suites was bolted, too.

The first flight I could get out of Rome was at seven the next morning.

"I'll take it," I told the reservationist.

"Eet will be seventy-five dollars to change your ticket, *signora*."

I couldn't think of a better way to spend seventy-five dollars. All I wanted was to be far away. Fast.

Hauling out my suitcase, I began to meticulously fold all of Karen's taupe-and-black ensembles. God, I thought, exasperated with my tidy packing behavior, why couldn't I just be in a forties movie right now? Then I could just yank the clothes out of the closet, stuff them hanger-and-all into the suitcase, slam the thing shut and haughtily stalk out with my cloche hat on. I've always wanted to do that at least once in my life. And if this wasn't the perfect time for a dramatic packing scene, then when?

But I never had done very well at anything movie-scene-like. In fact the one time I decided to bolt out into the night after a huge fight with Richard, I was a total failure at the dramatic exit. I remember slamming the front door, walking deliberately to my car, revving the motor and then realizing, pathetically, I had absolutely no place to go. Karen was out of town, Samantha was having some guy over for dinner and sex and Amy, my other good friend at the time, was at the assertiveness training class she attended so she could deal with her Neanderthal husband. Of course her Neanderthal husband *was* home, but what was the point of walking out on my own Neanderthal husband to hide out with someone else's? I sat there in the car with the motor running and no place to go for at least five minutes, tears of frustration slithering down my face. Then I realized the local library was still open and I could find refuge there. So that's where I spent the next two hours, sniveling and reading decorating magazines. It was not an evening of triumph.

But the good news was that this time when I slammed the door on Richard, I *had* somewhere go. I could go home to my safe, tidy, Richard-free world, where there were no deals, no deceptions and not much in the way of deplorability.

Zipping my two wheelless suitcases shut, I cursed myself for not traveling light, because I had to wait fifteen minutes for the bellhop to show up. The bellhop. God, my whole life would have been different if the bellhop had pushed the button on the right door.

But he didn't. He didn't ring the bell on *my* door. The front desk must have had Richard's and my room numbers grouped together as one continuous suite. So just as they had rung my door for Richard's cactus delivery, this time they rang *Richard's* door for my luggage pickup. And when Richard didn't answer, the bellhop knocked several times and then finally let himself in with the passkey. That's when I heard the blood-freezing scream followed by his hysterical cry for help.

"*Aiuto!*" the bellhop yelled. "*Aiuto!*"

The man across the hall and I flung open our doors and ran to see what was going on. The bellboy continued to yell into his walkie-talkie and as I stepped into Richard's foyer, I could see why. Richard was sprawled facedown on the lush Oriental rug.

It did not look as if breathing was one of his main activities.

If I live to be one hundred (which I only want to do if I can still drive), I will never completely understand why I did what I did next.

I saved Richard's life.

I don't know what part of it was a reflex action—you know,

you see someone crumpled on the floor, it's clear that the person is not breathing, you've taken a CPR refresher course every two years, so what are you going to do? You drop to the floor and begin mouth-to-mouth resuscitation.

But there's another part to it, too. The part that had to do with David's "life is messy" axiom. Because even as I was giving the embarrassingly labeled "breath of life" to Richard, my brain was racing through millions of psychological dark corridors in search of an answer to the obvious question: What the hell was I doing here? This was a man I detested more than any human on this Earth. In just the past hour I'd been given even more reason to detest him. But I kept coming back to the fact that the detested guy was most definitely on his way to dying and if I didn't do my best to rectify that, what would be the difference between me and a murderer?

Oh, God, how many times have I gone over the scene? Wondering if I could have ever mustered up enough inner Bette Davis to have merely stepped over the man and continued on my way down the hall. What possessed me to think it was a good idea to try to keep him on this earth? The guy was going to die anyway. He did nothing but use people. Every move he made was devious. I had no reason in the world to want Richard Farley alive.

Not to mention no reason in the world to want to be the one who had to ride with him in an ambulance to a hospital, where no one spoke my language, and where everyone thought I must have been his distraught and devoted wife. Clearly I didn't look young enough to be his distraught and devoted girlfriend.

By the time the emergency room had him stabilized, it was almost midnight. Oddly, I wasn't tired. No doubt because I'd just embarked on the biggest culture shock of the whole trip—Italian hospitals. Not that the hospital wasn't fabulous in several

ways. Ways like not needing to see your insurance card or passport or anything when you walked into the emergency room.
Nope, with socialized medicine, they just started taking care of
the patient—what a concept.

But the chaos. It was like *ER* meets Federico Fellini. They're
racing, they're screaming, then they run out for a cigarette
break. In fact the entire hospital was encased by balconies dotted with doctors and nurses and patients all smoking together—
even on the respiratory ward.

Our doctor, who was incredibly handsome and who displayed
pounds of chest hair from his barely buttoned shirt, insisted on calling me Signora Farley. He was, however, very patient explaining
Richard's condition to me. Fortunately I still had my pocket Italian dictionary in my purse, but it was significantly more useful for
culinary terms than it was for medical terms. "Catheter," for instance not being in the *C* section, while custard, cantaloupe and
chives were. Apparently Richard had suffered a serious heart attack—the kind they usually do bypass surgery on. But I had told
the doctor when we brought Richard in that he had some sort of
rare cancer (cancer actually being in the *C* section), and that he
had told me it was terminal. Oh, my God, the eyes of this man
when I told him that. Such pity for me as the widow-in-training.
When I finally got him to understand I was not the soon-to-be
grieving wife, the inquiries about our relationship stopped. I was
simply perceived as the courageous good Samaritan friend. The
kind who might know what family members should be contacted.

Only, of course, I didn't. And given that it was Saturday, the
two numbers I had for Richard at his office didn't answer. The
only other move I had was to call the hotel and have them send
over all of Richard's things. I figured maybe then I could dig up

an address book, or better yet, maybe there'd be a doctor's name on one of his prescription bottles. But I came up empty. No addresses, and no labels on his meds. Just a plastic travel container with the days of the week marked on seven compartments. Friday and Saturday were empty, but the rest of them were filled with colorful, unlabeled pills.

And all I could think of was this: Oh, God, am I going to have to sit in the hospital with this despicable man until I can reach someone in his office on Monday morning? With the time difference that would be almost two whole days and I wasn't at all sure I had that much more good Samaritan in me.

On the other hand, just leaving Richard alone and unconscious in the hospital for the next forty-eight hours to maybe die—well it didn't quite make me a murderer like the CPR moment would have, but it sure put me into a lifetime despicability category that I'd always hoped to avoid.

I know he deserved it. And some people might say that leaving him alone at that moment was my big chance for revenge. But honestly, I have always hated revenge stories. Those post-breakup stories where the breakup-ee figures out a way to sabotage the job of the breakup-er; or the Nobel Prize-winning student goes back to high school to lord it over the science teacher who said he'd never get anywhere. It always seems so Pyrrhic. So petty. Even the original plan to substitute Karen for me on this trip always seemed to fall in the category of a good practical joke—never revenge. Nope, to walk out on a man maybe dying alone in a foreign country would have been too pricey. I'd have had to live with it the rest of my life.

Of course, he didn't die. Nor did he exactly rally. He just lay there for two whole days, occasionally opening his eyes, and way too drugged to talk. Not that I could have deciphered his mumblings anyway over the general din of the hospital. Unlike American hospitals where the din comes from in-room TVs, in this hospital the din came from in-room relatives. I'd say the ratio of visiting relatives to ill patients was somewhere around eleven to one. And it went on day and night. There were no restrictive visiting hours. The hospital *had* visiting hours. Only everyone ignored them. The hospital had No Smoking signs. Only there were ashtrays all over. The hospital had doctors and nurses. But no one wore name tags, so you never knew if you were talking to the internist or the orderly.

There was no cafeteria for visitors, you had to go next door to a bar; there was no water for patients, relatives had to buy you a bottle; and there were no phones in the room—but then who would you call? Your entire family was with you anyway.

And for those two days, I was the entirety of Richard's family. The bitter irony of it did not escape me—being family to this man who'd abandoned his family. Karen was dumbfounded.

"I wouldn't have even gone in the ambulance with him," she huffed long-distance. "After finding out why he really offered you the money?"

"You weren't there, Karen, with an almost dead guy at your feet. You don't know what you'd do," I said, rubbing a towel through my hair. I was back at the hotel on Sunday to bathe and hopefully nap for a few hours. The temperature had cooled off immensely from the day before. It was only perfect out, and I wished I was going anywhere in Rome but back to the dingy, cacophonous hospital. Talking to Karen made it seem like an even more bizarre destination.

"What are you doing, Kate? Going for the Joan of Arc award?"

"Hardly. All I'm doing is staying here until it's Monday morning in Vancouver. Then I can call his office and Richard will be their problem."

"You could have gotten on a plane, come home and called his office on Monday from here," she said.

"I know. But what if he died between now and then?"

"What if he did?"

"I can't explain it, Karen. This just feels like what I need to do."

"For you or for him?"

"Definitely for me."

But David really understood. "You'd do this wouldn't you, David?"

"You mean with my own ex-wife?"

"Yeah. With her. The woman who lied to you and cheated on you. And even if she just did what Richard just did, you know, jerked you around again. If she had a heart attack in front of you in a hotel room in Rome, you wouldn't just do nothing. And you wouldn't leave her to regain consciousness in a room full of strangers speaking a foreign language either. Would you?"

"Kate, I don't know. I suppose not. But not because I'd want to stay. I'd do it because I wouldn't want to be the kind of person who would walk away."

"Well, that's the same reason I'm doing what I'm doing. At least until I can get hold of someone in Richard's office to find someone to fly out here."

"And then?"

"And then I am out of here."

"You're not going to wait around another day for the person to get there, are you? You know, all worried that he might wake up and no one will be with him?"

"No way. I'm not looking for a gold star here. I don't want Richard to thank me. I don't ever want to hear a word from that man again."

Only I wasn't so lucky.

On Monday evening, after having reached Richard's personal secretary from my hotel room, I had to go back to the hospital because I'd left Karen's black blazer there. It was a bit before eight in the evening and as usual the hospital was as bustling as a big hotel lobby. White tablecloths were being pulled up by the staff (they actually served patients on china and white linens at a table in the middle of some of the wards), family members had spilled out into the hallways and smoke drifted in from a few balconies. When I stepped into the intensive care ward where Richard had been monitored for two days, he wasn't there. For a second I thought he had died.

"*Carla, dov'e Senor Farley?*" I asked the woman who had become my favorite nurse these past two days. She was older than the others, and unlike most of the overworked staff, she occasionally even managed to smile. But she was very businesslike when she announced they'd upgraded Richard's condition and moved him. "*Il dottore e in camera duecento.*"

Apparently, all Richard's belongings—including Karen's black blazer—had been moved to room two hundred as well, so I took the elevator up to retrieve it.

Richard was dozing when I entered the green room across from the elevator. His color was decidedly better than when I'd left the hospital several hours before, and he seemed to be on one less IV. The blazer was draped over a steel chair next to the bed—the chair I didn't have to sit in anymore. I had just tossed the jacket over my arm and turned to leave, when I heard him rasp, "Kate, they say you saved my——"

I walked straight to the elevator. I never turned around.

The trip back to Chicago was the direct inverse of the chronic Sarah Rose inquiry, "Mommy, how come it's so fast to get home and it always takes so long to get there?"

"Anticipation," I'd say in my best Carly Simon imitation, even though I knew full well that word was too big for her and the concept too abstract. So after uttering it——I'm a big believer in vocabulary building——I'd go on to explain the "getting excited about something before it happens" definition.

But I understood the word just fine, and anticipation, which was definitely not part of the mix when I'd been on the plane going to Rome, was without question a big part of the plane ride home to Chicago. I couldn't wait to put every second of the past four days behind me, dive back into my real life and feel like a regular mom again. I wanted piles of laundry to do, I wanted to yell at Danny to turn down his music, and I wanted to make Rice Krispies squares with Sarah Rose. Granted, I'd never made Rice Krispies squares with Sarah Rose before, but I wanted to do it now.

Anything to inject the ordinary back in my life.

Blessedly I had a row of seats all to myself, so I was spared one of those airplane discussions in which you either exchanged brief comments about how vile the food was, or laid bare your innermost thoughts to a total stranger. So I had plenty of space to consider the central issue of my return——the question of Now What?

Because now that I'd gone on this highly secretive, emotionally convoluted, exceptionally disturbing, incredibly enlightening, hugely bizarre four-day journey, well, now what? Did my life just *pinggg* back into its former shape and texture? Or was everything already so inherently different that even though Dorothy may have gotten back from Oz, and Alice may have gotten back from Wonderland, was it possible that I would never, ever really be able to go home again?

I reached into my purse and pulled out my mirror just to check. Basically I still *looked* the same. But of course I looked the same after I had sex the first time and I'd found that amazing. Not to mention disappointing. This time though I was relieved. Because if I looked the same, then maybe I could act the same, and maybe my world would feel the same. Maybe it was possible to take these past four days and wrap enough bubble paper around them so they were insulated from the rest of my life. Maybe I could just pack them away and slide back into the groove, and no one—except Karen, David, Jack Meegan and me—would ever be the wiser.

Right, and maybe there's a Santa Claus.

23

Chapter Twenty-Three

As soon as I dragged my bags out of customs I spotted David straight ahead standing in that way he had with one foot a bit in front of the other like some sort of aw-shucks cowboy. Just seeing him was calming. But as I moved toward him and we both started to smile, I realized I had no idea what we would do next.

The choices, of course, were hug, kiss or shake hands. None of them seemed quite right for the two of us, so what we did was stand there goofily grinning at each other for a few seconds. At least until David decided to go for the hugging option.

"Oh, boy," he said, pulling me toward him, "that was a long four days, Ms. Lerner."

Ms. Lerner was what David sometimes called me on air when I got to sounding a bit pedantic with a listener. I'd finish what I'd been saying and he'd cajole in the singsongy voice of a grammar school student, "Yes, Ms. Lerner." The first time he did it, I'd bristled a bit, but over the past few months, he did it more judiciously and with more affection, so it had come to sound like a borderline term of endearment.

"You smell good," I said, unaccustomed to being quite this close to him.

"You don't smell so bad yourself." He laughed, pushing back a little so he could look into my eyes.

"I smell like airplane," I said, shaking my head and wondering if I would ever master the art of accepting a compliment. Not that I was one of those people who thought if someone said, "You look great today," that it must mean I looked like a moldy sponge the rest of the week. But I still had trouble just saying, "Hey, thanks," and letting it go.

"Here, give me your bags. I'm not parked anywhere in this zip code," David said, extending his hand to take both my suitcases.

By the time we pulled out of the parking garage ten minutes later, the sky had darkened and big fat raindrops were starting to fall. "Between the rain and rush-hour traffic, we might as well settle in for a long ride home," he said.

I leaned back and turned my face toward him. "It's fine. I don't care how long it takes. I don't care if it takes 'til midnight. I am just so glad to be back. Tell me what's been going on here."

"Are you kidding?" He reached in his pocket and pulled out some singles to pay the attendant. "You're the one who has been in the thick of the high-drama adventure, Kate. Not me. I've just been here—Mr. Worker Guy. Doing what I do, and..." His voice trailed off.

"And what?"

Keeping his eyes focused on the swish-swish of the windshield wipers he said softly, "Stewing about you. I tend not to be a man who stews. But man, you sure sailed off into some unknown territory."

I smiled and touched his arm. "I sure did. But you can stop stewing as of right now. Because I am back, and I am glad. Rome and Richard are behind me. As is my brief stint as an almost-rich woman."

"What do you mean?"

"I mean I'm not taking the money. Actually, let me amend that to be less self-serving. I'm not getting the money. Those were Richard's almost-last words to me that night right before his heart attack."

"Do you think he really meant it? Without paying you that money, he loses his big masquerade as the contrite industrialist."

"Who knows if he really meant it?" I shrugged. "It doesn't really matter. The important thing is that *I* meant it when I said I don't want any part of his money. I truly don't. I'm just grateful that I got back here in one piece and, with the exception of you, Karen and Jack, no one is any the wiser."

And they weren't. For at least an entire day.

David walked me into the house and set my bags down in the front hall. "Wait a second. One more thing," he said going out to the car and returning with a huge bag from Whole Foods. "I went to the store so you'd have stuff for breakfast." The bag was crammed with eggs, fresh-squeezed o.j., giant bagels, half-and-half for my coffee and some sunflowers all wrapped up.

"David, this was so sweet of you."

"I was glad to do it," he said, leaning over and kissing my forehead. "But I'm going to take off now so you can go call your kids and get them back over here." He hugged me again. "Yeah, it definitely feels better to have you back on this side of the ocean."

Before I even put the groceries away, I went right to the kitchen phone. Tim answered immediately. I'd only talked to him and the kids once since Richard had been in the hospital, and of course I couldn't tell them where I was really spending my time. God, I hated the way the lying felt—the lying about the trip in general and my sudden return in particular.

Clearly I'd been aware from the get-go that I was going to have to lie. But there is something about executing the lie in the specific that feels decidedly crummier than planning the lie in the abstract. Granted, I'd already lied to Tim and the kids by saying my trip to Rome was a junket for talk show hosts, but now I had to explain my premature homecoming by inventing a story that the people on the trip were a bunch of pushy radio jocks—and that I felt completely out of place with all the dueling egos. Then, of course, Tim asked me who was the most offensive person, so I had to make up a completely fake afternoon drive host from Denver. The whole thing felt swampy.

"Are you sorry you went?" Tim inquired.

"No, but I am very glad to be back. I missed Danny and Sarah Rose a lot. How've they been?"

"Great," Tim said. "Sarah's on the red team at camp and they're in hot pursuit of the blue team in swimming and softball. I just got the complete play-by-play at dinner. Now that the rain has stopped, she's down at the park with Danny working on her pitching. Danny's been working late, but I bribed him to come home for dinner because I was grilling steaks. He's quite the carnivore."

"I know. Listen," I said, starting to rifle through the jumble of catalogs, credit card applications and bills that were piled up, "can you send them home when they come back from the park? I can't wait to see them."

"Sure," said Tim. "I'm sure they'll be happy you're back early. Well, one of them will be anyway."

"What's that mean?"

"It means Danny seems a bit morose. Tense."

"I thought you said he ate well," I said sitting down at the table and absently flipping through my new Horchow garden catalog.

"How you eat and how you are are not always related, Kate. At least not when you're a seventeen-year-old boy. You need a lot of fuel to feed the machine. Whether it's a euphoric machine or a sulky one."

"And Danny was sulky?"

"Yeah, or preoccupied. Something."

Tim was right. I could see when the kids walked in that Danny was not in a good place. Not that I expected a seventeen-year-old to greet me with the same sort of leap-into-your-arms enthusiasm of a seven-year-old. Especially a seven-year-old who zigzagged between needing to tell you everything and needing to ask you everything.

"And so our counselor's name is Susan Malone and she has red hair like me—only straight—and then there was this gross food they made us eat for snacks—do they have snacks in Italy, Mom?—And can you get Nickelodeon there? And you should see this one girl on my team, Mom, she already knows how to dive...."

That was Sarah Rose. For at least an hour until she wound down and went off to bed. "Only one girl has been mean to me about my burn, Mom," she whispered into my ear when I tucked her in. "And when Cassie heard her, she told her to shut up and ever since she has, and now we're all friends. Her name is Ally. Can Cassie and Ally come over to play one day after camp?"

"Sure, honey," I said, hugging her close, thrilled to smother myself in her little girl smell again. "I'm so glad to be home."

"Me too, Mom," she said, kissing me with her toothpaste-slicked breath. "Sleep tight."

"You too, baby." I turned on her *I Love Lucy* night-light and closed the door behind me.

Danny had given me a perfunctory kiss and then immediately deposited himself on the couch to channel surf. Tim didn't have cable, and even though we only had the bare-bones package, I'm sure Danny was feeling ESPN-starved.

"Hon, can we lower that some?" I asked. "Sarah Rose is trying to get to sleep and I'm going to be attempting the same thing very shortly. I'm whipped."

He clicked off the TV and slammed down the remote.

"Danny, for Pete's sake! You didn't need to shut it off—just turn it down."

"Yeah, well."

"Well what? Really, honey. It's fine if you just leave it on lower."

"Forget it, Mom. No big fuckin' deal."

"Danny!" We hadn't exactly ruled out the f-word in our house. I mean I'm a big believer in picking your battles, and the occasional f-word hardly qualified as a deal breaker if your main goals were to produce a kid who didn't become a teenage parent or spend any time in drug rehab. "What's going on?"

"Nothing. That's the problem. So far summer sucks. I hate my job at the insurance company, but there's no place I can make better money. And Jamie is gone until August, so there's no one to hang with at night."

"You have other friends besides Jamie. Why don't you call one of them?"

"Jesus, Mom," he growled. "You sound the way you did when I was in seventh grade."

Danny's seventh grade year was the worst. Not only because it was the year that Sarah Rose had her accident and Tim and I spent huge portions of that year terrified and in hospitals, but also because it was the one year, the only year, that Danny had had a truly hard time in school. He had just started junior high, and whether it was because he was pudgy then, or shy, or what, he was coming up empty when it came to friends.

I handled it horribly, took it completely personally and wound up doing pathetic mom things like packing double desserts in his lunch so he could offer one to another kid and maybe have a crack at having someone sit with him in the cafeteria. I don't remember how he finally turned the corner, but he did. By the middle of the summer he had a whole crew of people to be with, as he has every single year since. At least until the past year, when he seemed to voluntarily whittle his options back down to basically only Jamie.

"Oh, God, honey, I'm sorry. I don't ever want anything to sound like it's being repeated from seventh grade," I said, trying to let him know that whatever was going on for him, I was on his side. "I'm sorry."

"Yeah, sure," he said staring sullenly into the blank TV.

"Danny, what's going on?"

"Nothing. Not a damn thing, Mom. Just chill." Then he

grabbed the duffel he'd taken to Tim's house and stomped up the stairs.

Welcome home, Kate.

24

Chapter Twenty-Four

The next day was hardly an improvement.

When my alarm went off at six, I'd already been up two hours doing that jet lag thing where your European body rhythms jangle you into fully alert mode in the middle of the American night. So you start doing laundry and paying bills and getting a jump start on your First Day Home List. My First Day Home List included hitting the supermarket, getting Karen's clothes to the cleaner, calling the bank to have them return Richard's money from the escrow account and apparently going to work. I hadn't planned on going in to the station, and David knew I was only a maybe, but it felt like the exact right thing to do to get my life feeling regular again.

His back was to me as I walked into our office. Clearly he hadn't planned on my showing up—magazines and newspapers blanketed the floor—and I knew he'd have made a valiant effort at domestic order if he'd thought I was coming in. "Honey, I'm home…" I mimicked.

"Hey," David swiveled around and grinned. "What are you doing here?"

"I don't know. Me and my overdeveloped ego probably couldn't bear another day away from the mike," I said, grinning back at him.

"You think you're ready for the airwaves?"

"As ready as a woman can be who hasn't seen the front page of a Chicago paper in days."

He handed me a pile of newspapers. "Okay, woman, then let's hunker down."

What a relief to be back, to not be anywhere near Richard Farley, dead or alive. To just be back talking to our listeners and reading car and restaurant commercials.

Next on my list was the bank. There were all kinds of papers to fill out so they could close down the escrow account and send the money back to Richard. It was a strange feeling, walking back into the bank parking lot with a piece of paper in my purse that said so long to more than a million dollars. I guess I should have felt poor, but I didn't. All I felt was relieved, and very excited to see Karen.

"You look beat," she said as she hobbled to the door on her walking cast. Her hair was back in a ponytail, which as a chronic professional she almost never let herself do—even though she looked great that way. Not to mention, about twenty-two.

"I guess I am," I said, realizing I'd forgotten to eat all day.

She hugged me and pulled me inside. "Hon, are you okay?"

"I think so," I said, following her through the hall arches into the parlor where she lowered herself onto the leather couch, and propped up her leg. The truth was, as soon as I'd fallen asleep in my own bed, in my own house, and replugged into my own life, an odd mental gauze began to come down and enveloped the whole trip. It wasn't that I couldn't remember everything about it, but for the whole day the entire Rome experience felt very third person. As if it had happened to some woman named Kate.

"What about you, Kare? How are you doing dragging around all that plaster? You don't look any the worse for wear," I said, nodding to what appeared to be a fresh pedicure.

"I'm fine. Bored with the inconvenience, but fine. Listen, I need to hear about you. I mean, here we tried to figure out contingency plans for all these possible scenarios, but, God, we never, ever considered that you might rescue the guy from the jaws of death."

"Jaws of death?" I laughed. "That's a little melodramatic, don't you think? Have you been watching trash talk shows this week?"

"No." She smiled. "I've had a lot of time on my hands, but I haven't sunk to that. I seem to have spent my days on the phone. I'm on this medication that makes me real wired, real chatty. One day I even called up your partner, David."

"You did?" I asked, feigning nonchalance. Karen had never once gone after or taken away a man I'd been involved with. On the other hand, I think we always both just acknowledged that she was the twin with the most guy clout. In every twin relationship there is always one twin who slays the opposite sex that much more readily than the other. In our relationship, that twin was not me. Mostly, I was always okay with it. This time I felt a little less okay. "You called David? He didn't tell me that."

"I doubt it was a highlight of the week for him. But he was

the only other person who knew what you were really doing. And in his own way, he sounded kind of concerned. More than radio-partner concerned, actually. I don't know, are you two kind of…?"

"We're kind of undefined at the moment. There's a lot of interest and a lot of baggage."

"Meaning…?"

"Meaning he looks at me and says to himself, 'Okay, she's got a couple of kids, a couple of ex-husbands and just made a really big secret trip.' And I look at him and say to myself, 'Where was it ever written that it's a brilliant idea to be involved with a colleague—particularly a colleague who has huge issues left over from his cheating ex-wife, and hasn't set foot in the romance arena with a new woman in twenty years?' That kind of baggage."

"Oh, boy."

"Right. Oh, boy."

I stayed at Karen's another hour, and when I pulled into the backyard at home, Sarah Rose was just being delivered from day camp. "Mommy, Mommy—" she popped off the bus and hugged me "—Cassie got a new puppy and she invited me over to see it before dinner. Can I go down the block to her house? Puh-leeze?"

She stuffed her soggy rolled-up towel and bathing suit into my arms. "Sure, honey, do you want some juice or something before you go?"

"Nope," she said, waving me off as she ran to get her bike. "I want to see the puppy. His name is Booger. Isn't that funny?"

I didn't think it was particularly funny. But it was a lot funnier than what happened next. Because next I walked into the kitchen and found Danny standing there, hand clenched around a piece of paper he was shaking at me.

"What the hell is this, Mom?" he yelled, the chords along his neck bulging with purple rage.

"What the hell is what?" I asked, setting down Sarah's wet towel.

"What the hell is this?" he roared, slamming the paper on the kitchen table. It was a heavy cream-colored card. The name Richard Farley was embossed across the top. It was the note Richard had left for me when he'd asked me to his room for a drink.

Chapter Twenty-Five

We've all had the nightmare.

You can't find the classroom where you're supposed to take the test. Or you find it, but you realize you forgot to study for the test. Or you take the test, but you discover when you take it up to the teacher, that you seem to have no clothes on. The point is, the nightmare isn't just about the *dreaded*. It's about the *unthinkable*.

And seeing Danny holding Richard's note in his hand was precisely that—unthinkable. It was beyond the bounds of comprehension. It was an over-the-top, cold-sweat, heart-racing impossibility. Such an impossibility that it had never even been a what-if. Of all the what-ifs Karen and I had considered, it didn't even make the top one hundred, so bedrock obvious was it that this COULD NOT HAPPEN. Maybe water could catch on fire, maybe men could finally get cellulite, but there was no way that Danny would *ever* find out I'd been in Rome with Richard Farley.

Only Danny had.

His face was twisted in pain and fury, his eyes glaring at me. I didn't think my heart would stay in my body if I moved toward him, so I just stood there in the middle of the most silent kitchen I've ever been in and stretched my hand out toward him. "Danny…" My voice felt like cellophane, all crackly and transparent. "Where'd you get that?"

He wrenched away from me, circled the table, and stood at the other side of it. "Don't come near me," he snarled. "I got it from your dresser. I came home early from work because I felt crappy. Then the Greenpeace person showed up and I went into your room to get your travel wallet to see if you had a twenty. This fell out," he said, tossing Richard's note card on the table in disgust.

"I see," I said, not even remembering stuffing it in there when I'd walked into the hotel after my first—and only—day of sightseeing.

"Well I'm glad you see. Because I sure as hell don't. Every time I read it, I say to myself, 'Naaah, no way. No way my mom snuck off with this colossal asshole I've been hearing about my whole life.' And then I go, 'maybe it's from another Richard Farley.' That could happen. Like I've got that friend Julie whose mom has been married to three different guys named Bob. Maybe it's just some same name coincidence or something. I mean, I'm really trying to figure this out, you know? But everything I come up with seems like kind of a stretch. Not as much of a stretch as you going to Rome— if you really were in Rome—with that motherfucker…whoa, ironic term to use, huh? Because I suppose you fucked him too, didn't ya, Mom?" And then he grabbed a chair and flung it back toward the wall behind him. Tears started streaming down his cheeks.

"Oh, God, Danny. Let me just explain. Please. This is just so complicated."

He made a sound somewhere between a snarl and laugh. "Yeah, I bet it is. Except it's simple, too. You went away with him, didn't you?"

"Well, it's not exactly like that...."

"Yes or no, you went with my father to Rome. YES OR NO?"

This went way beyond nightmares. Nightmares you could wake up from. "Yes," I said and sunk into the kitchen chair across from him. "But I need to tell you how and why it happened..."

"Oh, I'm sure there was a great reason."

"Danny! Will you just give me a chance to explain?" And so I began with Richard's letter....

I'm not sure how I thought Danny would feel when he initially heard that Richard was dying given that Richard had been dead to Danny for years. So I wasn't surprised when at first there was only silence. Then he cracked his knuckles and sneered, "So what are you saying? That this was his own personal Make A Wish thing? And you nobly decided to go off with a dying guy on some final request trip?"

"Hardly, Danny. There was nothing noble about it. It was a business deal."

"Right. 'Meet me for a drink in my room.' It really sounds like business."

"It was."

"What kind of business?"

"Your dad told me that if I would meet him in Rome for those few days he would give us all the back child support money he'd ever owed us, plus interest, plus seven hundred and fifty thousand dollars more. That's a lot of money, Danny. A whole lot.

Enough to change our lives forever. I didn't know what to do. I thought about it for weeks...."

"So how much did you sell out for, Mom? What was the big total that made this seem like such a great idea? I mean, do I at least get a car out of this? Or a spring vacation in Cancún?"

Now I was the one who was starting to cry. "That isn't what this was about, Danny. You don't get cars and trips. You don't get anything. I don't either. Not now. I decided not to take the money."

"What?" he yelled, actually even more furious than before. "He offers you money to meet him in Rome. You actually go and meet him. And now you're not taking the money? Some businesswoman you are. What happened? Did you fall back in love with him or something? Boy that would be really touching. Right before he croaks. No, wait, I get it. You *are* a great businesswoman. You decided to pass on the money now, pretend you fell back in love with him, get him to marry you again, and then get to be the rich widow and get *all* the money! My God, Mom, I take it back. You are a great businesswoman. You're fucking brilliant!"

"Danny stop it. You're hysterical. You're crazy and hysterical."

"Maybe I am, Mom. And what are you?"

"I'm trying to explain to you what happened." And I went over it again. This time I included the part about Richard's self-serving motivation for his offer, my walking out, his heart attack and the next two days in the hospital. "He might even be dead right now," I said.

"I give a shit. This is so not about him. It's about you. Not just your willingness to be bought out, which in some ways I can understand, but your ability to completely lie to me. And to

Sarah. God, you really trumped the old spinach in the taco story. Who knew you were still such a master of deceit."

"Oh, God, Danny, stop it!"

"Stop what? Stop telling the truth? It was deceit, wasn't it?"

"Yes, it was, but it was deceit with love."

"Bullshit, Mom! Deceit with love? That's...that's like some surprise party or something. Not running off to Italy and shacking up with a guy who walked out on us."

"I didn't shack up with him..."

"Riiight."

"I didn't," I snapped, starting to get angry. "Not that my sex life is any of your business, but we did each have our own room and we did not have sex."

"This is fucking ridiculous," he said, throwing his hands up in the air. "I can't deal. I've got to get the hell out of here."

And for the second day in a row, Danny stormed upstairs to his room and slammed the door. Within seconds some CD was blasting.

I stood at the bottom of the stairs with no idea what to do next. For a moment it felt like my life was over. The same way you feel in the ocean when a wave sucks you under and your whole life flash cards in front of you. Every regulation mom moment I'd had with Danny—every car pool, birthday party, trip or laugh at the kitchen table—all of them were fast-forwarded through my brain cells under the heading, "Yeah, but none of that counts now." That's how it felt. As if seventeen years of trust and love instantly dissipated and all my years of mothering were now defined in his mind by this one duplicitous act.

"You should have thought of that before," said the smug, toga-clad, imaginary Greek chorus that suddenly showed up in my head to offer a little creative torment. But they were right. I should have seen how risky and fragile the whole scheme was, and how if my son ever found out—a possibility I had never considered—it was conceivable that I might lose him over it.

My whole body began to shake. This entire thing had gone too fast and in too scary a direction for me to even begin to absorb it all. I sat down on the bottom step with my arms crossed around my knees and tried to steady myself. There was a lot of stomping around and slamming of drawers going on in Danny's room. I hadn't heard him that furious since the middle of his freshman year when I finally decided it was no longer my job to try to wake him up in time for school. It was always such a horrendous struggle and he was so surly. One day I decided that from then on he was in charge of his own getting up. He had three alarm clocks and I was retiring from the reveille business. That first week was not very pleasant. He was late four out of five mornings. And he desperately wanted me to believe that it was my fault. But it was a No Sale for me. I felt perfectly comfortable in my position.

I didn't feel one bit that way right now. I felt shamed and terrified. And I had every right to be. Danny flung open the door of his room and came tromping down the stairs. I jumped up. He was carrying a big duffel stuffed with clothes.

"Where are you going?" I asked as he brushed by me, his face splotchy from crying.

"I'm moving to Tim's."

"You can't live with Tim! You live here. With Sarah Rose and me."

"I don't want to live with you right now. I don't even want to be in the same solar system as you right now, Mom. I think you suck."

"Oh, God, Danny, please don't do this. I understand that you're upset. I really do." I put my hand on his sleeve.

"Good," he said shaking off my hand. "Then let me be upset. I think it's—as they say in psych class—pretty damn 'appropriate.'" He opened the front door and started down the porch stairs.

"Danny," I said, following him out front. "Please don't go. This wasn't supposed to happen."

He turned and glared at me. "Which part wasn't supposed to happen, Mom? You sneaking off with my son of a bitch father or me finding out about it?"

Then he walked down the front steps and headed toward the bus stop.

26

Chapter Twenty-Six

Then there was Tim. Whose rage and level of righteousness didn't begin to approach Danny's, but who was profoundly upset with me nonetheless.

"You went to Rome with Richard?" he repeated in an obvious effort to comprehend what I'd just told him.

As soon as Danny had disappeared around the corner, I'd gone immediately to the phone. I wanted Tim to know Danny was headed there and I wanted him to know—well, *wanted* isn't exactly the word—I felt he certainly *needed* to know why Danny was so upset. Plus, at some level I was terrified that instead of actually going to Tim's, Danny might decide to just plain disappear. After all, he *was* related to Richard.

As a young teenager Danny had, in fact, orchestrated two moderately successful running aways—one when Tim and I told him we were getting divorced and the other was from Tim's house when the two of them got into some sort of curfew blowup. In both cases he'd wound up crashing with friends, but he was crafty enough to select the homes of really peripheral friends, so Tim and I had the pleasure of phoning at least six sets of strangers to explain that our child hated us and we had no idea where that child might be.

"Damn it, Kate," he sighed, clearly unable to grasp that his ex-wife had gone to Rome with her ex-husband and that she had felt that this was a creditable, intelligent decision. "I'm trying to understand. But the logic of this eludes me. I feel as if I don't know you," he said.

"You know me, Tim," I said, seated on the couch in the living room. The very living room he and I had painted, the very living room he and I had vacuumed, the very living room that still had bunches of his CDs and books in it because we could never remember who had bought what.

I got up to adjust the front shutters against the late-afternoon sun. Whether it was a huge stress headache or a dose of jet lag, it suddenly felt like an industrial-strength vice had just clamped itself around the sides of my head. "It's just that you weren't with me as I went through the decision-making process on this one, so from the outside it probably seems like surprising behavior."

"Surprising is hardly the word. The first word that comes to mind is 'shocking.' It is so out of character for you."

"Out of character because you find it reprehensible? Or out of character because for my whole life I've always played by the rules?"

"Both. I don't know. Jesus, Kate, why didn't you come to me to discuss this? For God's sake I'm an *ethics* professor…"

"I know, Tim. But the fact that you know about the history of ethics doesn't de facto make you the arbiter of all that is ethical. And anyway, you're my ex-husband—with a distinct dislike for my first ex-husband."

"A dislike I thought you shared."

"I do. I do even more than before I left."

"Then why did you save his life?"

"Because I did not want to be the reason for his death."

"Which you wouldn't have been if you hadn't gone in the first place. God, Kate, I only wish you'd talked to me first."

"And what would you have advised me, Tim?"

"The truth? Actually I'm not sure," he said thoughtfully. "I detest hearing that you went on this trip with Farley. I detest that you lied to the children and me. On the other hand, I don't live in such an ivory tower that I think the world is ruled by ethical absolutes. At Danny's age one is ruled by absolutes. At our age, one is ruled by an awareness of gradations. The financial motivations you had are valid. We both know that Sarah Rose will run out of insurance money. We both know that Danny had that money coming to him and he has a long tough road ahead if he wants to be an artist..."

"So what are you saying?"

"I'm saying, Kate, that if I'd been in your situation, I honestly don't know what I would have done. As an ethics professor, I'd like to think that I'd have passed up the offer, but as a father, I'm not one hundred percent sure that is true. And I intend to share that with Danny."

"You do?"

"I do. I think it's important for him to hear that."

"Thanks, Tim."

"You're welcome," he said. "Um, Kate?"

"Yes?"

"I'm sorry about all of this."

"Me too."

"I'm sure. I also have to tell you that I'd rather you didn't get into this with Sarah Rose. I know there's some irony again in the ethics professor saying let's perpetrate a deceit on our child, but that's just further proof that I meant what I said. I do not for a second believe in absolutes."

I was on the swing in the backyard when Sarah Rose showed up an hour later. Swings and I have had a long, soothing history. As a kid, the swing was always the place I'd retreat to if I needed to assuage my soul. Whether it was because a cousin of ours had just decapitated my favorite doll, or years later when I had to tell Karen that I didn't want to apply to the same colleges as she did, or years after that when the police finally located Richard in Canada, swings had just always provided me with solace in stressy times.

Even Sarah Rose knew that. "Why are you swinging, Mommy?" she asked when she wheeled into the backyard on her bike. "Do you have a problem?"

I scuffed my feet on the ground to slow the swing to a stop and held out my arms to her. "Want to get on with me?"

"Nope. I want to watch Nickelodeon. Cassie's puppy is really cute, but he chews things. And he piddles."

"That's what puppies do."

"Is Danny home? Are we eating soon?"

"Sarah," I said, reluctantly separating myself from the swing even though I'd hardly begun to destress yet, and taking her hand as we walked in. "Danny and Mommy had a big fight. And when it was all over, Danny was so upset that he decided to sleep over at Daddy's. Maybe even for a few days."

"Are you mad back at Danny?" she asked, tilting her head up and fixing me with her brown eyes.

"No. I'm not mad, just really sad about it," I said squeezing her hand.

"Then maybe we should make some happy food. You know, the kind you make when we're sick. Let's have French toast with powdered sugar faces on it for dinner."

"Sure," I said, as the kitchen door slammed behind us. I took the bread and milk and eggs out of the refrigerator while Sarah pulled out the wire whisk. She loved the whisking part.

"Did you have the fight with Danny about his allowance?" she asked pulling the step stool up to the tile counter. "Danny always says he doesn't get enough money for allowance."

"No, honey. It wasn't about his allowance. Danny works. He doesn't get an allowance."

"Oh. Well, I still do. You know what, Mom? I'd like to get what Cassie gets. She gets a whole dollar."

"What would you do with a whole dollar?"

"Maybe give it to poor people. Maybe save it up for a trip. Could you and me go on a trip sometime? I bet you'd have a better time with me than the icky people you went to Italy with."

"I bet I would too," I said, cracking open the first egg.

Chapter Twenty-Seven

I slept in a fetal position that night.

Actually, I slept in a fetal position that whole week.

Because other than getting the call from Tim confirming that Danny had indeed landed safely, I had a son who was completely incommunicado. Not that I expected any big reunion to take place between us in the first twenty-four hours, but I was kind of hoping for contact after four or five days. I'd phoned and e-mailed him every day and I'd gotten zero response. Tim said Danny was just processing a lot of adult information through an adolescent brain, and that the best thing to do was to give him space.

"I think Tim is completely right," Karen said when she came over for dinner on my third night without Danny. She'd been going stir-crazy after nearly three weeks in her place, so I'd picked her up and brought her back to my house to graze on an assortment of our favorite foods—giant steamed artichokes, anchovies, crusty French baguette, really smelly Reblochon cheese and a bottle of cabernet.

"God this tastes fabulous," she said, smearing more of the ripe, creamy cheese onto her bread. "Do you think our loving this meal is God's way of punishing Mom for always feeding us from the five basic food groups?"

"I think God's too busy punishing me for having met Richard in Rome to worry about nailing Muriel on unimaginative food selections."

"Since when did you become My Sister The Victim? That's not your usual M.O., Kate."

"I know," I said, pouring her another glass of wine. "I'm sick of the self-flagellation myself, but it's kind of hard to get this hair shirt off, as long as the one male person I love most in the world thinks I am only a slightly less reprehensible mom than Medea."

"Medea killed her kids, for God's sakes. You only mortally wounded one."

"Gee, Kare, thanks for the support."

"I'm sorry. I'm just trying to put it in perspective. I know you hate it when I comment on the kids."

"Why do you say that?"

"Because everyone who has kids hates it when those of us who have no kids say anything. There's this silent rolling of the eyes that says, 'And what the hell qualifies you—a person who has never endured projectile vomiting on a regular basis—to make any observation about me and my children?'"

"I'm not getting into this now," I said, getting up from the table to clear our plates and start some decaf. "All I want is to figure out a way to regain a relationship with my son. I swear to God, Kare, having Danny hate me is more agonizing than anything I have ever been through."

"What about when Richard left?"

"I was angry, not agonized."

"What about when Sarah Rose had her accident?"

"I was terrified, not agonized. No, this is bleedy stuff. This feels like my skin is being scraped away every couple of minutes. The only time I feel semi-normal is when I'm on the air."

That has always been an odd thing about radio—its ability to yank me out of myself so no matter what kind of day I'm having in real life, on the radio, it never feels worse than mediocre. The people calling in are generally too interesting, or too quirky, or there is just something so funny and electric about the exchange that for the most part, having my job is almost my own daily dose of Prozac.

The truth is, there are some *crummy* jobs out there—jobs where people have to wear shower caps all day because they work around food, or jobs where people have to smell other people's armpits because they're testing deodorants—those kinds of jobs. So if your son decided he hates you and you are a professional armpit sniffer, well it just seems you don't exactly have an opportunity to lose yourself in your work. Not like I did.

Then there was the other reason that radio felt like such an emotional reprieve—David. Suddenly he was so *there* for me. His stepson Michael was twenty-five now, so it had been nearly a decade since David had actually faced off with adolescent rage, but that didn't muddy his understanding of the emotional morass a parent could plummet into.

"I remember one summer of almost daily blowups with him," he said when we were getting ready to go on the morning after Danny had moved out. "Michael was behaving so erratically that Jeannie and I made him take a drug test."

"Was he on drugs?" I asked, lifting the lid off my morning Starbucks.

"No, he wasn't. Of course, insisting on the test only exacerbated things with him, but Jeannie and I needed to know for sure that he was clean."

"So how did it resolve itself? It did resolve itself, didn't it?" I asked, desperate to know that there was, for sure, a happy ending.

"It didn't right away. Michael was pissed off for most of the summer."

"Most of the summer? God, I'll die if Danny isn't talking to me for most of the summer."

"Kate, he might not." He pulled off his reading glasses and looked at me soberly. "It could take even longer. Danny has walked into way more information than a seventeen-year-old can handle. He needs time to rage and sift through it. And he needs plenty of distance from you. If he didn't have Tim's place to go off to, believe me, it would probably get a lot uglier around your house."

"You don't mean violent, do you? Did Michael get violent?"

"It depends what you consider violent. He did wind up in the emergency room one night after smashing his fist into his bedroom wall."

"Did you ever find out what all the surliness was about?"

"Yeah," he said, shaking his head as he remembered. "Some girl he was hot for was giving him a real hard time. Jeannie and I probably never would have found out if one of his other friends hadn't told us. Michael has always played the love life thing pretty close to the vest."

"God, David, what am I going to do?"

"You're going to *do* nothing. You're going to *be* calm. Danny has just had his foundation rocked to the core. Right now he may feel he can never trust you again. He'll get over it. He's seventeen, Kate. He has no antenna yet for nuance. No antenna for the 'yeah, buts' of life."

"The 'yeah, buts'?"

"Yeah. The, 'Yeah, Mom's a good person, but she made this *one* badass move...' Or the, 'Yeah, that move she made seems pretty badass, but she must have felt she had a pretty good reason.' Right now Danny can't do the yeah-buts, he can only do the 'yeahs.'"

"So how long until he can factor in the 'buts'?"

He laughed. "If I knew that, I wouldn't be in talk radio. I'd make a fortune privately consulting with parents and then predicting for them the exact day, hour and minute their teenager would stop behaving like an asshole."

I had to smile. Because the truth was, if someone could have told me that in two months Danny would finally be able to deal with me again, even though I'd hate the intervening sixty days, I'd at least be comforted by knowing this part would finally end. But, of course, no one could tell me that.

Not even David, who was being pretty wonderful. "Listen," he said, after we'd finished our show that day and were dumping our newspaper clippings onto our respective desks, "how are you doing on the jet lag?"

"I'm not sure. It's a little hard to distinguish if my jagged sleep pattern is from that or from the Danny stuff, or maybe even some of the Richard stuff."

"Don't tell me you're worried about Richard, too. I thought you'd let go of that once his company sent someone over to Rome."

"I have let go of it. Believe me, I'm not worrying for a second about whether Richard is dead or alive. It's just that this past week obviously stirred up a lot of old Richard stuff. And I suppose that's contributed to my inability to sleep."

"No doubt. Well, I'm asking because I wanted to know if maybe you'd be up for dinner tonight. About twice a year I get fried chicken fever and I'm going home to fry up a couple batches of it this afternoon."

"You run, you garden and now you tell me you fry chicken, too? David," I said, duly impressed, "you're the Renaissance guy extraordinaire. I love fried chicken, but I'd like to stick close to home in case Danny calls or shows up."

"I understand." He began to pack up his briefcase.

"But I'll tell you what," I said, realizing I had just said no to the first official date David had ever asked me out on, "if you want to bring the chicken over—I love it cold—I'll put together some potato salad and slice up some beefsteak tomatoes. We can have a picnic on the back porch. Sarah would love it."

"Me, too," said David.

"Here," said Sarah Rose proudly handing the paper cup of lemonade to David that evening. "I made it all myself. I sell it on weekends. It's my Mom's secret recipe."

"Thanks," he said, taking it from her. "What's the secret?"

Sarah wiped her hands down the front of her T-shirt and looked at David with considerable seriousness. "If you tell a secret, then it's not a secret anymore."

He grinned. "That's true, Sarah Rose. And this is very good lemonade. But let me ask you this question. I liked what you said about secrets, but you've got me wondering something."

"What?" she said, sitting down on the porch steps looking up at him with her elbows on her knees.

"I think it can be true that if you tell a secret then it's not a secret anymore. But, can there *be* a secret? I'm asking can a secret even exist, unless one person tells something to another? Because if you don't tell it to at least one person, then it's just a silent thought. What do you think?"

Her little forehead furrowed on that one while she scratched her head and pondered. "I think grown-ups are very serious. Being a kid is better."

"You could be right, Sarah Rose."

We had a fine evening.

28

Chapter Twenty-Eight

Actually, David and I had several fine evenings that week. At least as fine an evening as is have-able when your firstborn refuses to talk to you since he has decided that you are a few substrata below toxic waste.

The time David and I spent with each other was low-key and easy. One night we hadn't even planned to get together, but he dropped by with a couple of rare hostas that he'd dug up and divided from his garden. When the doorbell rang I was upstairs taking a bubble bath with Sarah Rose. It was several minutes until I got us both out, and by the time I got downstairs, David had already given up ringing and was back at the curb about to get into his car.

"David," I called out, standing at the door in my formerly white terry cloth robe, "what's all this?" There were several plants wrapped in damp newspaper on the porch.

"Those hostas you liked so much. I was dividing a lot of my

plants tonight and I figured I'd bring them over right away. The quicker you get them in, the better."

Then grinning mischievously, he added, "Sorry about not calling. I know how you feel about drop-ins."

David and I had had a huge disagreement on-air a month before over the loveliness (his take) or the rudeness (my take) of the drop-in visit. David was almost wistful about it. He saw it as a harking back to a sweeter, less frenetic time, when people would get in their cars on a Sunday afternoon and go "visiting."

I, on the other hand, am not a drop-in kind of a girl. I don't do it, because it usually feels like someone is walking into *your* space at *their* convenience. I was pretty adamant on-air that I was a phone-first kind of person.

And then there he was at the curb, a flagrant drop-in who knew full well that, speeches to the contrary, I'd be genuinely pleased to see him. I had to laugh. He'd nailed me. "You know what? If you'd set those hostas in back for me, as soon as I dry Sarah's hair, I will reward you lavishly."

"What's your version of lavish?" he asked.

"The beer of your choice."

"Sold."

One week with no word from Danny soon became two. And then three. I checked in with Tim every day to get a read on Danny's rage-o-meter, but Tim was giving Danny a lot of space. He said Danny was being perfectly polite—albeit remote—over at his place, but that he was seldom around.

"What do you mean?" I asked one night when I'd dropped Sarah there to sleep over. "Isn't he ever home for dinner?" We were sitting in Tim's extremely beige, extremely tidy living room.

Tim's house always looked as if the cleaning lady had left twenty minutes before. It had been a sticking point in our marriage. The man was hyperfastidious—he even folded his dirty laundry.

"Nope, hardly ever. He's just been working overtime a lot at the insurance agency."

The ceiling was being pounded from above. Sarah was upstairs in her room singing and strutting to *Annie*. Like every little girl with curly red hair, she thought "Tomorrow" was her own personal theme song.

"God, I just wish he'd make some sort of contact with me."

"He will, Kate," Tim said, squeezing my shoulder paternally. "But I keep saying over and over. This is going to take time. That boy really loves you. If he didn't, he wouldn't be this white-hot. You can understand his fury, can't you?"

"Of course. But what if he never talks to me again?" I wailed. "What if in fifteen years Sarah winds up being one of those people that writes into some advice lady? 'Dear Advice Lady—I'm getting married in six months, but my mother and my brother haven't spoken since I was seven. I'm afraid there'll be an ugly scene between them and it will ruin my wedding. Can I flip a coin and not invite one of them?'"

"Here's how she'll answer." Tim laughed. "'Dear Sarah— Don't flip a coin. Just don't invite your mother. It'll be okay. She's been worrying about this for fifteen years.'"

Sometimes even Tim was funny.

More than anyone though, David was committed to getting me to laugh.

"Look, you just have to sit tight and do your best not to fixate on your anguish," he said as we stopped for the light across from the Fourth Presbyterian Church. We had gone for a long walk after our show. The church covered nearly a half block up on North Michigan Avenue and its massive gothic arched courtyard looked like the set from *Romeo and Juliet*. "Even though anguish can be very attractive, very sexy."

"What does that mean?" I asked, taking my foot momentarily out of my shoe and wondering how our moms spent their lives in heels. I couldn't do ten blocks in flats without feeling a deep, abiding need for a podiatrist.

"It just means that anguish sells. It can be torch songs, Shakespearean tragedy—whatever—most of us can be very good at suffering. I think we're hardwired for it. In fact I've often thought that each of us has our own personal anguish quotient that we always manage to fill."

"Anguish quotient?"

"Yeah. Say you have an anguish quotient of five and I have one of seven. You can fill your five or your seven with anything you want to anguish about. It can be the Cubs, it can be cancer, it can be finance problems. No matter. Your five and my seven will always be filled. Obviously if you're walking around with your five completely taken up by the Cubs and then you get diagnosed with cancer, the cancer knocks the Cubs out of there. But—and here's the point—it does not compound the Cubs. It doesn't go from five for the Cubs plus ten for the cancer to make an anguish quotient total of fifteen. It just stays steady at five. Tops it goes to six."

"David, what on earth are you talking about?" I asked, completely perplexed.

"I'm just saying, Kate," he continued as we crossed the street, "that right now your five is completely wrapped up in Danny pain, but that as soon as the two of you find your way out of this—and the two of you will, I know it—your anguish quotient of five will fill right up again with something else."

"So you're saying no matter what, a person is never completely happy? Boy, that's a pretty cynical perspective."

"What's cynical about it? I think it's somewhat soothing. I'm saying that no matter how grim a situation is, you'll probably keep it contained in a manageable-sized arena and not become overwhelmed with it. For instance, even though you are grieving right now over this freeze-out from Danny, you're not completely immobilized. You're functioning. Sarah Rose still has a very involved mom, our listeners aren't aware that you're in any pain..."

"David, if you think for one second that I feel normal, that I'm not dying here. That I feel happy or even okay..."

"I'm not saying you're happy or even okay, but..." He stopped walking and put his hands on my shoulders. "Hey, Kate...what are you doing for the rest of the afternoon?"

We had stopped in front of Crate and Barrel. I've always wanted to live a Crate and Barrel kind of life, but it seems destined to elude me. The one time I ever brought something from there—it was a tweed chenille throw reduced from one hundred dollars to twenty-two dollars—as soon as I brought it home to my place, it morphed from looking really stunning in the store to looking like a ratty attic hand-me-down. Even so, just wandering through there usually lifted my spirits.

"Well, I thought I'd go in just take a look around for a bit. Sometimes twenty minutes in the Crate makes me feel better."

"Oh," David said, in the tone of a kid who had just been told there was no more dessert left.

"Why?" I asked, surprised at his disappointment.

"Because I just had this great idea. Remember last week on the show when we were talking about doing something a little outrageous that we've always wanted to do?"

"Huh?" I can hardly remember what happened on a show we did this morning, much less do rapid recall on one we'd done a week ago.

"You know, the one when listeners called in and finished the sentence 'I've always wanted to...'"

"Oh, yeah. I remember." It *had* been a fun twenty minutes of radio. Some of the memorable endings to the "I've always wanted to" line were "have a penis for one day"; "finish a whole Sara Lee German chocolate cake by myself in one sitting"; "tell my boss he has terrible oral hygiene"; "learn to figure skate backward"; and "watch two horses having sex." Our listeners had nothing, if not range.

On the other hand, so did David and I. My finish to the "I've always wanted to" challenge came from a lecture I once heard on the art of persuasion. I've always wanted to get on an empty elevator and, instead of facing front, I want to face back. Then I'd like to see how other people at stops along the way deal with this—whether they'd ignore me, or flee, or whether they would simply face backward, too.

David's "I've always wanted to" was a bit less perverse. He just wanted to see three sunsets from the same spot on the same night. Apparently you can do this, if you lie down on the beach and watch the sun set from that level, then as soon as it disappears beyond the horizon, stand right up and because of your angle of elevation, watch it set again. And then right after it sinks that second time, leap into the nearest lifeguard tower for the final encore. I suppose if people were on the beach at the time, there would be some potential embarrassment involved in his little event, but not nearly as much as there would be in mine.

"I was just thinking it might be fun for us to do what we'd actually talked about."

"I suppose it would."

"No, I mean now. This afternoon."

"Do what? The elevator thing and the sunset thing?"

"Yeah. What do you say?"

"I say you're crazy, David."

"I say you're chicken, Kate."

Which would explain how, even though I had about as serious a situation at home as I'd had in a long time, I found myself facing the back wall of the elevator in the Foote Cone and Belding Building, a building that houses some of the more highly paid creative people in the city. But not so creative that, as they stepped into the elevator and saw the two adults facing the rear, each and every one of them didn't think it was a real good idea to step right off that elevator and wait for the next available car. We completely freaked everyone out.

David wanted to do it again.

That's how much fun it was.

Our sides still ached from laughing fifteen minutes later when we got back to the station parking lot.

"Okay. Now the sunset part," I said, opening my car door and tossing my purse on the front seat. "How about we go home and change and head over to the beach around 7:30? Sarah's at Tim's for the night, so I'll pick you up and we'll go over to Montrose Harbor, okay?"

He smiled oddly. Like an about-to-make-fun-of-me smile. "And what do you propose we do at Montrose Harbor?"

"What do you think—the three-sunsets-in-one thing."

David shook his head. "Not gonna happen, Kate. Not at Montrose Harbor."

"Why no—" but I couldn't even finish the word "not." Because suddenly I knew why not. Chicago faces the wrong way on the lake for sunsets. Chicago faces east. Which is great for sunrises. But for sunsets, you had to drive around to the other side of the lake. You had to drive over to Michigan.

My hands flew up to my face in full *Home Alone* fashion. "Oh, my God, David. I feel so stupid. I'm horrible in science, but still, this is over the top."

His smile wasn't making fun of me anymore. It was tender, almost protective. "It's fine, Kate. Just a little geographical quirk of our fair city. You're allowed to get a C in geography."

"Actually, I was praying for a C when I was in college. I still don't understand how they invented latitude and longitude."

He laughed, closing the door for me as I slid in behind the wheel. "So like you were saying. How about we both go home and change, and then drive over to Michigan in about an hour? We can still get out of town before rush-hour traffic and it only takes ninety minutes to get to New Buffalo. Are you up for a triple sunset in another area code?"

Chapter Twenty-Nine

Going with David to *another state*—well, it felt different.

Not like an official trip, but not exactly like just heading over to Lake Shore Drive and the beach either.

It felt like enough of a trip, though, that I did one of those "I've got to square my life away before leaving town" projects. For some people it was drawer straightening, for others it was bill paying, for my friend Roberta it was an "if the plane crashes and I die, here's some words of wisdom for the kids" letters. Every time Roberta left town she'd go to her computer to update the letters in case she had any more Big Life Insights since her last trip. But all I did before leaving for Michigan was send off one more e-mail to Danny. I resisted saying anything melodramatic, like, "Who knows if I'll make it to Michigan alive." I just said that twenty-five days of not communicating didn't feel like a wise or satisfactory way for us to co-exist.

"Danny, you and I are as connected as two people can be," I

wrote. "We have always been able to hash things out. Even if you didn't like a rule or a restriction that I was imposing, I usually felt you understood where it was coming from. And vice versa. Even if I didn't like a certain behavior on your part, I'd want to get some input from you and understand where it was coming from. We have done that for each other for a long time. We need to do that now. Please come home. I love you a lot."

I knew the chances were slim to none that he might answer. But it still felt better to send the e-mail and to tell him—without using the words—that this distance felt close to intolerable. We absolutely needed to talk. Not so I could apologize, not so I could explain. But just so he could *hear* what my thought processes had been and why I finally made the decision to go to Rome for the money. I didn't need him to approve. I needed him to be able to live with it. And to live with me.

God, I missed him.

David picked me up a little before four. He'd changed into a pale gray T-shirt and faded old jeans. The legs I'd never seen were still not on view. He had a camera on the front seat, but when I climbed in he set it in back.

"You're going to document this on film?" I asked, nodding to the camera.

"That's the plan. I'm a little pissed I didn't have a camera with us when we were in the elevator this afternoon. It would have been a great shot."

"Of us, or of the people's reactions when they saw us?"

"Both." He grinned and popped in a CD of old Eagles tunes.

I slammed the door of his car and buckled myself in. "Do you think we'll get fired for this?"

"For driving over to Michigan?"

"No," I said as "Hotel California" came on. "For not listening to our station while driving there."

"No, I think they just take away your dental benefits on a first offense."

"What about the second?"

"Castration," he deadpanned, doubling up and pretending to grab his crotch. I can't say it was the first time I'd ever considered that David had a crotch, but it was the first time either of us had even vaguely referred to it. And for a brief moment, it turned me into a guy—a visualizer. It's a known fact that men are genetically wired to be mental undressers. Someone says to a guy, "Hey, Tom, this is Susie," and while Tom's mouth is saying, "Nice to meet you, Susie," his brain has managed to remove the complete outfit that Susie worked forty-five minutes to put together. Girls don't tend to do that. Not usually. Except there I was sitting next to David after his castration remark and my mind was going, "Whoa, not so fast with the castration comment, not until I can at least imagine what you look like intact."

The pathetic truth was, I hadn't been with a naked man in over three years. I was lucky I could still even visualize one. The last man I'd slept with was a terrific guy named Jason Marks. Jason was lanky, blond, boyish even, and was the first man with facial hair I had ever kissed. I'd always thought I'd hate facial hair if it got up close and personal. I didn't hate it. It felt cozy. No matter where he'd put his face. And he put it in a lot of places. We had a very intense four months, followed by a very amicable breakup. But with the exception of some visits to the Art Institute, it was true I hadn't seen a naked man in an awfully long time.

"What's in the bag from Whole Foods?" I asked, trying to shake myself loose from the land of mental porn.

"Dinner," he said. "I decided to feign sophistication and just bring bread, pâté, cheese and wine."

"You're sure that will be enough for you?" I asked, somewhat dubious that a man could make a whole meal out of appetizers.

"If it's not, I'll just slay a wild buffalo on the way home."

The drive out of the city was gorgeous. Some days Chicago just wows you with its glory. Skimming sailboats and catamarans dotted the lake on our left and on our right we passed Grant Park and Buckingham Fountain and then all the stunning gothic buildings on the University of Chicago's Hyde Park campus. After that it got nasty for a while going through the smelly, smoky gray of Gary, Indiana's, factories, but soon we were passing the turnoffs for the grassy flatlands of the Indiana Dunes and finally we crossed over the state line into the village of New Buffalo, Michigan.

We had plenty of time before sundown, so David and I decided to poke around the village for a bit. The stores and galleries were still open on Whittaker Street and then we wandered into a lovely garden behind a restaurant called Miller's Country House. The Millers sat us down on their deck by the lily pond and tempted us into having something called Michigan margaritas. The concoction delivered the gentlest of buzzes, so by the time we got over to the public beach, we were feeling indisputably glowy inside and out.

Lake breezes were being tempered by the still toasty sun. Most of the families had left the beach to go home to their cottages, but there was still a handful of people and dogs scattered about.

"It looks like we'll probably have a few witnesses to our upcoming event," I said to David as we spread his old Ohio State blanket on the sand.

"You know what? I think I don't care," he said, unpacking our food. "If it feels half as exhilarating as our elevator gig today, I'm going to want other people to watch. Maybe we'll inspire them."

"Yeah, to call the cops," I said, opening two bottles of water and handing him one. After the margaritas, neither of us was interested in wine.

We clinked our plastic bottles together and David toasted, "Here's to completing our 'I've always wanted to...' sentence."

"How long have you wanted to do this sunset thing," I asked, turning over on my stomach and looking back across the lake toward Chicago.

"About two months," he answered, stretching down beside me on his back. Putting his hands behind his head, his T-shirt pulled out of his pants and I could see about three inches of his flat, tan, reddish-brown furred belly. I've always loved men's bellies.

"I read about it one Sunday in the science section of the paper, and it seemed like such an obvious thing to do, even though I'd never thought of it."

"So if we had asked the 'I've always wanted to...' question six months ago, we wouldn't be here, right? You'd have wanted to do something else."

"Yup."

"What?"

"Well," he said, sitting up to spread some pâté on the coarse white bread and handing me a slice, "we'd be taking a little exploratory voyage inside some composer's head—probably George Gershwin's—so we could understand whatever the process is that makes music get written."

I started to laugh. "Sounds like a trickier trip than just driving to the other side of the lake."

"No question. But figuring out how music gets made is something I've always wanted to do, ever since my parents would spend all day Sunday in our living room playing records and talking about the music."

"Were they musicians?"

"Nope. They were music appreciators. And I think I must have been five or six when I first started asking them how music gets made. My mom says I'd ask, 'But how does the music get *borned?*'"

I smiled. It felt odd to think of David as a little boy. I don't think any of us do that with each other very much——brain trip back to when our boss or our colleague was sitting in a little plaid shirt and corduroys with a runny nose and scuffed shoes. It's a sweet image, and something of a leveler.

David continued. "Music has always confounded me. I can understand the process of a blank canvas being filled in with color and images. I can understand the process of a blank page being covered with words. But to this day I do not understand how silence becomes rhythm and melody and sound. Have you ever thought about it?" he asked, his black eyes squinting against the sun.

"No. I'm too shallow for a thought like that. Have you ever tried to write music?"

His smile was self-deprecating. Actually, it was a little bit sexy and self-deprecating. Maybe the sexy thing decided to creep in when we crossed the state line. "Sure. But——" and he held his hand up in a policemanlike "stop" motion "——don't ask to hear it. Not unless you're willing to show me your high school yearbook or something. It's only fair to shoot for a little parity if we're going to humiliate ourselves. Okay?"

I thought of my graduation photo, with the full Farrah Fawcett 'do and granny dress ensemble. Letting anyone but a blood relative look at that would not be a smart move. "Okay, fine," I acceded. "No song requests. We'll just have to settle for sunsets."

"Settle? What do you mean settle? This is going to be sensational."

And it was.

David and I had walked down the beach so we could be within steps of a lifeguard stand. And then we took our positions, lying flat on the sand, readying ourselves for sunset number one. He had his camera set on a timer behind us, so it would shoot the two of us prone like human worms on the ground with the sun going down. I volunteered to take a shot of him standing and looking at sunset number two right after, but getting photographic evidence of sunset number three was going to be trickier. There really was only room for one of us at a time up on the lifeguard station.

"You know what the problem is here?" I asked. "The problem is we're focusing on getting this documented rather than just doing it. It's so symptomatic of how screwed up we all are. It's the video screen theory of life."

"The what?"

"The video screen theory. I mean if you go to the ballpark, more people are looking at the video screen than at the actual players playing the ball game. For most people, their reality has become the reflected reality, not the real reality."

"And you call yourself shallow?" He laughed.

"I call myself lucky. I'm about to see three sunsets in one night and have at least two of them documented."

* * *

We were quiet driving home. Quiet and comfortable. Not old shoe, married couple comfortable—how could we be, without ever having had our first kiss yet?—but comfortable knowing that we were probably about to have it. And it was going to feel important.

It did.

It was a front porch kiss. The kind where if the porch light is on the whole world can see. I don't think we cared. We were sitting on the top steps watching the fireflies and trying to stretch the evening out just a little longer.

"What's the longest date you've ever been on?"

"You mean besides this one? Or isn't this a date?" I leaned back on my hands and supported myself from behind.

"For me, this has definitely been a date," David said, running his hands through his hair. "I asked you to do it, I picked you up, I got the food, I used up gas—I even showered before I came over to pick you up. It feels like a date to me."

"You showered?" I smiled. "Well I guess that cinches it. It was definitely a date."

"Was it a fun one for you? Go ahead, you can tell me," he teased. "Be brutally honest."

"It was definitely a fun one. What about you?"

"Definitely a fun one," he agreed.

"So?"

"So?" he repeated. "So do you remember how fun dates generally end here in America?"

"Well," I said, turning to face him, "I think I do. But it's been a long time for me." And then in an effort to halt all our snappy banter—sometimes I hate snappy banter—I took David's face in my hands and kissed him.

I think he was surprised. I think he thought he was going to be the kissing initiator. I don't think he minded being usurped though. In fact it was clear from how he kissed me—soft to hard, tentative to exploratory, polite to tonguey—that he was having as amazing a time as I was.

"Wow," I said as we reluctantly pulled apart. "Just wow."

"You have incredible lips," he said, tracing my mouth with the tip of his finger. "I bet you hear that all the time." I think I blushed. I flashed on all those years Karen and I felt ashamed of our mouths because they were so pouty and full. When all we had to do was wait for Julia Roberts and the collagen-obsessed twenty-first century.

I took hold of David's finger and kissed the tip, then took his hand in both of mine and said, "We have to talk."

"Oh, God. The four most dreaded words a man can hear." He laughed.

"But you know we have to."

"Kate," he said, covering my two hands holding his with his other one, so our arms were completely intertwined, "not tonight. We both know things have been changing between us. We both know that kissing makes it even more changed. But we're adults. Adults who like each other a lot. And adults who like each other a lot are allowed to kiss without each kiss launching some big policy statement. Sometimes they even kiss a lot without any words passing between them."

Which is what we did. About a hundred more times.

Chapter Thirty

We waited a whole week to sleep together.

It was an extremely rough week.

For all sorts of reasons.

Some of it was the sexual tension. A huge hormonal flood-gate had opened that night on the porch. There was no getting around that. The next morning at the station I was terrified we would go on air and it would sound like mating dance radio. But the sexual tension was only part of what made the week so scratchy. The biggest part was the Danny situation. And the newest part was that Cassie, the girl who had defended Sarah Rose at camp against the she-bully of bitchy burn remarks, was out sick for most of the week and Sarah Rose became the temporary magnet for some prepubescent brutality.

"Every time our c-c-c-ounselor was far enough away so she couldn't hear," Sarah Rose sobbed one afternoon as she sat on my lap and clung to me, "Ally would call me 'wrinkle neck' and all the other girls would laugh. It was so mean, Mommy. I hate camp. I'm never going back. Please don't make me, please."

Oh, God. It was my worst thing as a mom. I could be strong in the burn ward of a hospital, and I could even be strong in the face of this communication limbo with Danny (though I was feeling increasingly crumbly), but when either of my kids was being picked on in the playground, I became a quivering mass of not-quite-congealed Jell-O.

And that's how I remained all week—gelatinous and looking longingly at the phone even more on behalf of that other kid. Wednesday of that week happened to be Danny's eighteenth birthday, a birthday I'd always figured we'd commemorate under the same roof. But, apparently, it wasn't going to happen, and sad as she was about her camp situation, Sarah Rose felt as bereft about Danny's birthday as I did.

"I asked Danny if he would come home just for that night, Mommy, and he said no. He doesn't even want to have ice cream or cake with Daddy and me on Wednesday. Do you think it'll be okay if I make him a birthday card?"

"Oh, honey, I think that would be really nice." Of course, I'd sent him a card earlier in the week, but there had been no response. And of course, I called him on his cell all day but, again, there was no response. The phone loomed fairly large that week as something of an instrument of torture.

Not with David, though. The nights he wasn't at the house with Sarah and me, he'd call just to check in. He knew I was having a rough week, and rather than try to mollify me, which was Karen's approach—"the teasing *will* stop;" "Danny *will* come home"—David was good at just listening. Not that "mmm-hmm… yeah…can you just let me get back to ESPN" kind of listening that men—even kind, developed men—have perfected over the years. I mean *caring* listening. The kind where your fears and pains were not just being perceived as a litany recorded on a continuous tape, but were being heard and felt in a fearful and pained way. That's caring listening, and it's not all that easy a skill for a woman to develop, much less someone who happens to be a man. But David had it for sure, and it was a huge comfort that week.

Actually, by the end of it, some of the pain had let up. Sarah's seven-year-old protector still hadn't returned to camp, but Sarah apparently had decided to take matters into her own hands and instead of crying when the teasing started again, she yelled back, "I am not a wrinkle-neck, I just almost died in a fire accident." Apparently the "almost died in a fire accident" grabbed the attention of the assembled tormentors, and suddenly Sarah morphed from being the group outcast to having the lead role in a movie-of-the-week drama. I'm not a big fan of children— or adults—with Sarah Bernhardt tendencies, but if that was what it took to get everyone to back off, then so be it.

Friday evening I drove a much happier Sarah to Tim's for the weekend. He was glad to hear about the turn of events in the land of seven-year-olds, and while I was catching him up, I found myself standing in his kitchen, looking for signs of my other child. Had the Coke can in the recycle bin belonged to Danny? What about the Birkenstocks in the mudroom? Was he really going to walk through this back door in a matter of hours and spend the weekend right here with Sarah?

For the past five weeks, I'd resisted the temptation to put Sarah Rose in the middle and ask her anything about her time with Danny. She wasn't seeing him a whole lot less, but she was see-

ing him at a very different address. If she volunteered something—"Daddy, Danny and me, we went to the Chicago Cubs
place, Mom, to see baseball!"—I devoured it. But I didn't push.
I didn't ask any coy questions about Danny or his behavior. It
wasn't fair to her. And it wasn't necessarily going to be helpful
to me. How Danny behaved with his sister, whom he adored,
had nothing to do with how he felt about me. I knew he'd never
punish her by pushing her off, just because he needed to do that
with me.

I was extremely glad the week was done and extremely glad
that David was about to come over. I'd picked up some steaks
and fresh tomatoes and corn that afternoon and told him his
only job was to show up and be boss of the barbecue. "Whenever I grill, I smell like lighter fluid for two days," I said.

"I've never heard of that." He laughed. "Maybe you just stand
downwind and get as smoked through as your burgers. Would
you like me to observe your technique?"

"Nope, I just want you to cook," I said, kissing him quickly in
the parking lot before leaving the station that afternoon. Neither of us had made a single speech all week regarding where
we were headed—which we both knew was bed—and how we
were going to handle it on air and off. It wasn't that we weren't
thinking about it, but given that we made our living from talking off the top of our heads, I think both of us wanted to reflect
a bit before issuing edicts and rules of this extremely new road.

I thought the shows we'd done so far that week sounded remarkably regular, but then people who work together in offices
and have affairs always think they're fooling everyone and in the
meantime there's generally an office pool going on about when
the woman is going to get pregnant. But then David and I

weren't officially having an affair. At least not until after we'd had a great meal and split a bottle of wonderful pinot noir that Friday night.

Even so, it was a surprise—not that we wound up in the bedroom, but that we managed to wait until dinner was over. And that what happened between us was so remarkable.

What is there about first-time, long-awaited, hungry, blushy sex between two experienced adults that makes it both hot and tender at the same time? Why is it initially so tentative and subsequently such an implosion? All those cravings and discoveries about each other's bodies and each other's responses all folded into such sweet and sweaty hours.

Yes, hours. David and I were at it for hours. Me on top. Him on top. Doggie style. Gymnastics style. Front sides, back sides, breasts, tongues, privates, fingers, insides of knees, eyelids...we were wondrously devoid of self-consciousness. Our lovemaking was damp, fragrant and noisy. We were both moaners, unbridled and unrelenting moaners.

Who knew? Who knew that your favorite sentence from a man you'd talked to for a year and half would wind up being, "Turn over, I love your ass." And that your second favorite would be when he came up from a leisurely visit between your legs to kiss you and said, "taste us." Oh, we were good at getting to each other's centers. And even though each time it was a little different, and a little better, ultimately, I had to beg for respite.

"No more," I said, finally rolling away from him. My lips were bruisy-feeling from hours of kissing and nibbling and licking. "I give up. You win."

David pushed my hair back from my face and tracing my jawbone, he whispered, "What do I win? I'm not looking to compete with you."

I took his hand from my face and kissed his open palm. "I'm not competing. You just have to let me stop. You're too much."

"*We're* too much," he said, moving our hands to his lips.

"Yeah, maybe we are." He must have heard the fear in my voice. The little glitch alert that told him I was moving toward that "Oh my God, what have I done" zone.

"Kate?" he said quietly, preemptively. "Don't. This is about *us*. Not me with an echo of anybody, or you either. I haven't been with a woman since Jeannie. No one. Because everyone I met, I still kept relating to through the prism of Jeannie. That hasn't happened with you. You've had your own place in my life. In my heart. You own it. And what just happened between us—this incredible explosion—is about us. This isn't you with someone who is just the next guy. And me with someone who is just the next woman."

"Oh, David," I said, aching for him to be right, "how do we know that? I can't speak for you, but I do not have a great track record in the love zone. What if all this is about the fact that I'm in a really vulnerable, shaky place and could really use a safe warm haven right now? Are you ready to finally be someone's safe, warm haven?"

"I'm not."

"You're not?"

"I'm not ready to be *someone's* safe, warm haven. I'm ready to be *yours*."

I knew I was going to start to cry. Not big hiccupy crying, but the tears were almost two-thirds down my cheek when his arms went around me and I buried my face in the still sticky warmth of his chest.

"Oh, baby," he whispered. "It's okay. Don't worry. I know your secret."

I pulled away to look in his deep black eyes. "What secret?"

"You know."

"No, I don't. What secret do you know about me?"

Very gently he put his lips to my ear and pulled me even closer. "I know you're not perfect. And…"

"And?"

"And it's okay. I'm still going to love you."

31

Chapter Thirty-One

I was beginning to feel as if my life was nothing but tabloid head-lines. What I mean is, usually my life read like a small-town weekly. The headlines might be Kate Gets A Four Percent Raise. or Kate's Kid Passes His Driving Test. But now my life read like 64-point headlines in *The National Enquirer.* Kate Sneaks Off To Europe For Paid Tryst With Ex. Devastated Son Discovers Truth—Walks Out On Kate. Kate Breaks Workplace Vow—Gets Naked With Radio Partner.

I needed a recess from my life.

I didn't get one.

Instead, I got another banner headline. A cataclysmic, impos-sible-to-believe headline that read Kate's Son Arrested For Bank Fraud. Actually, the technical charge, according to the federal officer who did the physical arresting of Danny was *conspiracy to commit* bank fraud. The word *conspiracy* made me think the crime sounded more nefarious but less actionable.

I was wrong. Conspiracy to commit bank fraud is plenty actionable. Four to eight slammer years of actionable.

My Danny.

The federal agents rang my doorbell at seven o'clock on Saturday night. It had been storming all afternoon and David and I had decided to acquiesce to the crummy weather—not to mention our hormones—and spend most of the day in bed. We woke up and had a lovely co-ed shower, followed by an even lovelier co-ed nap, followed by decidedly co-ed lovemaking, then another nap, another shower, more lovemaking and somewhere in there was an excellent salad niçoise that I am famous for making—if you define fame as having at least one person ask you for the recipe. It had been a steamy, languorous day, but by seven that night, some sort of excursion requiring our getting vertical, dressed and out among the living seemed like a good idea.

We'd decided on a movie within walking distance, and David had gone home to change. So I assumed it was him when the doorbell rang.

"One second, I just have to grab my rain slicker," I said, flinging open the door and being confronted by a man who definitely wasn't David. Actually I was confronted by two men who definitely weren't David.

"Ms. Lerner?" he inquired.

I nodded.

"We're from the Secret Service," said the taller man, flashing a beyond-official-looking set of plastic IDs. "I'm Special Agent Thompson and this is my partner, Special Agent Mattingly. May we speak to your son Daniel please?"

"Danny?" My heart fell to my stomach, my stomach to the floor. "There's nothing wrong is there?"

Our dialogue was like some outtake from an old *Dragnet*. So, of course, he said, "Well, yes, there is, ma'am. Is your son home?"

David came bounding up the porch stairs right on cue. "What's going on?" My face must have terrified him, given that all the blood had drained out in the past minute.

I grabbed his hand and pulled him to my side. We were all still standing on the porch. "David, these are Secret Service agents. Officer...?"

"Mattingly and Thompson."

"Mattingly and Thompson. They want to talk to Danny."

"What about?" he asked. Not addressing me. Addressing them.

"Um, ma' am, we'd like to come inside," Officer Thompson said. "Is your son home?"

"No, he's not," I said, letting them in the door. "Can you tell me what's going on?"

There are two ways in which a person's life can change. Most of the time it changes incrementally—information is gathered, experiences are integrated, feelings gradually deepen or gradually erode—it's a process. Other times it changes swiftly. In a nanosecond. And that's what happened when Officers Thompson and Mattingly told me they had a warrant for Danny's arrest. Apparently Danny was part of a corporate payroll check-counterfeiting ring operating out of the insurance office where he did the data entries. Where he ostensibly did nothing but data entries.

"The way it works, Ms. Lerner," said Officer Thompson almost wearily, "is that your son scans a blank check into the computer. Then once it's in there, he can use the computer to redesign the check—put in wavy lines, move stuff around, change or create the logo—whatever. He can make it a payroll check from anywhere—Coca-Cola or a local jewelry store—most people working in a currency exchange don't know what a particular company's payroll checks look like. He can also make it for any amount—two hundred and fifty-four dollars or twelve hundred and eighty dollars—it doesn't matter. Some other guys he's involved with from the Secretary of State's office make fake driver's licenses to go with the checks, and then they can be taken to any exchange in the city and cashed."

"How do you know my son is doing this?" I whispered, incredulous.

"We have him on tape talking to one of his pals in the Secretary of State's office. We don't know who the guy is yet."

"How can you not know his name, but know Danny's?"

"Because this guy calls from a cell phone. But your kid isn't allowed to use a cell at his office, so he always answers on the same land line at work."

"How does Danny know this man?"

"That's something we want to find out. All we know now is that your son is very good at following this guy's directions. Daniel agreed to cut two checks last week—one from an insurance company and one from a local grocery store. You used to need to be an artist to do something like this. Now you can do it with a good laser scanner and a good laser printer…."

And an amazingly bad moral compass, I thought, completely aware that my own moral compass would probably be described in the exact same words by Danny—my extremely righteous child who was now being accused of committing a federal crime.

I didn't even realize I was crying until I put my hands over my mouth and nose and felt the tears. "Oh, God, David, what is going on?"

He'd been next to me on the couch the whole time, but for the past three minutes I hadn't been cognizant of anything in the room except Officer Thompson's bushy mustache moving up and down as he was giving me this horrible information. David's arm went around me instantly. "Just breathe deep, Kate. Don't jump to any conclusions. Danny is being arrested for something. Not convicted. It's completely possible that the agents here have made a mistake."

"Not likely," said Officer Mattingly menacingly, who, unlike his partner, had a wanna-be, wispy mustache. "Like we said, we've got your son on tape and we've got several sets of these phony checks and drivers' licenses he and his pals have manufactured these last eighteen months."

My heart soared. "Eighteen months? Danny has only been working at this insurance agency for ten months. He couldn't possibly be at fault."

"I wish you were right, Ms. Lerner." Officer Mattingly squinted his eyes a bit and moved a toothpick from the right to the left side of his mouth. It was like he'd been sent by central casting. He was even wearing a brown suit. "We're not saying he was in on it from the beginning. Who knows? But we do know that your son was making something like ten percent off the face value of every check he created. The kid must have a pretty hefty bank account somewhere."

The irony of discovering Danny was stashing money away illegitimately while I was off in Rome acquiring money for him somewhat less than legitimately was not lost on me. I got up from the couch and walked to the window. The Geracis, our neighbors across the street, were backing out of the driveway in their monster van. It was filled with their monster children. Though maybe I needed to revise my definitions of monster children. Luke and Tony Geraci may have been two of the biggest bullies in the entire middle school, but to my knowledge no officers of the federal government had ever knocked on the Geracis' front door looking for them.

"So what do we do now?" I locked my eyes with David so he knew I considered him part of the "we."

"Well, first we need to find your son. Can you tell us where he is?"

"He's been staying at his stepfather's. I can give you his address. Officer, can you give me any idea how serious this is?"

"Ms. Lerner, it's very serious. Conspiracy to commit bank fraud is a federal crime. Since this has been going on, it looks like your son and his cronies have cashed over $500,000 worth of phony checks."

"But Danny doesn't have all the money does he?" I asked.

"No. I'm sure not. But the way the law works is that each and every member of this ring can be hit with the full half-million dollar charge."

"So what does all that mean," I asked, even though I was terrified to hear the answer. "Can Danny go to jail?"

"Yup, he could be locked up easy for a couple of years." Officer Mattingly said this calmly, as if informing parents of their kid's potential prison sentences was a pretty routine way to spend a Saturday night.

"Oh, my God!" I gasped. "Is that likely? Can Danny really go to jail?"

"I don't know if it's likely or not. But it's certainly very possible."

I grabbed on to the edge of the couch to steady myself. "What do you want me to do? Am I supposed to come with you to get him?"

"I don't think that's a good idea, ma'am. It only complicates things—for him and for us."

"Why shouldn't I be there," I asked, my other hand holding on to David. "Don't you think he's going to be terrified?"

"Probably." Thompson nodded, shifting his weight from foot to foot, obviously familiar with Mama and Papa Bear protective feelings. "But that's okay for him to be. Also, Ms. Lerner, in my experience, having a parent along sometimes deflects our ability to get a straight story. The kid is worried about clearance from you and clearance from us and we may be putting heat on him for different things."

"I don't want to put heat on him, Officer Thompson."

"You don't now. But you will. I've never met a parent yet who, once they were assured that we weren't going to hang their kid, didn't—at least for a little while—want to hang the kid themselves."

32

Chapter Thirty-Two

But I didn't want to hang Danny. I just wanted to protect him and extricate him from this horrible morass. Even though the Secret Service men told me not to try and reach Danny, I ran to the phone.

Tim didn't answer his home phone or his cell, and even though he was terrible at checking messages, I left them at both numbers. Next I left one with Jack Meegan. Danny was in desperate need of a lawyer.

True, Jack was primarily a divorce lawyer and if he got a call on Saturday night, it was usually from some estranged husband who had found his entire wardrobe srewn on the driveway. But I needed his recommendation for a criminal defense lawyer. Pronto.

When I hung up, David took my hand and pulled me into his arms. All I wanted to do was burrow in there and make today go away. "How are you? Because I'm not expecting you to be okay."

"I'm very not okay," I said into his shirtfront as I started to cry. "I am so sad, and so scared for him. Oh, my God, David, what is going to happen to him? What has he been thinking? Or feeling? How is he going to deal with all this? I can't even imagine."

But of course I could. I had a ton of scenarios running through my head. In one Danny sat stony-faced in a jail cell, icy vibes radiating out from him, and saying to me through clenched teeth, "I don't want to talk about it. Especially not to you." In another he was racing toward me in slo-mo, arms outstretched, tears coming down his face, sobbing, "I'm really sorry, Mom, really sorry." And in yet another, he was swaggering toward me, all disdain and mock bravado, announcing, "Welcome to the land of high crimes and misdemeanors, Mom. I guess the apple doesn't fall far from the tree, does it?"

I had a million of them. David did his best to disabuse me of my tendency to buy trouble, but there were five thousand years of Jews before me continuously refining our genetic predilection for trying on tragedies. "I'm planning to stay close to you as you go through this, you know," he said two hours later as he was clearing away the sushi we'd ordered in, but that I couldn't touch. There was something about mixing raw feelings with raw fish that just did not work for me.

I continued to sit at the kitchen table while he made himself comfortable, looking for the plastic wrap and putting everything away. The clock read 9:40 and I couldn't believe I hadn't heard from Tim or Danny yet. Didn't they allow you one phone call? On *N.Y.P.D. Blue* they at least give you that.

All I could think of was how Danny used to beg to play Monopoly with real money because he said the game money looked so fake. And now he was about to be arrested for making a different kind of fake money.

Both David and I froze when the phone rang a little after ten. "Hello?" I said tentatively.

It was Tim, who sounded as rattled and scared as he had the night we were with Sarah Rose at the hospital after her accident. "Danny just left with the two agents," he said hollowly.

"Is he all right?"

"As all right as you can be when you thought you were coming home to watch two movies on video and instead you're being escorted downtown by two Secret Service guys."

"Do you know where they took him?"

"Hang on, one of them wrote it on the back of his card. Here it is. The Metropolitan Correctional Center."

"How was he?" I motioned David to pick up the phone in the living room. I wanted him—I needed him—to be in on everything. "Was he scared to death?"

"Yes, he was scared to death," Tim said over the phone, while my eyes were drawn to a crinkled picture on the refrigerator of Danny. In the photo everything about him was quintessential third-grade boy—cowlicked hair, grimy T-shirt, skinned knees—but on his feet were a pair of red glitter Wizard of Oz shoes. He had loved the movie and after seeing it, all he wanted was a pair of these shoes. Tim and I equivocated about them a bit, but ultimately like all things kids develop a passion for, we determined the glitter shoes phase would probably have a beginning, middle and an end. And it did. Four or five months tops. By the time Danny had outgrown the shoes, he'd also outgrown the passion. But I had always loved the photo and the fact that, in spite of the stares he got in the supermarket and the taunting he endured at school, we had all lived through it.

As we would live through this.

God willing.

"What exactly did the officers do when Danny walked in?"

"He didn't walk in by himself. Sarah and I were with him," Tim said. "We ran into him at Blockbuster. None of us had eaten yet, so we walked over to that tapas place on Clark and had dinner. Danny dared Sarah to try the octopus—he said he'd pay her ten dollars if she would—and she loved it."

"Ten dollars?"

"Yeah, I was a little surprised by that too. But I guess we know now where he was getting his money."

"Tim, do you really think he did this?"

"Kate, I know he did it. He admitted it to these guys. He broke down in tears and told them. It was awful."

"Awful that he told them?"

"No, that was bad. What was awful was seeing him fall apart like that. And knowing he's been in such a different psychological place than I'd ever thought—than you've ever thought, too."

"Did he say why?"

"Kate, these guys don't ask you *why* you commit a crime. They just want you to admit that you have."

"Well, if he's confessed aren't they going to go easier on him? Isn't that how it works?"

"I don't know. I would hope so. But I deal in ethics. This is the law. They don't always overlap. The agents kept trying to get him to give the names of his contacts at the Secretary of State's Office, but he wouldn't say a word. Have you done anything about getting Danny a lawyer? I think we have to take care of that right away."

"I've left a message for Jack Meegan. But it's conceivable I won't hear from him tonight or even tomorrow."

"Well, they aren't going to even set bond for Danny until Monday morning. They told us that already."

"What? You mean he's sleeping in jail? For two nights?"

"That's what the officer said. They're taking him downtown for questioning and fingerprinting. And then they have to hold him there until federal court opens on Monday and the judge can set his bail."

Of course I was crying again. There had been way too much surrealism in my life these past ten weeks, but these last few hours went beyond surrealistic. They were more like a bad drug trip. I'd never even had a bad drug trip, but it couldn't be worse than this. "Kate," said Tim solicitously, "I know this is killing you. Me too. But we have to stay calm and clear. Sarah is in the bathtub now. Obviously she was pretty upset when the agents took Danny with them, but I got her calmed down. She wants to talk to you before I tuck her in. Can you pull yourself together to do that?"

David walked in with some tissues. He was still holding the phone and I was glad he'd heard it all. At least that way we were learning about everything together. I tried to smile at him as he handed the tissues to me.

"Of course I'll call her. Oh, God, Sarah Rose. Was she terrified?"

"Yes and no," Tim sighed. "I think there was a part of her that felt as if she was watching a TV show starring her brother and a couple of policemen. She knew it was real, but in some ways she related to it as if it were something on cable. When Danny left she cried briefly, and then she asked a whole host of questions. You know how she is. I did the best I could to answer, but when she gets out of the tub and you call, she'll no doubt ask the same ones of you."

"That's fine. I want to talk to her."

Fifteen minutes later I was on the phone with Sarah. She was up way past her bedtime and was clearly fragile, but her questions were pointed and direct. "Is Danny going to live in jail? Was the thing he did like robbery? Does Danny have a gun? Is Danny a bad guy?"

It was a heartbreaking conversation. She was struggling so hard to reconcile her love for her brother with the facts she was trying to absorb.

But her last question was the hardest. "Mommy," she said, "I'm not going to be scared. You know why?"

"That's good, honey. Why?"

"Because I know you won't let anything really bad ever happen to me or Danny. Right?"

I couldn't say a word.

So she repeated it. "You won't ever let anything really bad happen to us, right?"

"I'll sure do my best, honey."

I just couldn't say "right." It would have been the biggest lie of all.

33

Chapter Thirty-Three

There have always been buildings that scared me. When I was little, it was Mr. McMichael's house down the block. Mr. McMichael was the Boo Radley of our neighborhood. He was a lanky and grizzled man who never raised his window shades. Mr. McMichael also never cut his grass—the rumor was that this was because his two pet boa constrictors liked to slither around in there. Thus, due to our fear of a potentially escaped boa, we always crossed the street when we got near Mr. McMichael's house.

Now that I was an adult though, different buildings terrified me—like the battered old high-rises of the Cabrini Green projects, sad shells of abandoned concrete testifying to the triumph of rage over hope. Another ominous structure that always undid me was the narrow, triangular Metropolitan Correctional Center—the very same Metropolitan Correctional Center where my only son had just spent the night. Looming high out of the South Loop, with its skinny, slitlike windows, it was a horrifically menacing structure, one that seemed to glower at you rather than just gaze. It had always been an unnerving edifice to drive by.

But it was four times as unnerving to walk into.

Think granite, concrete and prison bars—everywhere. Even in the lobby, where I was given a visitor's pass after signing in with the marshal and confirming that I was bringing in no explosives, Uzis or chocolate chip cookies. The marshal also offered me a key, in case I needed to check my electronic devices in their conveniently located gray lockers. Apparently I was one of the few visitors with only a cell phone that Sunday morning.

"Then just sit over there and wait." The marshal scowled, nodding to a row of tan plastic seats in front of a long picture window. I didn't know it at the time, but it was the only real window in the whole building. The rest, those hundreds of narrow vertical ones I had stared up at all these years, were completely opaqued out, ultimately giving everyone inside this eerie feeling of being surrounded by a permanent blizzard. Ten minutes after sitting down I was called over to a metal detector where my purse and I were scanned, X-rayed, patted down and scanned again. Then I was asked to display my hand so it could be stamped with ink visible only under a special light.

Ink-branding completed, I found myself facing a gray barred door that was electronically opened so I could step into what looked like my own personal jail cell. The barred door behind me clanged shut and for a few moments it *really* was my own personal jail cell. Until the other side opened up and I stepped into an elevator that took me up to the eighth floor visiting area.

The room wasn't anything like I'd thought it would be. I guess I pictured it like the ones in those slammer movies where someone is always visiting Sean Penn. There would be long tables with telephones on either side of a bulletproof window. Bunches of people would be seated there, whispering dramatic dialog into the phones and their hands would be pressed against the glass futilely trying to touch.

In actuality, the visiting area looked like your average office lunchroom. One whole wall was lined with vending machines dispensing snacks, soda and coffee. Unkempt dusty plants were plunked together in the adjacent corner. Curiously, the room had a play area for small children, though it wasn't supervised. The guards obviously had bigger fish to attend to. But, on the whole, the room was surprisingly spacious and brightly lit. It was lined with rows of brown veneer picnic tables with orange plastic seats attached. Even though it was only ten-thirty in the morning, maybe twenty people were already in there, holding hands with the inmates they were visiting, some even kissing. Whether the kissing was allowed or just ignored was unclear, but the guards obviously had no problem with it. All the inmates and visitors seemed to be speaking quietly, even gently, to each other. God, I thought, I hope Danny and I won't be the one exception.

David had wanted to come along with me, but it hardly seemed the best place for him to meet Danny for the first time. Particularly since another man he didn't know was coming over to visit him at one—Lou Bosco, his newly acquired defense lawyer.

Jack Meegan had called at midnight the night before and been terrifically reassuring when he gave me Lou's name. "I've known Lou for twenty years, and I can say the same thing about him I hope people say about me. He's a clean guy in a dirty business. That doesn't mean he's ineffective—to the contrary, he's a skillful and respected negotiator. And compared to some of the clients he deals with, believe me, your son sounds like a veritable pillar of society."

"Oh, God, Jack, do you think he'll get off?" I asked, my insides constantly alternating between floating away and freezing solid. David had been semiasleep next to me in bed, but looped his fingers through mine when he heard me ask the question.

"Kate, I'd love to say yes, but I don't know jack shit about this end of the law. Lou is your man for this. He's expensive, real expensive, but you've got Farley's money now to pay his bills, right?"

"Actually, Jack, I don't."

"What do you mean you don't? We set up that escrow account. Didn't the son of a bitch pay you?"

"It's a long and complicated story and I want to tell you, but tonight is not the time. Just give me Lou Bosco's number."

"Kate, I'm telling you, this guy is the most expensive in the city. Let me rethink this and give you another name."

"Is he the best?"

"The best."

"Then don't rethink anything. Just give me his number. I'll find a way to pay him, Jack."

I sat up and turned on the light so I could find a pen. David managed to locate one first from the nightstand on his side of the bed. *His* side of the bed. Oh boy, that was fast. Just like everything else had been all summer. Except for these interminable weeks when I was cut off from Danny. "Can I call this Lou Bosco now?" I asked.

"You'd better call him now. Otherwise you won't get hold of him until after his golf game tomorrow. He tees off religiously at 6:00 a.m. You'll want to talk to him before that so he can get over to MCC and meet with your son before bail is set on Monday morning."

"Bail? Oh, my God," I gasped, wondering how I was going to pay bail and this lawyer, too. "Do I have to go there with a lot of cash?"

"Lou will know. I think they may take a check. It's probably the only place left in America where they don't take Visa. No Advantage miles yet for felons..."

"Jack!" I yelled, pulling the covers up around my shoulders because the air conditioner had been a bit overzealous.

"I'm sorry. I know this is serious. I've been at a dinner party all night and am still feeling the aftereffects of too much repartee."

There was no repartee with Lou Bosco, however. The man was all business. No sentence he uttered was longer than ten words. "Bank fraud for $500,000? Ambitious kid."

He asked a few more questions and then announced, "Okay, my fee is $25,000 up front and $500 an hour after that. If he gets acquitted, I get a $50,000 bonus. I don't negotiate. Not with clients. Only with the district attorney. Don't worry, I'm great at it. Great. You got any questions?"

"Yes. The Secret Service men said this was serious. Were they trying to scare me? Is it serious?"

"It's about as serious as it can get with no dead bodies. In some ways the government would rather deal with dead bodies. Financial crimes are insidious and much easier to hide."

"Oh, God," I whispered.

"Okay," he said, signaling the end of the conversation, "Let me know by eleven tomorrow morning if you want to hire me. If we're on, I'll see your kid at one. Then I'll call you at four."

"I don't need to think about it—you're hired. Just please help Danny."

"I'll call you at four tomorrow," he said, offering no more reassurances than punctuality.

* * *

So there I sat the following morning in a room full of civilians and men in orange Ted Kaczynski jumpsuits. I almost didn't recognize Danny when the security guard clanged open the heavy metal door and escorted him in. In the five weeks since we'd seen each other, he'd lost weight, and he'd grown a touchingly scraggly goatee. "Oh, honey," I said, my arms reaching out to him as soon as he was uncuffed from the acne-pitted security guard who led him in, "are you okay?"

His body stiffened as soon as my hands touched his shoulders. I couldn't tell if it was hate or terror. But everything about him telegraphed clenched, wary feelings. "I guess so," he said in a monotone. "How come you're here?"

"Did you think I wouldn't be here?"

"I don't know what I think," he said lifting my hands off his shoulders and folding himself down into the orange chair. "I haven't had a whole lot of sleep."

I moved around to the opposite side of the table and sat down to face him. It was obvious he'd feel safer with some physical distance, and I'd be less tempted to reach all the way across and risk his recoiling. We needed to proceed very slowly.

"Where did you sleep? Do they have you in a room?"

"It's a cell, Mom. I spent last night in a regulation jail cell with two other guys, all the lights on, people yelling up and down the hall, and a mattress about as thick as my driver's license. Speaking of which, if you ever need a fake one, I can get one for you. Though you've probably heard that already from the creeps who dragged me down here."

I just let him get it all out—all the contempt and fear and shame that were coursing though him—he needed to put it out there. I got that. I got that he had to go through some sort of emotional detox before we'd ever get to a place where we could calmly deal with the issues at hand—his legal situation and our relationship situation. Because both were in peril.

I let him take the lead. "I guess you're pretty pissed at me, huh?"

"I'm not pissed, Danny," I whispered, restraining myself from touching his hand. "I'm overwhelmed—by everything that has happened between us and at the two completely out-of-character acts we each seem to have been capable of doing."

"Yeah," he said, eyes cast down, but his face still grimly held in check. And then like the child who was still very present inside all the teen trappings, he muttered, "But you started it."

Oh, God, he so needed to be right. Caught buck-naked in the legal headlights, just as he had caught me in the moral ones, he still craved some unattainable-for-either-of-us chunk of righteousness.

"Honey, I didn't start anything," I said softly. "I got found out by you first, before you got found out by them, that's all. But what each of us did had nothing to do with the other. You didn't get involved in this because I decided to meet your dad in Italy, and I didn't decide to meet your dad in Italy to stop you from getting involved in this. In fact, if we'd known what the other one was doing, I'm sure it would have made each of us stop cold and take a look at our own actions. It's like our own version of that O Henry story *Gift of the Magi*."

"What are you talking about?"

"That story by O Henry. Don't they teach it in your school? It's about this wife who cuts off her hair to pay for a fob for her husband's watch and at the same time, the husband sells his watch to buy her a comb for her hair. Don't you see the incredible irony in all this?"

"I don't want to see the irony in this," he snapped, and then leaned forward on his elbows and held his head in his hands as he slowly, finally, began to cry. "I hate this! I hate that you thought it was okay to go off with my dad for money. And I hate that I got busted for something that seemed so simple. Mom, I had no idea I could get in this much trouble."

I pushed a packet of tissues across the table to him. Reluctantly he took one and blew his nose. Then he slammed his hand down on the table while he continued to rant, "And I mostly hate that nothing is clear-cut. God, when I was little, everything was so clear. You were either a Han Solo good guy or a Darth Vader bad guy. But then I get to real life and nothing is clear. It's all fucked up, Mom. It's really fucked up."

I got up and went over to put my arms around him. This time he let me. It didn't matter that there were thirty other people in the room—they were all going through their own dramas. God, life was weird. Two days ago when I had no idea my son had committed a serious crime, I was in more pain about him than at that very minute, a minute in which we were standing in the middle of a federal prison, both of us terrified that he might go to jail.

Because at least when we were standing in the middle of that federal prison, we were standing there together.

Chapter Thirty-Four

My visit with Danny was limited to an hour, and then I drove directly to Tim's to collect Sarah. On the way home I did my best to convince her that Danny seemed to be doing all right. I also did my best to convince me.

We pulled into the driveway and found David in the back doing some volunteer weeding in the garden. Sarah ran over to kiss him hello, and then grabbed his hand as he strode over to me. "How did it go?"

I let Sarah in the house, and then spent the next half hour filling him in. "Oh, man, Kate, I wish there was some way I could make this easier for you."

"Just keep being here." I squeezed his hand.

Sarah ran back outside, bursting into the middle of our discussion. "Mom, do you think we could go to the zoo, Mom?" she asked, apparently recovered for the moment from her concern about her big brother. "They said at camp that the mom lion had baby cubs and you can see them now. Could we do that? Could we?"

David knew I wasn't going to be capable that day of being more than ten feet from the phone, so he said, "I could take you today, Sarah. How about the two of us go and see the baby cubs?"

Sarah spun and looked at me. "Is that okay, Mom? Could I go with David?"

"Well, sure, honey," I said, hardly able to believe my daughter was so determined to look at creatures in cages on the very same day my son was being housed in one.

While David took Sarah to the zoo, Karen came over to babysit me. She'd called in the morning when I was downtown seeing Danny, and David had filled her in on the whole story.

"Oh, Kate," she said, hugging me when she walked in, her cast finally off. "Danny must be so scared. I tried to call him earlier this summer at Tim's and then again this week for his birthday, but he wouldn't return my calls. I'm sure I'm too connected to you for him to perceive me as neutral, and—"

The phone rang. It was Rob Fitzgerald from the *Sun-Times*. Rob was without question the most powerful reporter on electronic media in the city. He loved radio and TV and it showed in his work. Rob was thorough, generally fair and hard to dodge. If you were being fired, sometimes he knew it before you did. It apparently hadn't taken him much time to get tipped off to the news about Danny.

"I'm sorry to bother you at home, Kate. I know this is a tough time for you, but what can you tell me about your son's arrest?"

Karen got up and returned from the kitchen with leftover sushi from the night before. I wasn't hungry, but she dove in.

"Rob, I'm speaking to you off the record right now, okay?"

"Okay."

"Are you sure you have to cover this? Isn't there any way you can take a pass on it? I mean, it's not like I've got the number one drive-time show in Chicago or anything."

"Kate, your ratings aren't the point. You're a presence in Chicago radio, people are involved with you..."

"Rob, please. Can't you just this one time..."

He sighed. "I can't Kate. There are two papers in this city and I can't risk the *Trib* running this while I take a pass. I'm sure, as a professional, you understand."

I did. Which is why when he asked me once more what I knew about Danny's arrest, I behaved as professionally as I could. I referred him to Lou Bosco, who, as good as his word, phoned our house promptly at four o'clock.

Sarah and David came home midafternoon from the zoo. It was the first time he met Karen. And of course, he did that thing most people do when they've formed a relationship with one of us, but then are confronted by the physical reality of both of us—he looked for a second as if he thought a trick had been played on him.

"Jeez," he said extending his hand toward Karen, "I had no idea you two were so identical."

"*So* identical." She laughed. "I had no idea identical came with gradations. Hello, David."

"Hello." He smiled somewhat tentatively, his eyes shifting between my face and Karen's.

"Don't worry, David," I said, making room on the couch for him to sit down, "I'm still just me. The twin who is waiting for a call from her son's lawyer."

The call came promptly at four o'clock. As soon as Karen heard me say, "Hello, Mr. Bosco," she went into the kitchen to bring the portable handset back so she and David could listen in.

"I spent about two hours with him, Ms. Lerner, and I've just printed up my notes. We've definitely got a situation here."

"What kind of situation?" I asked, pulling the soggy lemon out of my iced tea and sucking on it the way I always have since Karen and I were kids.

"It's a bit unclear. Not that we can't get some potential breaks. The fact that your son turned eighteen only last week is a big point in his favor, because we can argue that the crimes he committed were committed when he was a juvenile."

"Does that mean they'll let him off?" I asked, catching the hopeful looks on Karen's and David's faces.

"Hardly. What it means is that in lieu of the worst-case scenario—which is that Danny could be incarcerated for up to eight years—they could only keep him locked up until his twenty-first birthday."

Being told that Danny could be jailed for only three years instead of eight was like being told you'd never get Alzheimer's because the cancer would kill you first. "Is that the biggest break we can hope for?" I asked, my heart desperate to hear a "no."

"No. Absolutely not. The fact that your son has never committed a crime before will help. The fact that he apparently has all the money he received illegally and is willing to return it will help. The fact that there were no drugs or guns involved will help. All that will help considerably."

"Considerably enough to keep him out of jail?" I asked, scooping a fresh wedge of lemon out of the iced tea pitcher. "Can you get Danny some kind of probation? I hate to be so dependent on TV for my reference points, but last month on *The Practice* there was this minor who was awarded probation…"

"Ms. Lerner, do me a favor. Leave TV out of it. I make more as a lawyer than those writers in Hollywood make for those scripts. We'll just stay with real life, okay?"

I brushed off his abrasiveness and said, "Fine. Can you get him probation?"

"Maybe. It'll depend on whether your son is willing to tell the government who was instructing him to cut those checks."

"What are you saying?"

"I'm saying we should probably be able to get the charges dropped in return for full disclosure."

"Oh, my God," I gasped, the hallelujah part of my heart exploding. "That's really possible?"

"Possible. Not at the moment, necessarily probable."

"Because…?"

"Because I've heard your son's sentiments about naming other people who were involved. Even naming them to me."

"And his sentiments are…?"

"Adamant. Sanctimonious. Naive."

"What do you mean?"

"Your son said he has no intention of revealing any names. I told him that was a stupid decision, but he said not telling the whole truth is a genetic trait in his family. He said you could explain that. Do you want to help me out?"

I sure didn't. But Lou Bosco needed to know everything. So I sure did.

He didn't say anything until I'd finished telling him the story about Richard's offer, the trip and Danny's finding out about it.

"And that's why your son has been living with his stepfather? Because he found out about your little Roman holiday?"

I had not had an easy day. "Little Roman holiday?" I exploded, jumping up and knocking over my iced tea. "Listen, Mr. Bosco, that remark is way out of line."

David motioned me to calm down, but I was having none of it. "Let's get straight about something. Your business is to defend Danny—not to make flip editorial comments about my personal life. It's been hard enough to deal with Danny's judgmentalism all summer. I don't need any from you. Not from a man who makes his living defending drug dealers and who knows what else? Jack Meegan said you were a good lawyer. So fine, be a good lawyer. I know I don't have to like you, but I'm not paying you to insult me, either."

Karen and David were incredulous. I was incredulous. I was also shaking, but I was glad I'd said what I'd said.

And ever so glad Lou Bosco said what he said. I could hear him take a deep breath before he did, the kind of deep, belabored breath that made me wonder if he was fat. "You're right, Ms. Lerner. Yes, I am a good lawyer and no, we don't have to like each other. But I do like you. You're decisive and clear. Most people I deal with aren't. And you're right about my remark. It was uncalled-for. I apologize."

"Thanks," I said, having learned years ago that accepting apologies was much more gratifying than sulking if you were of a mind to get on with your life. "I appreciate that. Now, do you think Danny understands that his best hope is to give all the information he has to the government?"

"I can't say. At the moment he seems very resolute. I don't know him, so whether it's real or some false sense of bravado,

I can't say. But, according to him, the agents did their best to unnerve him, and he stayed pretty unruffled."

"What do you mean, 'unnerve' him?'" I asked, as I watched Karen use a paper towel to sop up my spilled tea.

"Oh, the usual things they generally pull. They fingerprint you with this nasty black ink but never give you quite enough cleanser to clean it off, so every time you look down at your hands you feel tainted like a criminal. And they continually hammer away about the gravity of your predicament, telling you that it's an open-and-shut case."

"Is it?"

"I doubt it. But they say things like, 'You've got one foot on the banana peel, and the other in the penitentiary door.' They watch too much damn TV, too."

"They don't physically push you around do they? Danny didn't seem like he'd been…"

"No, Ms. Lerner. They work on your brain. But, yeah, generally, their big finale is to let you know that if you go to federal prison, how many new male friends you will make—whether you're looking for new male friends or not."

"Oh, my God."

And suddenly Lou Bosco turned into a human. "Don't waste your time thinking about it now, okay?" he said in as close to a conciliatory tone as I'd heard from him. "Your son is a long way from being locked up. We just have to make sure that he understands that this notion of silence with honor will backfire. His best ticket out of there will be full cooperation."

"So, what are we going to do?"

"We're going to do one step at a time. The first step is to show up at 9:45 sharp tomorrow morning at 219 South Dearborn.

That's the Federal District Court. Then we'll post bond and get your son out of that orange jumpsuit."

"Then what? Can he come home?"

"I imagine so. Then we'll get to work on the second step."

I didn't even ask what it was. All I heard was that Danny was going to come home.

35

Chapter Thirty-Five

Lou Bosco may have sounded fat. But he wasn't. However, he *was* very disheveled. No matter that Danny's bail bond hearing was his first appointment on a Monday morning, Lou looked like he'd just exited a 5:00 p.m. rush-hour subway after a long, hellish week. His tie was loosened, his remaining strands of hair were sweatily adhered to his forehead, and his briefcase was not the briefcase of a man who had tidied up and gotten ready for the workweek on Sunday night. Danny never could believe that on Sunday nights a lot of us grown-ups operated as if we were preparing for the first day of school the following morning, but I was a grown-up who had never gotten out of the habit.

Lou Bosco looked like he had never gotten into the habit. The minute he pried open his old leather case, his files nearly exploded out. "Hold on just a minute, Ms. Lerner," he said, rifling through his papers. "Michael O'Malley is the assistant U.S. attorney handling the case. He's a bastard, but I've worked with him before and done fine. We'll get your son released to you. Just hang on. This morning is all pretty routine."

Routine was the last thing this morning had seemed to me so far. For starters, I had to be absent from our show, and David wasn't going to be able to pretend his partner was just sick. As David had warned me, both papers had carried stories—thankfully brief—on Danny's arrest. There was no way David would be able to dodge listener calls on that. Secondly, Sarah Rose had had a huge meltdown once she found out that they'd written about her brother in the newspaper and she begged me not to make her go to camp. And thirdly, I was terrified that the magistrate for some reason wouldn't release Danny.

Only that's not what happened. Danny was released to me, but the bond I was asked to post was not just a cash one. The magistrate also asked me to put up the deed to our house. Granted the house was tiny and in disrepair, but it was still the main asset in my life. Only now, if Danny ran off I'd have no house and I'd owe Karen the money she'd loaned me for the bond. I hated the feeling of the financial limb I was on.

There wasn't a lot of discussion in the car going home. Both Danny and I were aware we were going to have to feel our way back toward each other. I didn't want to gushily overwhelm him and, in spite of the seriousness of his situation, he wasn't sure he was ready to forgive me. My crime was ethical, his crime was legal and while neither of us stood on high moral ground, both of us were feeling the bruises of having been deceived. The only difference was, my day-to-day world didn't unravel and Danny's assuredly did. Suddenly he had no job to go to; suddenly he had a pre-trial officer to report to; and suddenly he had acquired the kind of unwelcome notoriety that turned even mowing the lawn into a potentially awkward encounter with a neighbor. It was not an easy time to be Danny.

The only one who didn't notice was his baby sister. Something remarkable happened between the two of them during those three weeks between Danny's return from the MCC and his preliminary hearing. Not that the two of them hadn't always been enthusiastic members of a mutual admiration society. Sarah Rose was enough younger than Danny that she didn't even have the skills to annoy him in the full-blown way a preadolescent could have. Instead, Danny was as protective and adoring of her as she was worshipful and adoring of him. And that only intensified during those first weeks when Danny moved back home.

"Mom, Danny says he'll set up the tent and we can camp out in the backyard tonight—can we?" she asked, diving onto my bed about four o'clock on the day I'd brought him home. I'd retreated to my room to phone David and Tim, after seeing that Danny had fallen asleep outside in the midafternoon sun. Sarah must have been unable to resist rousting him out there, and he no doubt had bribed her to let him finish sleeping by offering her this big camp-out plan. I actually had no problem with it whatsoever—it struck me as good a way as any to nourish the illusion of normalcy in our abnormal-feeling household. "Can we have a cookout too? Just me and Danny? With marshmallows and everything?" Sarah asked jumping up and down in her gleeful seven-year-old fashion.

"Absolutely," I said, somewhat relieved that Danny had figured out a way to circumvent an awkward dinner his first night home. It was fine with me if he needed to get his grounding via tightening his bonds with his sister. He and I would find our place in time. I hoped.

Plus, it made it easier to say yes when David asked to stop by that evening. "I don't want to intrude if things are real delicate over there," he'd said on the phone after I'd told him what had transpired in court. "But on the other hand, I miss you. Danny *is* going to have to meet me at some point."

"I know," I said hesitantly, wanting hugely to see him, but sensitive to the fact that David's showing up might compound Danny's feeling that I had a partner, and that he was alone in this mess. He wasn't alone, but he might be feeling that way. "Danny *does* know who you are, David. He knows that we've worked together for a year and a half."

"Kate, Danny knows who I *was*. But now I'm not just a radio partner. Not unless something has changed between us since yesterday."

"Nothing's changed," I whispered. "You know that."

"Good. Then let me pick up some dinner. The kids can make s'mores and hot dogs outside and I'll bring something equally artery-clogging for us to eat inside."

He brought hot Italian beef sandwiches and cheese fries—a horrible combo, but wonderful comfort food all around. We parked ourselves in front of the TV so we at least looked like we were watching the Cubs. Mostly, though, we talked and did our best to do no more than hold hands. In spite of everything that was going on, or maybe because of it, I felt a huge compulsion to just burrow into David.

"Were there a lot of listener calls about Danny today?" I asked, ready to hear the worst.

"Yeah, enough. Mostly at the beginning of the show."

"You put some of them on, didn't you?"

"Definitely. We had to." He took a gulp of his beer. "Most of them were very empathetic—people who'd had kids who'd gotten into trouble, people who had done dumb stuff as kids themselves, and only now realized what it must have been like to be on the parents' end, people who…"

"What's the score?"

It was Danny. He'd come in from the kitchen to see why his mom had a baseball game on. It was something of a sports first. "Danny, this is David. I don't think you two have ever met."

"We haven't," said David, getting up and extending his hand. "But I'm glad to meet you."

For a moment Danny looked confused about what to do. Then he remembered and shook David's hand. "Yeah." He smiled tentatively. "I heard you and Mom have been hanging out."

"You did?" I asked. "How do you know?"

And then in the first glimmer of a grin that I'd seen from him all summer, he tilted his head toward the backyard and said, "The kid out there is not exactly a great secret-keeper."

Unlike you and me, I thought.

Chapter Thirty-Six

Our world those next few weeks before Danny's preliminary hearing was suddenly densely populated by three men we hadn't even known at the beginning of the summer.

Granted, I had known David, only not in the way I knew him by that August—not as my most close-in, partner-y person. But in addition to David, Joe Hampton, the pretrial officer Danny had to check in with, and Lou Bosco, who I was actually beginning to like, had become huge factors in the warp and woof of our daily lives.

Every morning by ten, Danny had to show up in Joe's Loop office and sign in with him. "Why can't I just check in with this guy by phone?" Danny had asked Lou that first morning after his bail bond hearing.

"Why do you think?" Lou said, stuffing four or five manila folders back into his briefcase as we left the courtroom. "They want you to check in face-to-face because it's a bigger pain in the butt for you. What the hell. You're going to have to be downtown with me anyway. We're going to be spending a lot of time in the U.S. Attorney's office together."

"Doing what?"

"Answering the same questions a hundred times over. And—with any luck—starting the process of trying to strike a deal for you."

"I told you—" Danny turned to Lou "—I'm not going to tell them anyone else's names."

"Yeah, I know. But things change, Danny. In fact, I'm counting on it."

"Well, don't," Danny growled, as he pulled down his Cubs hat.

During the following weeks, Lou worked tirelessly with Danny at the debriefings going on in the assistant U.S. attorney's office. As Lou explained it to me, he and the assistant U.S. attorney were operating on two levels. On one, they were beginning the long tentative dance around each other in which Lou had to feel out how willing to strike a deal the government really was just in case he could get Danny to cooperate. On the second level, given Danny's transparent claim that he knew no one else who might be involved, both sides had to prepare as if there was going to be a trial. But before a trial date could be set, Danny had to appear at a preliminary hearing and then be officially indicted.

Lou called the night before the hearing to touch base with Danny, but he and David had gone to a Cubs game. David had been spending a lot of time with us at the house, but none of it included any adult overnights. We had enough complications in our highly bail-bonded home without tossing in a mom who had a new man sleeping over. Plus, David and Danny seemed to genuinely like each other, and I didn't want anything to rock the boat.

In the beginning they circled each other somewhat gingerly, but over the weeks they seemed to be forging their own ways of connecting. Baseball was one and, oddly, cooking was another. Both of them liked killer-spicy food, so David bought a *Make It With Chilies* cookbook, and a couple nights a week we dined— make that, *they* dined—on some pretty challenging recipes. Sarah and I ate pancakes.

Danny's preliminary hearing was held in the same room that his bond hearing had been in. This time, however, when he stood before Judge Hartman, he cut a decidedly more impressive figure. The scraggly goatee was gone and so was the orange jailbird jumpsuit. As per Lou's instructions, Danny was clean-shaven and blue-suited.

Karen had come with us to court this time, and having her there was very calming. She watched me during the hearing, I watched Danny during the hearing and Danny watched his shoes during the hearing. The whole thing took no more than twenty minutes and, as Lou predicted, Judge Hartman found for probable cause. Two weeks later Danny was officially indicted.

The night after the preliminary hearing was a very somber one at our house. Danny had gone over to Jamie's for the afternoon. She had just returned from her job as a summer intern on a newspaper. This was the first time they were seeing each other face-to-face since Danny's arrest and I knew it would be very emotional for both of them.

Judging from Danny's behavior at dinner, their reunion that afternoon had not gone all that well. He was edgy and remote. And he stayed that way until he and Jamie mended fences two days later. But when school started the following week, things went south for him all over again. People kept their distance. I suppose you might expect that when you're the only kid in the senior class with a federal trial date on your calendar. Not to mention, most of his classmates were preoccupied with their own concerns—like getting into college, a topic that was decidedly a moot point for Danny, given that he could actually be behind bars by the time the rest of them were attending freshman orientation.

But I did my best not to think of that.

In fact, Lou Bosco *insisted* that I not think of it. "Look, I still haven't stopped trying to persuade your kid to give us the name of his contact. The government is dyin'. It's making them crazy they haven't nailed the main guys in this fraud ring. I keep telling Danny they'd drop the charges if he'd just give us the names that he's protecting."

"Why doesn't Danny get that?"

"I don't know. The kid is fixed on going down with the ship even though we're standin' out there with a lifeboat."

"Oh, God, this is making me crazy."

"Don't worry. Whatever happens we'll handle it. That's why you're paying me the big bucks."

The big bucks I didn't really have.

I tried not to worry about that part, too. And David was a big help. He even offered to loan me money when I'd gotten my second not-completely-payable bill from Lou in late October. But I already felt horrible enough that I'd borrowed money from Karen for bail and from Muriel for Lou's retainer. And I knew eventually I'd figure something out. One way or another we'd get the legal fees covered.

There were times, of course, that I thought about the money I could have gotten from Richard. But that never turned out to be a very helpful line of thinking. So I worked very hard at banishing Richard and his offer from my mind. Which worked fine. Until October 30 at nine in the evening, when the doorbell rang.

And Richard Farley was standing there.

37

Chapter Thirty-Seven

At first I thought the man on my porch was someone who was twenty-four hours early for Halloween. He had hollowed-out eyes and thatchy hair. His face was gaunt and gray. And there was a decided rasp in his voice when he said, "They said you saved my life. Or what's left of it."

"Richard!" I was stunned at how the cancer had savaged him in these past four months. "My God. What are you doing here?"

He hung on to the doorframe for support. His breathing was labored. I could see a big white limo idling at the curb. "I'm here because…" And then he stopped and was racked by coughing. "Kate," he said when he was able to speak again, "I need to sit down. Can I come in?"

"No, Richard you can't," I whispered. "Danny is here and I don't…"

"Danny is the reason I came here. You didn't answer my e-mail and you didn't return my call…."

It was true. Two weeks before I had gotten an e-mail from Richard. For the past four months he'd apparently been undergoing some kind of experimental treatment in a Mexican clinic. His e-mail was the first indicator I'd had that he was still alive, and reading it had left me feeling a thousand ways. All of them unsettling and none of them anything I wanted to reflect on. So I didn't answer.

Four days later he'd left a message on my phone at work saying, "Kate, I just met with my lawyer for the first time since I've been back. Why did you send back the money?" Again, I didn't answer.

But I did answer the doorbell. And now here was Richard, on my porch. "Please, Kate. Let me in. I just want ten minutes."

"For what?"

"For chrissakes, I need some water. Will you just let me in?"

"No," I said, pointing to the green porch furniture we still hadn't hauled in. "Sit there. I'll get you some water and I'll be right back."

I was trembling as I walked back into the house. Music was blaring from Danny's room, so I was fairly certain he hadn't heard the doorbell. Even so, it did not make me feel one bit calm to have Richard two hundred feet away from him down on the front porch.

"Here," I said, closing the front door behind me and handing Richard the water. I'd put on an old leather jacket to ward off the crisp night air. "Please say what you have to say and then go. Sarah isn't home, but I really don't want Danny to find you here."

"I'm sure not," he said, sipping the water, and then setting it down on the porch floor.

"First of all, I want to thank you for what you did for me in Rome. I was..."

"Richard, don't thank me. I have no idea why I did it. Please, what do you mean you're here about Danny?"

"I want to help if I can with this court case. Money, anything you need."

I was stunned. "How do you know about Danny's court case? Or did your ex-girlfriend reporter call it in to you?"

"I haven't ever heard from her again and her piece still hasn't aired."

"I don't care about that. I repeat, how do you know about Danny's court case?"

"It's not that hard to find out anything if you're online, Kate. You can read any newspaper you want. Even when I was in treatment, I'd scan six or seven a day. The *Trib* has always been one of them. When they wrote about Danny's arrest, I made some calls to see who this lawyer you hired was—turns out he is very respected."

"I'm so relieved you approve," I said testily. "God, Richard! The nerve of you just showing up and sweeping in here! How could you do this without asking me first?"

"I'm a dying man, Kate, I don't waste my time asking for permission."

"You never were big on asking for permission. So don't use your dying as an excuse for that."

"Damn it, Kate, back off for a second, will you? I've come straight from the airport and, as you can see, the 'miracle cure' wasn't exactly a success. So just cut me some slack, okay? Now, where do things stand for Danny legally?"

Why didn't I send him away right then? Why didn't I say, "It's not your problem. Just go." Why did I prolong his visit by even two minutes? "His trial has just been postponed until mid-January," I said. "His lawyer is still hoping we can get the charges dropped, but..."

"Is that possible?"

"It would be—if we gave Danny an emergency lobotomy. He's being very hardheaded. He won't give the government the names of the other people who were involved. And he's rationalizing his behavior by saying that since I lied to him about meeting you in Rome..."

"He found out about that?"

"He did," I said softly.

And, as if on cue, Danny flung open the front door and said, "Mom? Why are you out here? There was a phone call for you, and I told them..." His eyes swerved to Richard.

"Hello, Danny," he said calmly, greeting his son fifteen years after the original scheduled pickup.

"Hello..." responded Danny, clearly unaware who this haggard, cadaverous guest was.

I was rooted to the planked floor.

"Oh, I didn't know you had company, Mom. Sorry. Just call Mrs. Thompson when you come in. I left the number on the kitchen table. See ya'." He nodded to us both.

Danny turned to go inside and Richard croaked, "Wait!"

Danny turned back, confused as to why this strange man was calling to him. "Excuse me?"

"Danny. I'm your father."

Danny froze. "Mom?" his eyes sought mine.

I nodded.

"You're my father?" he asked incredulously, opening and closing his fists. "What the hell are you doing here?"

Richard didn't bat an eyelash. "I'm here because I want to help you. But your mom tells me you've decided not to cooperate with the government. I'm not sure that is a wise decision."

Danny exploded. The chords on his neck popped out as he screamed, "Are you for real? Where the hell do you get off questioning my decisions? I never got to question yours. God, you are such a dickhead."

Richard was not a close personal friend of remorse. He didn't back down. "I'm merely saying, Danny, not telling the government everything you know is a pretty stupid move."

"Funny, I think it's kind of an honorable move. I know that's kind of a concept, but how about one person in this family behaving with some honor?"

"Are you always this sanctimonious?"

"Sanctimonious? Maybe you just can't tell the difference, mister, between honor and sanctimony."

"I can tell the difference."

"Yeah, *Daaad?* So what is it?"

"Honor is a way of behaving. Sanctimony is congratulating yourself for that way of behaving."

"Brilliant," Danny sneered.

"Listen, Danny, I have no stake in this. I'm dying."

"Like I give a shit that you're dying."

"I'm not asking you to give a shit. Just tell the government the names."

Tears started streaming down Danny's face. "You are such a fucking hypocrite. Why should I play straight with these guys? You never played it straight with me or Mom. And last summer Mom didn't play it straight with me. Maybe deceit is just a family trait."

"Deceit is an inherent part of nature."

"And what's that supposed to mean?"

"It means if an animal can't deceive its enemies, it doesn't survive. But the difference between humans and animals is our capacity for self-deception. We can take plain and simple deceit, and ascribe noble motives to it so we deceive ourselves about what we're doing. Like you're doing now. Like I did when I walked out on you. I convinced myself that I was doing you a favor—that it would be easier on you not to deal with the constant disruption of an every-other-weekend dad. I actually deluded myself into thinking I was protecting you. Just like your mom did when she wasn't straight with you about meeting me. Protecting someone isn't always honorable."

"Shut up! I don't want to hear any more. I know most lies aren't for honorable reasons. Most lies are for ass-saving reasons. Well, I'm not trying to save my ass. So can you just leave me alone? I'm going to bed."

And he walked inside, slamming the screen door behind him.

"Wait!" Richard pulled himself up out of the chair.

"What now?" said Danny from behind the safety of the screen door.

"Nothing. Just, uh…goodbye."

"You're saying 'goodbye'? Man, that's a big change in my life…."

"Listen Danny, I'm sorry."

"Sorry? Sorry for bailing on us? Or sorry for reemerging? Look, I've got enough going on in my life right now. I don't want some belated Kodak moment with my biological daddy, okay?"

"Okay. Just know this. Know that I truly regret the decision I made fifteen years ago. And that I'm wishing with every fiber of my being that you will not regret the one you're making now."

"Don't worry, mister, you'll get your wish. Now why don't you get out of here," Danny said, gesturing toward the curb. "Your limo is waiting."

Chapter Thirty-Eight

Two weeks later, Rebecca, the Canadian journalist, called.

I had no idea why it had taken her five months to find me, but there she was. I hated her as much as I hated Richard.

"I know that he abandoned you and your son without a dime," she said in a voice drenched with faux sympathy. "But he claims to have offered you every cent back plus more. Is that true?"

Oh, God. It was my second chance to nail Richard—the first one obviously being to let him die on that hotel floor. I mean, I could have told her I had no idea what she was talking about. There was no way Richard could prove me wrong. Sure, he could show her the receipt from the money transfer to the escrow account. But with a bit more digging she'd find out that the money was never withdrawn and the account was closed down, so she'd probably figure that *he* had just set the whole account up as a ploy. It would have been so, so easy to say, "He never offered me a cent."

But I hadn't gone through all of this with Danny to lie one more time.

No way.

So I told her, "Yes."

"How much money was it?"

"I'm really sorry, but I am not doing this with you."

"Listen, Kate—can I call you Kate? I'm on your side. There is nothing to admire about this man. I'd like to come down there with a camera crew and…"

Oh, boy. I know there are jillions of women who would have killed for an offer like that. I mean please…an offer to have a *Dateline* or a *Sixty Minutes* do a story on the despicability of your ex? Not to mention the opportunity to trash that ex on national TV and get your hair and makeup done for free? Oh. My. God.

But the truth was, I wasn't one of those women. Not now anyway. Maybe I would have been if she'd called me on that day I was furiously packing up in Rome. There were definitely thirty minutes in there when I'd have joyously cooperated with her. But that was before. Before Danny, and to a lesser degree before seeing Richard so totally savaged by cancer and chemo. "I'm sorry, no," I said calmly.

"No, what?"

"*No* to your cameras and *no* to any more questions."

"Kate, I just want…"

"Rebecca, I'm going to hang up now."

She called back every day for a week. And then she stopped.

Which was a big help. Because suddenly it was *crazy.* Not in a criminal trial way, but in a real-life way. Sarah came down with an industrial-strength case of chicken pox, the holidays were in our face and bless her little pacemakered heart, Muriel decided to come up and "visit" with us.

Muriel never came up for Christmas, a holiday that in our house was decidedly secular considering that we were Jewish and all. That didn't mean we didn't have some Christmas traditions, however. Ours was to sleep in on Christmas morning; have a huge brunch of scrambled eggs and salami, broiled tomatoes and cheesy hash browns; drive out to Evanston to pick up Tim and go to a feel-good "opens-on-Christmas-Day" movie; and then, like every other Jewish family I've ever known, stuff ourselves in some Chinese establishment—given that they are the only restaurants in America open that night.

This year though, instead of going out for Chinese, David insisted we eat at his house—Tim, Karen, Muriel, the whole crew. Talk about your odd gathering. I mean, it was Tim's first encounter with David. It was David's first encounter with Muriel. And it was Muriel's first meal with Danny since he'd been indicted. Other than that, everyone was real comfortable.

David truly outdid himself. There was turkey, three kinds of potatoes—sweet, mashed and roasted with garlic and fennel— a chilled cranberry soufflé, creamed baby onions and a wonderful endive salad. But a glorious turkey dinner wasn't all David had done. He'd set up a huge tree ("In honor of having a real seven-year-old in the house") that was laced with popcorn, cranberries and pinecones—but only halfway down. David had left the bottom half for Sarah to decorate. It was her first tree ever.

I'd gotten my real present from him the week before—a yearlong membership in the Orchid-Of-The-Month Club, as wondrously indulgent a gift as I'd ever gotten. But at dinner that night, David had a token gift on the table for everyone—me, Muriel, Karen, the kids, even Tim.

Only it was the gift he got Danny that was the biggest hit—a book called *From Concept to Cash: How to Get Your Book/Movie/Music to the People Who Will Buy It*. Danny grinned ear-to-ear when he unwrapped it. I hadn't seen that kind of a smile on his face in months. "Wow, David, thanks. This is some vote of confidence."

"Yeah?" David smiled back, as he passed the bowl of stuffing to me. "I already told you I thought it had real potential."

"What are you guys talking about?" I asked.

"Nothing, Mom. I was just telling David one day about this idea I have for a sort of book. I haven't completely figured it out yet. Though I guess if I get sent to the slammer, I'll have plenty of time to work on it."

"What's a 'slammer,' Danny?" asked Sarah Rose, looking expectantly at her big brother. Oh, God, we'd done such a good job these past months not to have any *what's-going-to-happen-to-Danny* discussions in front of her. It was harder at the beginning when everything exploded around us. But ever since Danny had been back in school, Sarah must have figured he was completely back in the land of the normal, because most of her inquiries had stopped. Until tonight.

She repeated her question to the blaring silence of the table. "What's a 'slammer,' Danny?"

Danny's eyes darted from Tim's to mine. To dismiss her question, or to tap-dance around it was not what he was about these days. On the other hand, I knew he didn't want to frighten her. So there it was—Danny's first preview of parenthood—the old damned if you do and deceitful if you don't moment. He took a deep breath and said, "'Slammer' is another word for jail, Sarah."

The tears were instant. "Are you going to jail? Mommy, is that true, is Danny going to jail?" She jumped up from her seat and threw her arms around Danny's neck. "Danny, don't go to jail. That's where bad people go. You can't go to jail..." And that was it. The beginning of a total family meltdown. Danny started crying, I started crying and then we were joined by Tim, Muriel and Karen. David was the only one who didn't cry. Not that he didn't have reason to—we'd ruined his whole Christmas dinner.

Chapter Thirty-Nine

The preparations for Danny's trial went full speed ahead just after the first of the year. With the court date only weeks away, and Danny still intractable about revealing any names, Lou had no other choice but to start rehearsing Danny so he'd be ready for his testimony and for the government's cross-examination. Danny came home from Lou's office completely drained every evening.

"I picked up a chicken pot pie for you," I said one night when he was walking in and I was headed out to collect Sarah from Karen's house. The two of them were making some sort of birthday present for me that I wasn't supposed to know about. Sarah had already made something for Karen that she had hidden down in our basement. Poor kids, they always had to do double duty on our birthdays.

"Fine," he said distractedly as he peeled off his old ski jacket. "Mr. Curland was walking up our driveway with this. Says it came by mistake in his mail."

Danny handed me a pale ivory envelope that was a little damp from the snowfall. The return address read McPherson, Rogers and Whitson, Attorneys-At-Law, Twenty-One LaSalle Place, Vancouver, BC, Canada. The envelope didn't weigh much, but I had a feeling that the document inside would be pretty heavy.

It was.

It was a three-paragraph letter informing me of two hugely irrevocable facts: 1) Richard had died on November twentieth, and 2) he left Danny and me $750,000 apiece.

"Oh, my God," I gasped, holding the paper out to Danny and lowering myself to sit on the bottom hall stair. "Danny, look!"

Danny read the letter slowly, emotionlessly and then set it down on the stair next to me. I stared straight ahead not quite able to speak. "Don't tell me you're sad about him dying, Mom. How can you even care?"

"Oh, God, Danny. I'm not sad. Not about him per se. It's just that so much in our lives is such a waste. So much time is spent posing as one thing and actually having the capacity to be another."

"Posing? Seems to me he was a dick to us pretty much through and through."

"Not just him. All of us. Yes, Richard posed as a guy who thought he could operate with no ties or obligations to anybody. In the end, I wonder how true that really was of him. I posed, for a while at least, as a woman who could accept a large sum of money to take a secret trip and yet, in the end, I wasn't able to do it. And then there's you. And the posing you're doing."

"And what kind of posing is that?" I could sense he was on his way to getting prickly again.

"Oh, Danny," I sighed, so depleted about Richard, so tired of

Danny's whole drama. "The whole 'bite the bullet, take your punishment like a man' thing. I can't believe you don't go to bed at night and think, 'What am I doing? Why am I risking three years in jail? To protect people I barely know?'" I began to cry.

Then Danny did an amazing thing. He sat down next to me and wrapped his arms around me. "Come on, don't," he whispered into my hair. We hadn't been that physically connected in nearly six months.

"I'm sorry," I said, honking my nose into a tissue that was stuffed in my coat pocket. "I'm just unraveling. I know you are fixed on not telling any names, and..."

Danny kept his arms fastened around me, almost like I was a life raft as he said softly, "It's not names, Mom. It's just *a name*."

"A name? You mean one name? Are you saying you are one name away from having the charges dropped? Oh, Danny...for God's sake! Is this someone who you think might hurt you? Is that it?" I pulled back so I could read his face.

"No, Mom." Now his eyes were welling up.

"Danny, who is it? I don't understand. For heaven's sake, who are you protecting?"

"Jamie," he whispered, tears coming down now full force.

"What?"

"Jamie," he sobbed. "She was the one who got me involved in all this. Actually, she was the main one I was doing it for. The money was mostly for her."

"Danny, what are you saying?" The phone began ringing in the kitchen, but the machine was just going to have to get it.

"I'm saying Jamie used to work at the insurance company, remember? She was the one who gave me the lead on the job."

"Right...so?"

"Well, she quit to take the newspaper internship this summer because she thought it would help her get into journalism school."

"I don't understand. What does this have to do with you and what you did?"

"Mom, Jamie was the one who was originally working with these guys at the Secretary of State's office. I don't even know their real names. When they called they all just used the name 'Al.'"

"You don't know their names?"

"Nope. That's what I'm saying. They set this up with Jamie. And when she got the internship, she was torn between staying on at the insurance company, where she could get all that extra money to help to *pay* for school, or taking the internship, which would help her chances of *getting into* school. So I told her she could have both. That I'd work there and get cut in on the money like she did, and then I'd split the money with her."

I couldn't believe what I was hearing. "You did this for Jamie?"

"And me. I mean I *was* keeping some of the money. Obviously I don't have any of it now, because we turned it all back when I got arrested. But the deal Jamie and I cut last spring was that I was going to give her half."

"Why were you willing to do this?"

"Because otherwise Jamie would be screwed for college. Her parents don't really have the money to send her."

"What about scholarships?"

"Jamie wasn't going to get any scholarships. Her grades were okay, but not great. At best she could maybe get loans. So when this internship at the paper in Boston came along..."

"How did she get an internship if her grades weren't that great?"

"Because of her sports columns on the school paper. Remem-

ber she won a state journalism contest last year? Anyway she figured having that internship on her applications would be a major
help."

It was a lot to digest. On one hand we have Danny's quiet girl
pal, writing award-winning sports columns for the school paper and counterfeiting checks in her spare time. On the other
hand, we have Danny thinking this all makes such perfect sense
that he is willing to sign on as the summer replacement coun-
terfeiter for fifty percent of the proceeds.

"Oh, my God, Danny. You've been sitting on this for all these
months?"

"Pretty much." His lower lip continued to tremble.

"Jamie's really hoping to get into Northwestern for next year.
If I give her name to the State's Attorney, that's it for her. She'll
never get in. She'll probably never be able to get in anywhere.
Or go into journalism at all."

"Probably not. But I'm not worried about Jamie. What about
you? You aren't going to have any easier time trying to get into
school. Especially if you spend three years in jail."

"Yeah, but I only want to be an artist. I can take classes anywhere. I can draw anywhere. I can become what I want to become with or without a degree. Jamie can't."

"Danny, you can't give up three years of your life because Jamie wants to be the next Diane Sawyer. Journalism is a very
competitive field. Jamie may not be good enough to get anywhere. She could go through four years in journalism school and
still wind up as a beat reporter in the wilds of North Dakota.
There are no guarantees on any of this."

"I know. That's what Jamie tells me."

"What do you mean?"

"I mean she says she would understand completely if I gave the prosecution her name."

"If she'd understand it so well, then why doesn't she turn herself in?"

"Because then I wouldn't have any leverage with the government. I wouldn't be giving them anything in exchange for their dropping the charges. Don't you see?"

"Oh, Danny," I said handing him my Kleenex because it was his turn now, "all I see is my son struggling to figure out the difference between being loyal and levelheaded. You are an amazing human. In eighteen years you've survived one desertion, two divorces, a slew of household moves and the added humiliation of a very public arrest. But I don't know if you can survive three years in jail. Three years that you can completely avoid by giving them Jamie's name, and she has already given you permission to do it. What's holding you back?"

"What's holding me back is why should Jamie have to go to jail for three years if I did the same thing and I'm going to get off? We both did the same thing. What difference is it which one of us goes?"

"How do you know she'll have to go?"

"If there's a chance I'm going to go, why wouldn't there be for her?"

"There might be. But if she got good legal counsel, she might be able to get off."

"Jamie can't afford good legal counsel. If she could afford good legal counsel, then she'd have had money and we'd probably never have gotten into this situation in the first place."

"Danny, you could help Jamie afford a good lawyer. Even a lawyer like Lou Bosco."

"How?"

I pointed to the letter on the stairs. The one that said Danny had just inherited $750,000 from his father.

40

Chapter Forty

We've been through a lot of lifetimes in the three years since I opened Richard's initial letter. I don't have that letter anymore, nor do I have the one sent six months later from Richard's lawyer, but the events that took place between those two letters have, without question, radically altered the paths of Danny, Sarah, David and me.

For starters, David and I broke up.

Not in real life. Only on radio. I left the station almost six months after Danny's case was dismissed. I just felt talked out. I think lots of people on radio do, but they're afraid to tear themselves away from the microphone. Something of an "I talk, therefore I am" mind-set. But Samantha's delight in her new restaurant world showed me there is indeed life beyond the airwaves, and when the designer at my favorite flower shop on Sheffield Avenue told me the store was going up for sale, it took me about three days to decide to buy it.

Obviously, David and I talked at length before I did it. I didn't want my leaving to jeopardize his future at the station, but I needn't have worried. David had several ideas percolating about ways in which he could reinvent himself. He's now anchoring a news-oriented show that is the radio equivalent of *Politically Incorrect*—disparate people from disparate worlds colliding over issues for two hours a day. The show is smart, funny and fast-paced, and the talk is that it is a serious candidate for syndication. David says it's the second most fun thing he's doing.

The first is our new house. Our new/*old* house. It's just north of the city in Evanston. The first day we saw it two years ago was a messy, rainy March Sunday. Pulling up to the dowdy brick structure I remember saying, "Let's not even bother with this one. It reeks of hopelessness."

"Come on, Kate," he said, leaning over to kiss me. "You're just mad I made you get out of bed on a rainy Sunday and ended our weekend sex-a-thon." He was right. We'd had my house all to ourselves for thirty-six hours and had taken full carnal advantage. I loved David with his clothes on, but without them, we could get ourselves into a place that was pretty exceptional. I think we were blessed in that way. And yes, I was covetous of the time we could get when we didn't have to muffle all our moans and moves.

But we'd made an appointment to see this house because our Realtor was convinced "this could be the one." It was hard to imagine we'd ever find "the one," given that we'd been looking for several months and had come up with nothing. We weren't looking for fancy. We were just looking for something that spoke to us—something with heart and grace.

And this crumbly, center-entrance house most definitely did not look to be it. From the outside. Then we stepped in. Forget the gouged chartreuse walls and brown painted moldings, forget the nasty green carpeting, and linoleum hallway, forget everything but the amazing torrent of light—even on that gloomiest of days—that spilled into the house from window after window. Only the front was restrained in the number of windows it had. But the back and the sides were gloriously glassed and French-doored and gave off onto the huge, deep double-lot yard.

Of course we bought it. And for two years have poured our hearts and pocketbooks into it, having the best damn time, measuring, scraping, figuring out, building, arguing and tending. Oh, are we ever tending. We've begun three separate gardens—one country English, one Japanese and one nothing but antique roses.

But our most important rose, the fabulous Sarah Rose, has not had the easiest of times. Not only did our move mean she had to change schools, but she also had to go through two surgeries a year apart in Houston. The first was not only unsuccessful, it actually exacerbated her scarring. But the second involved a new product that encourages the patient's own skin to grow without scarring and it seems to be working really well on her. We aren't by any means out of the surgical woods, but we are at least out of the financial ones—all thanks to Richard's money.

Still, it has been Danny's life in which the money has made the most difference. It allowed him to pay all Lou Bosco's bills for his own case, which was dismissed once he gave the government Jamie's name. And then it allowed him to rehire Lou to represent Jamie. Lou worked tirelessly to get the charges dismissed against Jamie too, and when, after several months, he succeeded, Danny and Jamie were stunned. I was scrambling eggs for a giant frittata dinner that night when the two of them walked in and sat down at the kitchen table. They were ashen.

"Did the judge issue his ruling?" I asked, turning the flame off under my skillet so I could give all my attention to what they might tell me.

"Uh-huh," said Danny solemnly, "he did."

"Oh, my God," I said, pulling out a chair so I could sit, too. I was terrified of what he'd say next.

"They dismissed it," he whispered. "The prosecution argued really hard against it, but Mr. Bosco was amazing. He got the judge to dismiss all charges."

Tears were sliding down Jamie's face. "I can't stop crying. I feel so stupid. Oh, God, Ms. Lerner, thank you so much," she said, wiping her eyes with the back of her hand.

"Thank me for what, Jamie? I didn't do anything."

"Yes you did. You hired Mr. Bosco for Danny. And you persuaded Danny to hire Mr. Bosco for me. And neither of us would have been able to have Mr. Bosco be our lawyer, if you hadn't—"

She clammed up.

"What? If I hadn't, what?'"

"If you hadn't—" her eyes sought Danny's "—saved Danny's father's life."

"Is that what Danny said?"

"Yeah," she said hesitantly.

"Jamie," Danny said, "don't do that. Tell her what I really told you."

"Danny, I can't. I don't want your mom to be mad at me. Or embarrassed. Or anything."

"Don't worry. Tell her what I really told you. It's going to be okay. Honest."

Jamie looked liked a deer caught in the headlights. "Danny..."

"Go ahead," he said firmly.

"Okay," she said, breathing deep. "What Danny said was that his father offered you a whole lot of money to go away with him. And that you did it. But that you changed your mind, and then when you were leaving he almost died, and he didn't because you saved him. And that's why he left you guys the money."

"He told you all that?"

"Yes," she said hesitantly.

"Well, most of that is true," I said, looking directly at Danny.

"Most? What do you mean, most, Mom?"

"I mean it's all true except maybe the last part. Danny, who knows why your father left us the money? It might have had nothing to do with my saving his life. He might have planned it all along and then decided to make me come to Rome first just for the sport of it. Or he might have just read about your arrest and decided to do one, no-strings-attached thing in his life. You never really know why someone is doing something until they finally, finally decide to tell us. I think we have both learned that these past few months."

"Point well taken," he said.

"'Point well taken?'" I repeated, shaking my head and smiling. "You, young man, have been spending waaay too much time in court."

"No shit, Mom," he said, coming over to hug me. It felt great to laugh again.

* * *

Yesterday was pretty big around here.

Jamie and Danny were interviewed on the *Today Show*. Not because of the crime they'd committed. But because of a book they'd created.

After graduation both of them wanted to put off even thinking about college for at least a year. Instead they put together a little book called *Mom Lies*. Jamie spent six months interviewing people and culling all sorts of delicious stories. One mom desperate to get her daughter into a big bed, dismantled her daughter's crib, but told her it fell down and got broken. Another mom, intent on seeing her soap opera every day at noon, told her son that *Sesame Street* ended a half hour early, and then was busted one day when he came home and said, "How come *Sesame Street* is on for a whole hour at Brian's house?"

Jamie and Danny had a great time sorting through the mountain of mendacities they'd collected and then, after choosing their favorites, Danny spent several months creating whimsical pen-and-ink drawings to accompany each one. David and I weren't allowed to read or see any of it until the project was completed, and the night they handed each of us a manuscript, we were given specific instructions:

1. This is for you to enjoy and criticize. We are open to any comments.

2. Make them fast, because we are hot to send this off to a list of ten agents. We've been compiling this list for a couple of months.

3. Don't worry about our egos if the agents ding us. We know the odds.

The book couldn't have been more charming. But the fact

was, they didn't beat the odds. No agent wanted to take them on. And yet they were right about their egos. Because after getting rejected by all ten agents, the two of them decided to publish *Mom Lies* themselves.

"Danny, are you sure you really want to invest a chunk of your own money in this?" I asked the morning he told me. We were raking leaves in the front yard while David and Sarah were at work in the back. "You know I think the book is great, but self-publishing is hugely risky."

"I know, Mom, but this book just feels like it has such universal appeal." He shook open a big black plastic bag, so I could scoop a leaf pile in. "Every mom Jamie interviewed out there had a whole bunch of these lies to tell us about. I think this book will make people laugh, feel less guilty—I don't know—I'm just sure there are tons of people who will buy it."

And he was right. Right enough to have sold an astonishing 20,000 copies of the book so far and evidently right enough to wind up being interviewed by Katie Couric for a pre-Mother's Day feature.

Sarah, David and I hardly slept the night before Danny was on. We were completely clutched that we'd miss the alarm, or the cable would go out, or the VCR wouldn't record. So many techno-advances, so little confidence. But at 7:00 a.m. the three of us were huddled on the bed in our room eating day-old Krispy Kremes.

"Mom," Sarah said, licking the sticky sugar frosting off her fingers, "can I go with you and David to the airport to pick Danny and Jamie up tonight?"

"I don't know honey, David's big car is in the shop, and with Jamie's mother it will mean six people in the car."

"That's okay. I can sit real small in the back."

David leaned and kissed the top of her head. "Well, as long as you sit small. Want to practice now?" He and I moved even closer together so she was completely squeezed in between us.

Our laughter almost drowned out Katie Couric's introduction of Danny and Jamie. "And now we're joined by two young adults, who have something of a successful book on their hands...."

Danny and Jamie looked great. He was wearing a pale blue oxford shirt under an olive green V-neck and Jamie, who in real life shunned cosmetics, had been made up to look border-line glamorous. Even more important, the two of them seemed inordinately composed—no doubt facing a federal indictment can do that for you. Katie asked first about the genesis of the book.

"Well, when I was little," Danny began, "I caught my mom in this lie. It was this pretty stupid lie trying to make me think that the spinach she'd put in my taco was really lettuce. Anyway, when I caught her in it, I remember being completely furious. I couldn't believe that a mom had lied."

"And now?" asked Katie.

"Now?" He shrugged his shoulders. "Now I know that at some point, almost every mom in America has told some kind of lie."

"*My* lips are sealed." Katie smiled. "So, Danny, was that the biggest lie your mom ever told?"

I held my breath.

"Not exactly."

"What was the biggest?"

Danny smiled at her. "My lips are sealed."

Katie did not retreat. "Well, let me ask you this. When you found out about this lie, were you angry too?"

"I was. But not anymore."

"And your mom knows that?"

Danny looked down at his shoes and reflected a minute. "I don't know. But I'm thinking she's probably figured it out on her own. She's pretty cool."

I reached for the remote to turn off the TV.

"Hey!" yelled David grabbing it back from me. "What are you doing?"

"Are you kidding, David? My son just said on TV that I was *'pretty cool.'* I'm quitting while I'm ahead. It's never going to get better than this."

"You're nuts." He laughed. "Truly nuts."

Could be. But I didn't care. I just figured the smartest thing I could do was jump into the shower, shave my legs and get ready for whatever was about to happen next.